Go West

Young

F*cked-Up

Chick

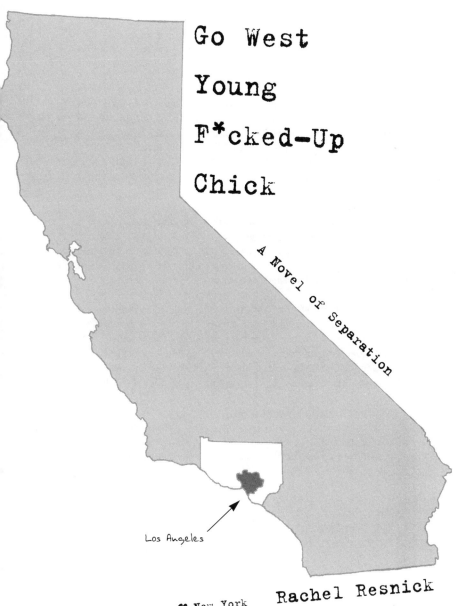

Go West Young F*cked-Up Chick

A Novel of Separation

Los Angeles

St. Martin's Press ≈ New York

Rachel Resnick

This book is a work of fiction. All of the characters and events portrayed in this book are fictitious or are used fictitiously; any real names are used solely as a literary device. Although aspects of this novel were inspired to some extent by actual events, those events have been completely fictionalized and this book is not intended to portray, and should not be read as portraying, actual events or individuals.

Portions of this book were originally published in *Absolute Diaster: Fiction from Los Angeles* (Santa Monica Review and Dove Books, 1996), *The Crescent Review, The Maryland Review, ART: MAG, Art Times, Chiron Review, West/Word, Pacific Coast Journal, Bakunin, Messenger, the minnesota review,* and *Chelsea.*

Design by Michaelann Zimmerman

Resnick, Rachel.
    Go west young f★cked-up chick : a novel of separation / Rachel Resnick.
       p.   cm.
     ISBN 0-312-19889-2
     I. Title.
    PS3568.E72G6   1999
    813'.54—dc21   98-40599
                                          CIP

First Edition: April 1999

10 9 8 7 6 5 4 3 2 1

In memory of my mother,
Jane Reidy

ACKNOWLEDGMENTS

I want to thank and acknowledge the following crucial people: Frances Kuffel, my witty agent, for having faith in me; Jim Fitzgerald, my hip editor, for taking a chance on this project; Rebecca Schuman, my enthusiastic pointguard at St. Martin's, for championing the book; Sonje Bolle, for setting the whole thing in motion.

Go West Young
F*cked-Up Chick

The first time I saw Ma after she died was on the New Jersey Turnpike, right near Exit 13A. A matted-haired mutt on the side of the road, sitting on its bony haunches so steady and forl orn on the shoulder, looking right at me. The mournful expression, the eyes, the mouth—my mother was trapped inside that dog.

I didn't stop though. Until I saw her again. Outside Baltimore. This time she inhabited the body of a hitchhiker, straw hair in his weather-beaten face but through that ragged curtain, Ma. Same eyes, same bulbous Irish nose, same alcoholic despair. "Gimme a ride, Rebecca." His thumb was jerking westward and he held aloft a sign saying CALIFORNIA BOUND.

I didn't pick him up. My mother told me not to ever pick up strangers. My mother was a vagabond, so I knew she wouldn't stay long in that hitchhiker. Ma wasn't dead—she was on the road. I was going to follow.

I got on 81 and headed for Nashville. There I hooked up with the 40. I sighted her in Oklahoma City, Shamrock, Tucumcari, Gallup, Kingman, Needles, San Bernardino. Ma in a trucker, Ma in a lizard darting across the highway, Ma in a Hopi souvenir shop clerk, Ma in a truck-stop state border waitress, Ma in a black Labrador retriever loose in the gas station. Sightings at first infrequent, increasing steadily, and all leading to one place.

When I got to Los Angeles, I saw Ma everywhere. In every face, every gesture, every melancholic smile, every deluded eye, every mad shopping-cart man, every Day 'N Nite clerk, every done-up whore, every slick man behind the wheel of a Benz, every wandering dog, every stray cat, every Central American woman with a bundle of laundry balanced on her head, all of them were her.

How generous. My mother had parceled out her spirit and given a bit to people all over town. Or she was slipping from one to the other fast as bubbles escape from submerged mouths. Or else she'd figured out some ghostly way to procreate and her spirit was spreading all through this disjointed city. Whatever the case, she was here, there, everywhere in Los Angeles.

I knew I was in the right place, this place I'd never been. Far from the graveyard in Bayshore, Massachusetts, and close to Ma's spirit.

Home at last.

Los Angeles.

Glitter-Gloat

In the universe of Hollywood, it's important to know your place and chart your course carefully through the sometimes lethal constellations. Avoid star burns. And never lose sight of the Milky Way, that faintly luminous freeway spanning the heavens cobblestoned with innumerable stars too distant to be seen with the naked eye. The path where all fellow travelers are stripped bare and bathed in starlight the way corpses are bathed.

Entertainment Tonight and Forever

How is it we learn to lick boots, and love it; the oily leather on our tongues. How do we know to welcome barked commands as excuses to sway this way and that, the tree the dog and our fever. And what of the desire to bend toward screams and frowns. The finality of manacles and locked hours. Employment and love one steady nightmare feed.

My first Hollywood job: slave to *ET*'s celebrity reporter, Darlene Comer.

It was summertime in Pasadena. Smog, string bikinis, Ray-Bans, cars with the tops down, the rush of heat-squeezed chatter, skin. So much bare skin, I was exultant. Even breathed the thick poison, liked the way it filled the throat. The sun hung there like a curved copper button, stitched into a thin blue cambric sky, burning up the clouds. Me, it was my body that burned, demanding immolation.

Isaac and I fucked all day in the deserted Caltech dorm. I scored a waitressing gig in the school's restaurant. We were broke, the dorm was hot, the few students around were suspicious of our presence. I was going to get a job in ENTERTAINMENT. Soon. And Isaac and I, well, I wanted us to always be together. I figured the more he wanted me, the harder it would be for him to leave. Sort of like my

4

desirability was a choke chain, or a type of collar. And Isaac was my dog.

The white button-down shirt tucked into a short black cotton skirt, nude drugstore panty hose, cheap black flats, and the swinging double doors leading to and from the kitchen of the Caltech restaurant. Isaac got a job working there too. When we worked at the same time and passed each other in the kitchen, we would kiss quickly before the doors swung shut.

Doors closed, the constant thrum of low-grade pain, these are the telltale signs of slavish love. When girls would proffer themselves on platters recently shined, and wiped, and generally made ready for the crowning delicacy of their own served-up head—severed, groomed, and perfectly dressed with candied eyes of adoration, boiled lips wincing at the ardent cut of head from neck. They are eager. They are volunteers. Have no pity.

After graduation I developed papillary conjunctivitis (tiny bumps on the underside of my eyelids) from contact lenses that prevented me from wearing them for a year. So it was back to glasses. I hadn't worn them since seventh grade, a time of oily hair, gawky limbs, braces, sexual unease.

"Still love me?" I said to Isaac, pointing at the offending frame resting on my face. I was also conscious of my breasts, the way they swelled in the lilac Warner's Sizzler Isaac liked because it was so flimsy. Slowly, imperceptibly, I jutted them forward. I was my own subliminal message, so I fancied.

"Sure, babe. You're like one of those secretaries in the commercials, y'know. Hair in a bun, glasses, uptight suit. Then they shake out their hair, whip off the glasses, throw off the jacket, and voilà."

Isaac gazed at the full-length mirror in the dorm room, arched his eyebrows, then tilted his jaw slightly upward. I did, followed his every move, though the trajectory did not always please me.

"What're you . . ." I said, vaguely disappointed.

"Nothing." Isaac stuck his tongue out like a gargoyle and wagged it at his reflection. He looked in the mirror more than any woman I knew. "Maybe, though, you could lose some weight."

"Lose," I whispered, freezing my body in its present position.

"What?"

"Nothing." I quickly sat down on the mattress, pulled my knees to my chest. I watched damp spots appear on the hose. Saw amoebas fattening, mini-maps expand and blur. I imagined Isaac's arms hugging me close, skin on skin, body pressed to body as it had been in the beginning, but he didn't move. Something had altered.

"Rebecca . . . you'll be late," he said.

The watch was a hand-me-down, a fake Rolex. In the heat, the gold scabbed off. The face was scratched. The second hand dragged, then flew forward. As if it had a tic. Toc. I shook it off my wrist into a softly puddling Japanese fountain and left it there.

"An educated girl," Darlene Comer said, glancing at my résumé. I noticed her feet only touched the floor because she was wearing heels. I didn't like short legs, never had. The higher the height from which to fall on bended knees, chastised and shamed, this was the unarguable advantage of long legs. The better to embrace one's wretchedness.

"Degrees don't matter," she said, speaking rapidly with her Delta twang. I nodded, taking in the stiffly sprayed hair, the pancake foundation, and the thick mascara. Would I have to dress like that? The phone rang and she answered it, putting up her index finger to let me know just a minute. I wanted to bite it, sever its authority. Pack it in my handbag for future use. Instead I focused on this woman's appearance. Her fingernails were long and coral pink and matched the shirt she wore under a Chanel jacket and skirt. On her breast was pinned a shiny gold star. Though in her late forties, early fifties, Darlene had a girlish quality. She seemed to be the complete opposite of the woman I knew best. My mother. The one with the sepulchral voice.

I looked around as she was talking. The reporters' den was crowded with desks, papers, file cabinets, posters, pencils, bags of take-out, typewriters. In the corner a stout older man in a sportscoat and turtleneck was smoking a pipe and tapping on a heavy-duty Smith-Corona. He winked at me. The nose was telltale red. I smiled, roughed up my hair, and wondered idly if he wanted to fuck me, the same way I had wondered with all my mother's come-and-go boyfriends. I liked the look of chaos, the sensation that business never stopped. I wanted people to want me. I wanted chaos.

"The stupid, he didn't."

I studied Darlene's work area—scribbled notes and snapshots of Darlene posing with celebrities tacked to the bulletin board along with an array of cocktail napkins, Hallmark cards, a sachet of candy bound by a satin ribbon, and a big yellow smiley sticker with dead black eyes. I smiled idiotically to mask the discomfort of waiting. Forced into limbo, a temporary invisibility.

"No, Joan Collins was divine."

Joan Collins. Who knew who I might meet? I was already thinking about introducing these people to Isaac, the glamorous part of the couple. The stars would recognize him as one of their own, give him a film part, and we would both be on our way. He'd see what I meant about L.A. being wide open. He'd change his mind. He'd change his mind, and I would eat the sugar-spun humility Darlene Fox offered with a deep throat.

"Kiss, kiss."

Darlene turned back to me.

"There's not much money, you'll have to work hard, seven days a week, hours are whenever I need you, but there's movies, TV, parties, celebrities, the whole shebang." The phone rang again. "What do you think?"

I didn't have to.

In the bathroom. Behind a metal door, I touched myself. Imagined Isaac wanting me, needing what I had, what I was. More than anything. Anything. Anything. Anyone. Flushed. My hands supplicating

7

beneath an empty spigot, then, the miracle of spat water. Too brief. My fingers, they smelled of sex, and something irreversible.

A hundred and twenty-five bucks a week is what I got as Darlene Comer's personal assistant, with a chance of getting raises. Less than half what I needed to live on. But with our savings and money from the restaurant, it was enough to put a deposit on an apartment closer to Paramount. We gave notice at the restaurant and began looking for places to rent.

There was no air conditioning in the car, no radio. Isaac had his blaster playing. We had the windows rolled down and the Beastie Boys whining. Isaac held the Thomas Guide, a map of the city that was thick as a dictionary.

"Hollywood first?" I said. Isaac shrugged. The sweat was already fanning over my back, sticking me to the seat upholstery. Instead of getting irritable at the weather and at Isaac, I luxuriated in the perfect press of heat that came equally from every side, and let it hold me.

Isaac was singing along to "It's Time to Get Ill," drumming on the dash. He hadn't spoken since we left Pasadena.

As I downshifted to get off the freeway at Highland, I remembered Isaac saying, "You'd rather grab that stickshift than me." He was right. Much as I desired him, the sense of power and freedom I got from being behind the wheel was, if not more basic than sex, then more self-contained. It didn't matter if Isaac was beside me once I was in the car, except that he was a distraction, whereas on still ground my need for him bordered on fanatic. Driving required no partner, no passenger, only a sense of purpose, a destination, a tank of gas and concentration. I never tried to explain this to Isaac because I was afraid the secret would be diluted or, worse, disappear. I had never told anyone what driving meant to me. It was too important. I was never more alive, more fluid, more present in my world than when I drove distances.

Every day I discovered new streets, new shortcuts, forgotten cul-de-sacs. One day we passed a weird little house with a rippled roof that looked like dripped sand, and another made out like a Buddhist temple with a red wooden pagoda frame over the porch and a shiny black Buddha on the stoop. Another day I saw a yard of carefully swept dirt and right next to it a yard dense as a jungle with vines choking the telephone lines and covering the door. There were mini-malls featuring three or four different nationalities—Jewish, Indian, Thai, or Chinese, El Salvadoran, and Armenian—in the middle of busy intersections. Things were for sale everywhere—in yards, on lawns, on sidewalks, at freeway ramps. On some streets, vendors sat on milk crates with their wares spread on card tables or leaned against brick walls—I spotted cheap china swans, hard plastic flowers, heaps of brown-spotted bananas, chestnuts, shiny tin rings and bracelets, huaraches, stuffed animals sealed in cellophane pouches, fat plastic-wrapped pillows, and aluminum-framed mirrors decorated with paintings of Jesus, Jimi Hendrix, lowriders, Our Lady of Guadalupe, palm trees. Over one "barata" bargain store, I saw the sign: NEWBORN • BIKINI • PANTY HOSE • BRASSIERE • SWEAT SUIT. How is a bikini born? A teeny-weeny yellow polkadot wet bundle popping out the snap crotch of a padded lycra one-piece.

I learned new, bolder driving maneuvers in Los Angeles: how to slip through yellow lights flickering to red to make left turns before oncoming traffic came surging in from the front and side, how to move into the right-hand lane at a stoplight, then when the light turned green, instead of turning right shoot forward in front of slow drivers. In these ways I began to achieve a communion with traffic, congested streets, bad drivers. The skill surface-street driving required was tight, precise, more poetic than the epic quality of freeway trips. I found my sense of exaltation and peace rose to new heights of satisfaction, and grittier states of grace.

"Hollywood's a dump," Isaac said the first day after we left yet another noisy overpriced miniature courtyard apartment with low ceilings, soiled off-white carpeting, dripping faucets, and peeling paint. I didn't bother to tell him the elegant faces I saw in the mottled striped wallpaper, or the way the paint peeled outward like flower petals radiating from a stained core.

9

We were driving west on Fountain when Isaac spotted a FOR RENT sign. Cochran Avenue. The manager, a five-foot-tall woman with a nasal voice and wearing a Japanese kimono, showed us around. She wore no shoes and she had hammer toes. It was a two-story white stucco building. The apartment was two-bedroom, with wood floors, sunlight, high ceilings. It was old, but cheery. At five hundred a month, it was more expensive than we could afford, but it was Saturday, my job started Monday, and I was tired of looking.

"Name's bad," I told Isaac at the Fatburger's that was around the corner from the apartment. I watched him eat a burger with chili fries while I sipped a seltzer water.

"Fry?" he said, pushing a cardboard carton filled with fries glopped with suspiciously orange chili.

"Cochran is just, you know . . ."

He licked chili off his fingers.

"I have a weird feeling about the name. Maybe it means we're making a big mistake."

Isaac said nothing, wiped his mouth.

On Monday, I started my job. As instructed, I parked on a dingy side street so I could enter the studio's B gate. Because I was hired by Darlene Comer personally and not by Paramount, I could not park on the studio's lot.

Friday night after my first week at *ET,* we went to The Formosa Café for dinner and drinks. I ordered egg rolls, a vodka tonic, and Isaac ordered Chinese spareribs and a Rolling Rock. The egg rolls were soggy and shiny with grease, the filling tasted like day-old coleslaw. The tonic was flat and the amount of vodka slight, but neither food nor drink was why anyone came. We'd been to The Formosa a few times and loved it from the start. The place was low-rent, dimly lit, crammed full of rickety brown tables, cozy round red leather booths, a dark bar with rows of bottles lit up behind the shadowed bartender, signed photos of celebrity customers tacked everywhere along the ceiling (a custom that extended in L.A. from restaurants to dry cleaners to gas stations), wobbly Chinese lanterns, and lit-up glass-case displays of Elvis dolls, statuettes, and memorabilia. And it was cheap.

"So?" said Isaac, gnawing on a rib. "The crazy hours worth it?" Isaac was wearing his baggy jeans overalls and a tank top underneath. I sighed at the sight of his torso and smiled at him. He looked better than any bust of a Greek god I'd seen.

"Excuse me," I said to the waitress, pointing at a tiny white cup of red sauce that sat on a saucer, "could I have some more of this red stuff?" She nodded without answering and bustled away. "You have to drench these rolls."

"That was fast, going Hollywood."

I frowned. The hard glint in his eyes ruined the Greek god effect. "I asked for more sauce? Big deal."

"Don't frown," Isaac said, pointing at my forehead where I had grown a small furrow.

I drank half my vodka tonic. They were small glasses. I still loved him, I repeated to myself. "You want to hear or not?"

"Shoot."

"I sit at a big fat typewriter, headphones stuck to my ears, listen to a tape on a Dictaphone, and type out the whole fucking interview. Every 'uh huh,' pause, 'hmm,' cough . . . takes hours."

"Huh." Isaac took my hand and kneaded the fingers. I glanced over at a ceramic Old Elvis with white bell-bottom jumpsuit striped with emerald green. The cock of his hip was right, but his eyes were flat and phony and the Chinese red paint around his trademark snarling lips was so sloppily applied it made him look like a transvestitic Kewpie doll.

"I answer phones and file, y'know, shit like that, but not every day." I took a bite of egg roll with a big smear of hot yellow mustard on it. The mustard stung.

"Sounds boring as hell. To your new job." Isaac clinked his beer bottle against my glass.

"Thanks. I didn't even get to Darlene . . ."

Isaac sighed.

". . . every day, she does herself up like Dolly Parton. All that deb training. I think she cakes the makeup on to compete with the younger anchors, y'know, try and fool the camera. They still use extra filters."

Isaac tossed the last rib onto the plate and grabbed one of my egg rolls.

"There's this high heel up on the file cabinet, and in the toe, get this, she's got a pint bottle of Rebel Yell. When we stay late, she takes nips or spikes her soda while she's writing."

"I could use some good weed," said Isaac, peeling the label off the Rolling Rock. Shreds of white fell to the tabletop.

"She's got a white Benz convertible, leather interior, car phone— and I drive. I figure out the directions to the interviews while she talks on the phone . . ."

". . . a chauffeur?" Isaac coughed. "You, Miss Ambition?"

"I'm paying my dues."

"For no bucks."

I drained the rest of my vodka tonic and nodded when the wait-ress pointed at it to see if I wanted another. "I met Bob Hope. We went out to his house in the Valley somewhere, this rambling ranch monstrosity. I was carrying Darlene's bags, and I saw the camera crew set up and watched Darlene chatting to this dried-up old man. I thought he was the gardener—but it was him, Bob Hope. He looked like a walking corpse. They sat him in a big wicker chair, the sun was beating down, and I thought he was going to die right there or was already dead. Then they turned on the camera."

Isaac leaned forward, stroked my arm.

"When the lights fell on Hope's face, he came to life. As soon as the camera started whirring, his face got animated, his nose got sharper, he started talking and didn't stop until they turned the cam-era off. Then he slumped back down and didn't say another word. Someone had to lead him away."

Isaac said nothing. I fished the lime out from the bottom of my empty vodka tonic and sucked the fruit off. The tartness calmed me.

"Sounds pretty damn lightweight to me." Isaac leaned back against the booth, stretched his arm along the top. His muscles rippled there.

"I'm learning. Jesus. It's my first fucking week."

"I gotta go to the john," Isaac said, getting up. I turned to watch, saw him glance at a woman in a booth by the bathroom door. She was sitting with another woman and a man. When he walked by, she waved, then covered her mouth with her hand. The woman was probably a model or an actress with high cheekbones, porcelain skin, and a revolting cascade of red Botticelli curls. She was wearing a filmy white lace midriff shirt and an armful of silver bangles. I turned back to the table and ran my fingers down the glass, streaking the wetness. Pushed my glasses up. Maybe Isaac was right and the job was bullshit. Isaac sat back down.

"There's something else I did this week."

The waitress brought over another Rolling Rock for Isaac. "I didn't order this," he said. The waitress winked.

"Gift from the lady back there," she said.

"Don't let me interrupt," I said, exhaling. "Go talk to her, go ahead."

"Don't start," Isaac said.

"I saw you looking at her."

"Rebecca."

"I sit in this cubicle, watch videos of movies to find clips for stories. This week we interviewed Claude Lanzmann."

"New heartthrob on *Days Of Our Lives?*"

"No. Directed a ten-hour documentary on the Holocaust from the point of view of present-day survivors. Darlene said pick out five juicy seconds." Isaac was gazing over my shoulder.

"I can't believe you," I said.

"I should at least say thank you. Someone's friendly, what's the problem?"

"Please. With blessings."

"Be right back." Isaac got up and went back to the booth. I didn't turn around. I took my glasses off and everything looked better. All the Elvises were blobs of white, silver, green, and red, the lanterns spilled warm light, The Formosa was a watercolor painting, a wacky Matisse, people's faces blurred and fuzzed, bottles shone. Behind me I heard voices. Laughter. Isaac said, "Hey, Brotherman," and slapped someone's hand. Then he was sitting down again.

"An actress," he said, his voice scornful. "Wanted to know if I was an actor. Guy was nice. Works carpentry down by the beach. Said he might be able to swing me some work. Other girl's a costume designer. They might join us."

"You didn't."

"Don't you want me to work? Pay you back?"

"I want to finish telling you about the documentary. I chose this scene with the barber." Isaac waved at the table, at the redhead. I kept talking. I needed him to hear the story, though I wasn't sure why.

"He's cutting a customer's hair and remembering how he survived the camps by cutting prisoners' hair before they were gassed to death. There's a close-up on his hands trembling as he shears away this guy's hair, hunks of it float down onto the floor behind him, slow, and the barber just breaks down." I paused. "I kept replaying the hair floating through his hands, through the scissors and onto the floor. Over and over. I couldn't stop. Are you listening? All Darlene said when I showed her the clip was did I think the director was sexy."

The waitress walked out from the kitchen with a slice of apple pie and a single candle burning in the crust. She brought it to the booth where the redhead sat.

"HAPPY BIRTHDAY TO YOU, HAPPY BIRTHDAY TO YOU . . ." sang the man and woman.

"It's Katrina's birthday," Isaac said. "The actress."

"Katrina. Like I give a shit."

"HAPPY BIRTHDAY DEAR KATRINAAAAAAA . . ."

"You are too fucking much," I said.

"HAPPY BIRTHDAY TO YOU!"

"What?" Isaac said sharply, leaning forward. "I heard your story.

What do you want me to do? Pat you on the back? Tell you how incredible you are? How smart? How you'll be driving a white Benz? I'm sure you'll be successful," Isaac said bitterly.

"HOW OLD ARE YOU NOW, HOW OLD ARE YOU . . ."

"Shhhhhhhhhhhhh . . ." the redhead motioned to her companions. A burst of laughter came from the booth. Tears slid down my face. I thought it was impossible, but The Formosa got even blurrier— reds merging with yellows and shadows and glinting ice cubes. Flesh blending with eight-by-ten glossies and smiling gold buddhas.

"Fuck," said Isaac. "Rebecca."

"Hey, Isaac!" yelled a female voice. "Come join us. Katrina wants you." More laughter. "Bring your friend!"

"Isaac," I whispered. "Isaac, I love you, I love you so much." Isaac kept his head down, toyed with one of the picked-clean bones on his plate. I reached out to grab his hand, but I must have misjudged the distance without my glasses on, because I only got my sleeve wet on the table and didn't manage to touch him.

There's this. The way the sky would rinse clean after a rainstorm. See the rooftops sharpen in the newborn air, edges poised to razor the blue? Their intent: to spill celestial guts on the hoods of cars.

One morning I came to work with a buzz cut.

Darlene raised her eyebrows but didn't say anything, just gave me another tape to transcribe. That night, when the reporters' den was empty except for us, Darlene tapped me on the shoulder. I took off the headphones.

"Rebecca . . . we need to talk," she said. Darlene never spoke to me that way. Nobody else had either when I was growing up. If anyone scolded, it was me. "Why don't you get a job? Pull yourself together." "Fuck off," is what my mother used to say.

Darlene sat on top of the desk next to me with her Styrofoam container of Thai food. We were eating invisible noodles, silver yum-yum, and mee krob. Try as I might, the noodles would not obey my chopsticks.

"You're only hurting yourself," she said, pointing a wooden chopstick at my hair.

"Don't you ever feel like . . . 'I'm a woman, screw me'?"

"I'm a woman and I do all right," she said.

She flashed a brilliant, manic smile. "You'll never get anywhere dressed like that," she said, pointing at my green Converse All-Star high-tops, magenta ankle-zip jeans, untucked shirt with a singed brown patch around the lowest button where I'd brushed against a lit gas burner. "Gotta show some leg," she said. "Didn't your mother teach you anything?"

She didn't really want to hear the answer to her question. She didn't want to hear about the Marlboro Mom, a woman who never wore high heels, who couldn't even keep a lousy job waitressing at IHOP or delivering newspapers. I kept the image of my mother in her daily uniform of Levi's, ragged T-shirts, jeans jacket, and heel-cracked cowboy boots to myself. I hated that jacket—Jackson Pollack–style visual violence complete with cigarette burns, wine stains like woozy flowers, holes fringed with white cotton threads, rips and faded strips like washed-out shorelines, etched creases from her elbows bent around the steering wheel, her elbows bent on the bar, her elbows bent on the pillow where she lay sleeplessly. After she died, I kept the jacket in my closet.

"I'll tell you a secret, Rebecca. I'd rather have beauty than brains," Darlene said, taking a large bite of invisible noodles. I watched her add a shot of Rebel Yell to the Thai iced tea before I left.

On the way home, winding through darkened streets with wistful Brazilian music on the new car radio, I thought maybe getting a buzz cut, dyeing a forelock purple or green, and wearing baggy long johns under ripped jeans didn't mean rebellion. Maybe it meant something else. With one hand deftly guiding the wheel and the other stretched around the passenger headrest, I thought about my mother. I saw her stumbling down the stairs in a cheap rayon K-mart baby-doll nightie, handing eleven-year-old me a book of food stamps, "Get me a six of Miller's and a pack of Salems." I avoided the scary ice-floe blue of her eyes. How did that square with the earlier vision I had of her—the lively brunette, hair bound back with a turquoise scarf, full lips laughing as men came up to her on the street and whispered what nice legs she had, and how pretty she was, me at age four or five trailing alongside, enraptured too and proud, as we walked through Central Park with hot dogs and I climbed the metal statue of Alice in Wonderland, perched on her shoulder with one hand grasping Alice's rippled cold metal hair and the other waving at my mother, the whole show all for her.

I sped through the last milliseconds of a yellow light and turned smoothly onto Fountain, executing a perfect, tight arc to the right. Revenge. That was my motive for wanting to make films. I stayed in the narrow right lane, squeezed boldly past parked cars, just missing their sideview mirrors.

Everyone thought my mother was a failure. Driving through the streets of West Hollywood, past shadowed palms and dimly lit bungalows, I reaffirmed I was on Earth to vindicate my mother's memory.

I glanced at my reflection in the rearview mirror and wondered how long it would take for my hair to grow out.

Hands grabbing, lifting, replacing hanger on rack, shoved far inside to the left. The jacket, hide it, no, revere it, just, give it a special place, a sacred spot deep inside the closet. Yes, sacred. Never mind that the jacket still smells of her. Feels of her. Against the wall, place the jacket, note the emptiness of sleeves, the way the shoulders poke in soldierly fashion. Wipe your hands on your pants when you step back out and shut the door.

Back at home, Isaac wasn't taking off anywhere except to the bookstore—maybe Samuel French Theater Bookshop on Sunset or Circus of Books on Santa Monica. Even though we were trying to save money for rent and other essentials and Isaac didn't have a job yet, he bought books and didn't read them. Philosophy, acting theory, anti-apartheid tracts, plays, literary criticism, poetry. He bought books when we had nothing in the apartment but a futon on the floor and all our belongings piled in the closets. The place was empty. Still, he couldn't stop buying them. And I didn't stop him.

Stack the cars. Thread the cars. Glue their bumpers together. Paint them all red, one long red line of cars cars cars. Doesn't matter. Traffic is unavoidable. You are one car among many, indistinguishable.

"Damn car phone. I didn't see him turning."

"Where are you?" I said. Darlene's voice was low and shaky. "I think Ivar," she said, pausing to look out the window. "Yes . . . north of Sunset. Transfer the phones up front. Hurry."

When Darlene climbed into my Toyota Corolla, I was embarrassed. There were cracks in the dash, paper scraps and dirt clods on the floor mats, stains on the cheap vinyl seat covers, dirt on the windshield.

"Sorry about . . ."

"Just drive." The aroma of Giorgio perfume filled the tiny car along with another smell almost as sweet. I realized, as I pulled onto Sunset Boulevard, that the other scent was bourbon.

Darlene didn't talk, except to give directions. She held herself stiffly in the seat, as if she didn't want to get dirty by moving around too much, or maybe that was my paranoia. I liked the sight of her Charles Jourdan heels on the wrinkled floor mat. Rare reversal.

As we drove along Sunset, the houses and shops got fancier and cleaner the farther west we went. I thought about all the accidents I'd been in with my mother. Thought about them with the same powerlessness as a common housefly watches its own wiry legs disappear one after the other in the spider's mouth. I remember the first accident—her hand bracing my body when the VW bug impacted a guardrail, or a curb, or something, was it another car? The song playing on the radio was "Echoes of My Mind," and it kept playing even after the crash. There were orange and yellow, green and blue stickers of daisies on the hood, so it must have been late in the sixties. There was a long wait in the police station. I sat on a large, uncomfortable, polished dark wood bench, sucking on Luden's cherry cough drops while my mother came in and out from different tests—Breathalyzers, lie detectors, alcohol-level testing.

I glanced up at the Marlboro Man billboard rising above Sunset, his cowboy hat peaking against the hills, and remembered how the people walked by where I sat in the cop station and looked at me sadly and how I furrowed my brow and stared them down. Every time my mother came out from another test, I pretended not to know her, instead studying a *Guns & Ammo* magazine I found on a table nearby while she chain-smoked and I coughed loudly.

When we turned north at Sunset Plaza Drive, Darlene perked up. "I can just hear Bliss. 'Again?' Married thirty years," she said to me, smiling too brightly. "We were high school sweethearts in Biloxi. Got hitched when I was twenty. Oops," she giggled. "Don't tell anyone."

"Twenty?"

"Had twins, and kept my career going, too. My kids . . . they're . . . special. They don't say that about me though," she giggled again. "I was a bad bad mother."

"Twins, huh," I said, winding through narrow, lushly green streets bordered by spacious houses.

I was disappointed. Success was fine. I admired that in a woman. Craved it for myself. Family, though, was a big blotto in my mind. Family was the missing jigsaw piece that ruined the interlocked picture of a daisy-dotted Swiss Alp and showed you the knife-gouged card table underneath. Family was fragments of busted beer bottles left jagged and piss-sticky on the kitchen floor.

"Not so fast," Darlene said, gripping the armrest. Enjoying her fear, I pressed on the accelerator. When I pulled into Darlene's driveway, I raced to the top. Her house was set at the edge of the hill and commanded a panoramic view of the city. I had never seen anything like it.

I wasn't invited in. Before she got out of the car, Darlene kissed me briefly on the cheek. "Bring your boyfriend by sometime." Then she was gone. I stayed for a few minutes in the driveway looking out at the tiny diamond lights of L.A. before I wound back down into the lowlands.

When I introduced Isaac to Darlene, the only thing she had to say about him later was, "Loser."

At the time, I thought she meant me.

We were in the Crystal Room of the Beverly Hills Hotel, it was five-thirty, I was in my one black dress, and we were waiting for the celebrities to arrive for the Contessa Foundation Fashion Show. All the proceeds would go to an animal rescue shelter. Before anyone with a *TV Guide* name showed, I raided the buffet table. I wrapped sandwich triangles, truffles, monster strawberries, and pâté in napkins, then placed the moist packages in my shoulder bag. Isaac and I would eat them later.

I picked up a glass of champagne and went to look for someone to help me spot stars. I had decided I didn't want to be a loser. I began to enjoy spotting celebrities with the help of tipsy Foundation patrons, even let myself fantasize about being invited to such an evening instead of infiltrating with the *ET* crew. Wasn't that what Darlene would call positive thinking? A little more champagne, and I was imagining what it would be like to don a clingy silver sheath and strut down the lit-up runway, knowing that every twitch of my ass and flex of my calf was contributing toward a dog house for some poor homeless canine. My idols Antonioni, Scorsese, Wertmuller, and Fellini tried to wave me back to them in a corner of the Crystal Room where they stood bad-mouthing the crowd and pooh-poohing Hollywood, but I was gone. I'd be up there on the stage cocking my hip for the sake of some outcast canary, fully inhabiting the shimmering skin of a star.

Every four-and-a-half months they come around to shave the palm trees. The city, that is. Special vehicles. Motorized pulpits lifting bodies up toward the shaggy bark. Great buzzing noises and roaring gears. Oversize razors in hand, they shear the dead brown skin. It falls in heaps on the street. Along with yellow, sickly fronds. All gets piled and swept to the curb. Scooped up and discarded in metal bins. Ritual sacrifice for the skyline. The fresh shave makes the palms look so goddamn vulnerable.

One morning near the end of my stint at *ET*, I arrived at Darlene's house to drop off some dubbed tapes half an hour early.

She opened the door in a terry cloth robe, barefaced. It was the first time I'd ever seen her without makeup. I was stunned. I never knew she had such enormous violet eyes underneath all the shadow and concealer and liner and mascara. Her skin minus heavy foundation was the biggest surprise. Smooth and supple and dotted with thousands and thousands of floating freckles shaping and unshaping like free-form constellations as I watched those eyes widen.

When she saw me, Darlene got flustered and fled back to the bathroom. I left the tapes on the front door mat and wound my way down the Sunset Strip, thinking of my first Hollywood boss. In that moment when she came to the door, Darlene looked like a little girl lost, but more beautiful than I'd ever seen her. A little girl lost who wanted more than anything to be adored.

Drunk, she reminded me of my mother.

With her naked face, she reminded me of me.

My First Abortion

During.

I remember a woman in there with me, on my right. She held my hand. Clamps. My body yawned open. She squeezed my hand. Cramps. All mine because I had refused any painkillers. I held on to her hand, this stranger woman. The sweetest hand I ever held.

Afterward.

In a recurring nightmare, I am a mother, complete with little boy and little girl and sort of a nondescript husband. We are all this dull gray clay color like when you're out in the sun and you open your eyes and all the colors have washed away. The setting is eye-hurting bright. Voluptuous silvery-black clouds appear and coalesce into terrifying gargoyle faces, bobbing and leering. They have deep-grooved sneers and smiling eyes with no pupils. These cloudy monsters menace me and my little clay nuclear family until we manage to flee into the street to mingle with other people.

We breathe in the air, thinking we are free, but nobody seems to see us. My family and I must return to the empty, dingy, brick apartment building. We crawl through long, dusty, dark basement corridors up the stairs until we reach the apartment.

Sleep is impossible.

I gather the children and clutch them to my sides, but the monsters appear everywhere wherever and whenever they want. In desperation, I run to the window. I see my hands struggling in close-up. The scraping of the sill and the squeaking of metal are deafening.

Finally I open it, grab the kids, and hurl us out. After a few minutes, the father emerges from the gloom and throws himself from the window too.

A Casa: This Too Is Hollywood

I hear the clumsy, insistent jingling of Paleteria Poncho, the ice man, and I wonder if he ever goes to the movies. I look out the window. He's wheeling his white cart down the sidewalk, a red baseball cap covers his eyes. Does a dream unspool for him under the cap's shade? I imagine the ice shushing inside, the bottles of colored syrup clinking against each other. How can he compete with the ice cream trucks? It won't be long now before they come. The upbeat music bleats in my ears, relentless.

Across the street, Father Armenia sits on the stoop, like always. He and his family are crammed into an apartment the size of mine, like clowns in a compact car. I don't know how many there are, but once I heard a cop say Father Armenia had nine sons, and eight should be in jail. The family fixes cars, and is the neighborhood patrol, so I don't have any complaints, even though sometimes they all scream at each other into the night, and other times wrestle on the street. Hard to believe this is the town that spins out all our dreams.

Where I live is called Little Armenia, so I figure I'm a guest of some sort. I live in a white Spanish stucco two-story building, and there's rot around my windowsills, stains from heavy rains that make the walls look weepy. There are cracks in the ceiling with dangling bits of off-white paint that spin around when there's a breeze. It's the natural art of deterioration, a paint chip mobile in progress. Who needs to buy paintings? I've got wood floors, high ceilings, a living room, kitchen, and bath. Not bad for five hundred nine bucks. The rent's gone up since I got here, but slowly. In L.A., it's a bargain.

Across the hall lives Jock Barger, a curmudgeonly actor/carpenter who plays a heavy in *As the World Turns,* and used to hang out with Charles Bukowski he says. He gets my mail when I'm out of town and I bring him back goodies—pistachios from Aegina in Greece, maple syrup from Vermont. He didn't tell me until recently that right before I moved in, three boys were shot outside our building. Two went into the bottlebrush bush and one landed on the lawn. I don't want to hear this, but I do. Living here, I see the eggshell fragility of it all.

Downstairs are the Krafts, Sandrine and Ted. They're the ones who told me about the apartment, five years ago, but I've hardly seen them since. I met her on *The Blond and Naked Angel.* Sandrine is now a big-time casting director. She cast *Dances with Wolves* and is such good buddies with Kevin Costner he gave her a camcorder after the movie was done. I don't know why they still live here, it's pretty much a boheme dive. Is a bargain worth hearing gunshots at night? I don't have a choice, and anyhow I think of the neighborhood as camouflage. Nobody's driving around scoping this street. A little car theft, a one-in-a-million chance of a stray bullet, I'll take those over premeditated break-ins, rape, muggings, murder. It's been quiet lately.

And anyway, I think the building is kind of charmed.

Mike Kelley used to live downstairs, right below me. He's an internationally famous artist now. When he lived here, I never imagined he was headed that way. I looked in his window and was disgusted at the upholstery-fabric curtains, lurid orange and brown swirls, and the painting of a pink penis floating through a muddy, turgid background that was tacked above his couch. His physical appearance wasn't much better. He looked unwashed, his lank dark hair was oily and stringy, his clothes shabby. I never spoke to him except once when he knocked on my door and I opened it. Thanks for folding my laundry, he said with a shy smile. He smelled like rancid butter and laundry lint. I smiled and shook my head. Wasn't me, I said. His face fell. Oh, he said, and walked back down the stairs. Some weeks later I saw him with a bottle blonde, and then he moved. Jock told me he struck it rich. Made the international art scene, got some big bucks, and bought a house. The other thing I remember about Mike Kelley is how he used to play conga drums at all hours, in the room right below my bedroom. I never minded. I remember thinking when the primitive pounding started up, the frenzied joyful slapping of drums, that Mike Kelley wasn't so bad.

After he moved out, I went to one of his shows. It looked a lot like a junkyard stuck in a gallery. One piece disturbed me though, the sock monkeys? He'd sewn two together like they were humping, and set them in the middle of the poured concrete gallery floor.

They looked claustrophobic, caught, and forlorn. Forced into an unfathomable adult act and frozen that way eternally. If Paleteria Poncho were there, he might have torn them apart, swearing, and given them as door prizes to the next boy and girl who bought ices from him. Convert them back from idea to entertainment.

Me, I just take solace in the thought that everything is possible in Los Angeles. Making movies, making monkeys fuck on gallery floors. Some people are stuck, but others break through the limits of their own perception. There's room here on the same street for being so poor you've got to roll a clanking cart full of ices all around town when everyone else is driving just to pay your goddamn bills, or doing your art and suddenly it catches on and you're hot and the world shifts latitudes and you move on into a warmer sea.

Phone Call with a Nineteen-Year-Old Artist Just Out of a Coma

All my paintings say OUTPATIENT on them. They don't take me longer than an hour. The doctors say not to do them, it strains my eyes. That's why I hate doctors. It's my life. Flea just called. We talked about spiders for hours. He's one of the Red Hot Chili Peppers. No, I couldn't even go out with him. One of the other Chili Peppers is married to my ex-stepmom. She's a starfucker. The other day I was eating with her and a friend, and they were talking about Drew Barrymore. Drew this and Drew that. I said, I don't care about Drew Barrymore. Oh, yeah, I need to go out with Flea. A star. Hollywood's gross. I tell people I'm a virgin since my coma. Someone talked about sex the other day and I said, "Ew, you're shocking me." When they told my ex-stepmom I was in a coma, the first thing she said, get this, "Kurt Cobain's in a coma!" My mom's not much better. She called on my birthday and left a message: "I can't believe I gave birth to you twenty years ago." She went on about that for five minutes, then said, "Oh, by the way, Happy Birthday, dear."

Yeah, right.

Passover Hangover, or Revelations and a Leaky Roof

Easter Sunday, rain and a hangover. (Darkness.) You are sitting on the dirty gray couch in the living room, doing nothing. Brown swill pours from cracks in the ceiling to six buckets strategically arranged below. Six five-gallon three-quart containers from Sonstegard Foods in Sioux Falls. These containers used to hold pasteurized whole eggs. Thirty pounds of them. Frozen. You realize this is as close as you'll get to Easter eggs today. Forget yellow-dyed sugar-frosted marshmallow chicks, crunchy bouncy beds of green cellophane grass, or chocolate bunnies wrapped in silver shrouds. Resurrection—of youth, of dreams, of death itself—doesn't come cheap. Maybe it doesn't come at all.

You stare at the labels on the white buckets. They are like epitaphs for a former life. Now these containers are filled with sloshing brown liquid, bilious waves of poisonous rain overflowing on the wood floor that used to be your living room. You want to vomit, but you can't move. If you had an Easter basket within reach, like the ones your mother used to buy from the local drugstore when she wasn't too drunk to remember what day it was, you would chew the head off a marshmallow chick.

The drops quicken. (Hail.) You listen vaguely at the window. It seems, miraculously, to be raining harder inside than out. This minor revelation distracts you only briefly. With every clangorous splash,

28

your stomach clenches. Inside, a cactus sprouts and blooms spines against the stomach walls. The spines retreat, the cactus uproots, thuds dully like a bowling ball against those same stomach walls. Sporadic, involuntary groans. Popped aspirin. Water. More water. It is an overboard weekend, with Passover squashing into Easter. Are you Christian? Or are you Jewish? Are you your mother's daughter? In your throbbing mind, a stuffed pastel bunny rising up from its grave gives way to a singing, dancing matzoh man. Through your hungover haze, you recall the Passover dinner of last night. The rain continues; the suburban seder floods back in. Inexorable. A riptide heralding apocalypse. Scattering all bunnies.

You remember driving down Liberty Lane, the Panorama City residential street where the Katzes live—parents to Anastasia—and not recognizing it. All the neat suburban ranch houses are newly painted, spruced, and pert. Fresh paint. Landscaping. Redone driveways. Motorized garage doors. Bright trim. Shiny gutters. You think there is a kind of dignity in dust, in faded paint and rutted drives, in lawns that speak of footprints, in roofs that hold in years of absorbed sunlight, smog, dandelion fuzz. Now the street is strictly Disney. Post-earthquake renovations. A sort of resurrection? And yet, you ponder, the neighborhood is Jewish.

Mrs. Katz, who greets you at the door in an apron printed with tumbling parsley sprigs, tells you all the women in the neighborhood are inviting each other to tea, each week a different house, to show off renovations. Hers is not done yet, but soon. Then she too will invite the women over. You enter where you used to bask in bland comfort. (Mrs. Katz is not your mother.) Things have changed.

No longer lived-in, the house is awash in sterile white paint, ominous pools of track lighting. The couches are reupholstered, stiff and crisp in muted mauves and peaches. The walls are bare and the chairs all match. Your brain hurts. The Katzes, Anastasia, and seven other guests blur into the sucking white background. You have to pry them away with great diligence. Restore them to three dimensions. At the table, everyone collapses again into cardboard facsimiles. Only when you stuff your mouth with a horseradish matzoh sandwich, and the stinging tears spring to your eyes, do you experience relief. Perhaps you are still flesh and blood, after all.

Nobody knows Hebrew. Including you. To maintain your necessary stupor, you sip more cherry Manischewitz, even when the Haggadah doesn't call for it; you do this surreptitiously at first, then with increasing abandon. The bright white walls are making you crazy. She was crazy, your mother. You are all seated around a table, many tables pushed together, covered with white cloth already stained with wine and food. One of the guests, the resident twenty-something, or is he the "stranger" called for in Jewish custom, shouts out the *Dayenu!* lines in good loutish Beavis & Butthead style, throwing the comfy room into a spin. You know she was crazy. Only Manischewitz rinses your mind, your palate, your unsatisfied craving for ritual, ceremony, even meaning. Your mother's blood. Is there any in these starched walls that used to sport long, jagged quake cracks, reminders of our fragility, tenuousness, stupidity?

Everything is too large, too tight, too bright, too. You don't fit. You know this. You are a pathetic pawn. The only god you know is the one your landlord told you to talk to when you complained about the floods coursing through your home. Is there a god on the fault lines, at the seder table? Why was she so plagued? Perhaps if you drain the entire bottle of cherry Manischewitz wine, drown yourself in sweetness, you will find at the bottom, with the dregs, not a dream-picked worm MESCAL (working its way through the freeways, through the fault lines, through the blue-glowing tubes that burn up every window), but a particle of god, even if it's only the memory that god, way back, even in Los Angeles, did once exist. And might take pity on your restless mother, if not you.

Happiness

A man takes a shit on the Saint James Hotel steps.

I watch him from my car. I am at a stoplight on the Sunset Strip. It is midday. His pants are down around his ankles. The shit coils out of his ass and onto the steps. The pile is a light caramel color. It is a cold day for L.A. and so his ass is pink and cheery. Like a baby's bottom. He has a beard, mustache, and a full head of scruffy hair. He has empty bowels.

What gets me though is the smile on his face. It's genuine. A smile of pure satisfaction. He's not looking at anyone. He's not shitting on the steps of the posh Saint James Hotel for attention. Or fame. Or fortune. Or even political reasons, like fuck fancy hotels, or fuck the government for not providing the homeless with sanitation facilities and roofs over their heads. It's simpler. This man needed to take a shit. Right now.

I walked into the *Invasion from a Dark Planet* art department to pick up the production designer's list of set dressing I had to seek and buy—futuristic lunchpails, Martian bedsheets, extraterrestrial dinnerware—and there was a man built like a Roman gladiator strapped into a pale green dentist's chair, his face covered in plaster, bald head gleaming. Three long-haired special effects guys were slathering gunk on his face. From up close I saw it was Helmut Grosskopf.

All that muscle like a comic book hero. I feasted my eyes on him. Best thing was he couldn't see me. Two women stood by, a couple of graphic artists in frumpy clothes with lined faces, freeze-dried hair. He'd closed his eyes with them in front of him, but when the mask was done, he was going to open his eyes on Rebecca Roth, production slave, decked out in snugfit jeans and a clingy T-shirt, hair gelled and shpritzed into a curly gold mane. Everyone knows he's a big flirt. I decided to play bimbo.

"Okay, Helmut," said Joe Blasky, his fingers flying over Helmut's square-jawed face, packing and molding and smoothing, "it'll only take three minutes to set this mask, then we got one more."

Helmut didn't say anything; he couldn't. But when the assistants popped two nostril holes in the fast-drying plaster, Helmut exhaled a bull snort of a breath and his massive chest heaved. I thought of my mini-refrigerator shuddering and shaking, exhaling gusts of frozen air.

Helmut was no grander than my kitchenette.

"Two minutes and counting," said Blasky.

I skated on those minutes, ran my gaze over every inch of the sedentary movie star's casually dressed body, from his cooking-stove-broad shoulders, long bulky arms, square-fingered hands big as skillets, to lobster-pot-lidlike pecs, cast-iron-tight abdomen apparent beneath a dishwater gray T-shirt, circled around his sweatpants-swathed crotch, and then, wondering if steroids had damaged the goods and hoping they had, I looked across those vast muttonous expanses of thigh, over those mountainous knees and down those rounded calves, down down down to his extra-wide duck-yellow canvas Docksiders: the tattoos of a neo-conservative. I heard he went to a wedding of a former Nazi war general, and unveiled his gift— a monstrous bronze statue of the general and his wife in lederhosen. Austrians. Worse than Germans.

"Remember to wrinkle your nose," said Blasky. "This is for the scene when you're inserting the miniature scanner up through your nostril and into your brain, so you've got to really contort your face"—Helmut wrinkled up his nose and raised his lips into a snarl of concentrated agony—"that's it!" said Blasky, while the two assistants rinsed their hands off in a bucket of water and wiped them dry with a towel. "Okay, one minute and counting."

I'd seen Helmut a couple of times before in the Max Factor building, briefly, always an imposing presence with his rock-hewn good looks, booming baritone voice, money-oiled charm, and bold, bright jackets of dazzling plum or electric blue, snazzy Italian shoes, and baggy silk trousers. He was definitely larger than life. Definitely immune to ethics. But this opportunity to watch Helmut for an uninterrupted stretch of time and him so deliciously vulnerable, well—

"Okay, Helmut, last one coming up," Joe said as the two assistants carefully pulled the mask from Helmut's face and placed it delicately on a paper-towel-lined shelf of the cart. Helmut blinked.

"Next one's simple. Just a straight face."

Helmut was looking at me. Eyes wide open. I grinned. Spar With The Star.

"Who are you?" he said, tight smile. "Where did you come from?"

So his Austrian accent was no put-on. It was thick as congealing schnitzel, each vowel bitten into, ripped off like crust on a baguette.

"I work here," I said, moistening my lips. "With Dan Wolf."

"Oh, ho," Helmut said, nodding his head, eyes over my body. "Dan's a good friend of mine. A wildman."

Blasky leaned over nervously. Time mattered. He had to finish his job or it would be his head blown to flesh-colored fireballed smithereens. He whispered in Helmut's ear, "We're almost ready," but Arnold waved him away.

"We met in Rome," I said, "Dan and I."

"My man Dan," Helmut said. His teeth were white as peeled garlic cloves, his cheekbones flat and fine as the polished teak of my salad bowl, his face flushed as a freshly washed plate. I knew, however, I was looking at yet another mask. The question was could I get beneath this one. I would use an ancient crowbar—cleavage. Helmut looked directly at mine. "We have fun in Vancouver. What were you doing in Rome?"

"Living," I said.

I don't think the two graphic artists were even breathing, at least I didn't hear anything. It was just me and Helmut, Helmut and me, carving out an electric playpen for that brief moment in time. Emphasis on brief. The idea was to make the encounter as brilliant as a spark-spraying jewel-bright fountain of fireworks before it faded back into the sky's nothingness. Those were my rules.

"What did you think of the Italian men," Helmut said, leaning forward slightly, his gaze lingering on my legs.

"Pussies," I said.

The two women gasped. Blasky busied himself with the drying mask, the tortured one. Helmut let out a hearty laugh.

"Neanderthals. They live with their mothers until they're fifty. I don't like," I said, "to be with men I can toss around."

Now Helmut strained his hands against the wrist ties with an exaggerated grimace.

"I wish I wasn't strapped in," he said, winking. "Can't you get me out of here?" he said to Blasky, who smiled wanly. The two assistants looked expectantly at their boss, holding the ready-to-dry-fast plaster. The boss gave an imperceptible nod "no" of his head.

"What's your name? Where are you from?"

"Rebecca Roth. I'm from all over."

"I mean, where were you born? What nationality?"

"Well"—I paused for effect, the Docksiders gleaming up at me with the insistence of egg yolks—"I was born in Jerusalem. Israel."

Now it was Helmut's turn to pause. His eyes gleamed, quickened, and seemed to pierce mine. Yellow-tipped coronas seemed to flare out around either iris, miniature solar eclipses behind the dark pupils. For that moment, the eyes no longer fit the mask that was Helmut's face. I imagined a carnival painting of Grosskopf's body on plywood with the hole where the head would be; instead of Helmut's mug, someone else's had just popped through—someone unknown. And ugly. "So you're Jewish, you don't look Jewish. Dan's Jewish."

"Yes."

"I'm Austrian, you know, a real Österreicher." Helmut swelled his neck and puffed out his chest, glancing sidelong at me—no trace of yellow flaring remained. It was back to pumped-up smarm. But I'd seen. He knew I'd seen. And I knew it excited him. It repulsed me.

"Yes," I said, pleased at having caused Helmut Grosskopf to pause. To acknowledge, even for a moment, the existence of an Other. Stars weren't used to average people dealing with them straight on, and I knew they were hungry for it, and often willing to play—or pay—but to actually penetrate their glittering eye-blinding ego-wrapping armor was always a coup. If they asked anything about you, well, that was no small victory. When you actually threw them off balance, made them reveal a private deformity, you knew you'd won a battle.

"What do you think of men in Hollywood?" he asked, and I think, but I couldn't be sure, I think he twitched his left pec. Was this a variation on the standard wink? Helmut had retreated into the role of woman charmer.

"On the whole they're not much better than the Italians," I said. "Maybe it's a man thing."

Helmut, I could see, did not get my meaning. Blasky leaned in.

"Last mask," he said, with a voice of composed pleading, and Helmut nodded once, leaned back into the pale green dentist's chair with his enormous snap-crackling dark eyes on me. The eyes of a would-be predator.

"Don't move," Helmut said to me. "I will be right back."

The two assistants positioned themselves on either side of Helmut's face like sentinels. Helmut waited until the last second to close his eyes.

"Two minutes to go, Helmut. You're a trooper," said Blasky. Helmut wagged a carrot-sized finger, but he wagged it straight forward, where I had been standing. Blasky shot me a dirty look, but I was busy studying Helmut. My specimen in straps.

His nostrils were like a bellows, his chest an impossibly smooth carving of two tortoiseshells rising and falling in the surf of his skin and T-shirt. He was an ego waiting to be stroked. With less than one minute to go, I did it, I touched Helmut, reached out and laid my hand on Helmut's leg.

His thigh quivered and jumped under my touch. The silky material steamed against my fingertips, heated by his humbled flesh.

Helmut unmasked.

Playing with stars as a peon is a dangerous pastime. With thirty seconds to go and counting, I slid out the door of the art department the way I'd come. I had another job to do. I was off to search out props for the movie's Martian laborers.

Fuori a Casa: My Anastasia

Late one afternoon I walk my friend Anastasia outside to her car after one more debauched Hollywood night out. She's spaced because she drank wine that doesn't mix with lithium, but I don't tell her what to do anymore. I try to give her dignity. We're moving in slow-motion and so is the man coming toward us. He is old, Slavic I think. Maybe Latvian. He wears socks and sandals, drab shirt and pants of indeterminate yellowish-whitish-grayish colors. Nothing to look at, except he walks so slowly, so deliberately, and then I see a large bright green thing moving up his leg and I think I'm hallucinating and that maybe I should cut down on the drink. I'm so fried.

At first it looks like a monstrous cicada, a grasshopper that's eaten Food of the Gods or radioactive garbage and turned mutant. Then the green moves up onto the man's shoulder and I see it is a parrot. Bright green with a throat of pure orange flame. A beauty.

The man pays no attention to me or Anastasia, even though we've stopped to watch—silence is a tacit understanding. All his attention is bound up in this tiny tropical creature that now picks its way down his arm, gentle clutchings in the fabric with her delicate black feet. Then I see the parrot flutter down and jaunt along the sidewalk, and how the man bends slowly, stiffly, down to her level to coax and compliment. I do not hear any sounds come from his mouth, but I see the way he follows this bird streaking tropical paradise and sassy promise along the broken sidewalk, I see the way he offers his bony finger up to her and she takes it, daintily, prettily, preens for a moment, then walks back up his arm to nestle on his collarbone, and I know when I see love. I put my arm around Anastasia's shoulder.

The gunshots we heard last night are forgotten. Anastasia is a frequent overnight couch guest when we've both been partying and staying out too late for her to drive home. A true Valley girl, born and raised in Panorama City on Liberty Lane, she was always the one in the photos who stared dark and unseeing with her left lazy eye wandering beyond the photographer while her parents and three brothers smiled pretty for the picture. Anastasia was the one who clenched her fists when the flash went off, the one who wore black in grade school, refused to comb her hair, the one who locked herself in the bathroom for privacy hours at a time and blocked her ears to her father's squealing violin, the one who painted lidless eyeballs with acrobatic legs kicking out of the irises. No torsos. No linkage. Not until college where her freshman roommates noted she said she would, but never did, go to any classes. She was sent to the school sanitarium and put on lithium for the first time. That's when her painted figures turned truncated. No heads, no legs, and breasts popping out everywhere—on goldfish, streetlights, trees, fleas.

"Bye, hon," she croons, kissing me on both cheeks, which sets her safety-pinned black sunglasses at an even more awkward angle. "Bye."

"See ya, doll. Be careful driving," I say as she clambers into her dust-caked, ding-pitted Dodge Dart. The bumper is tied up with rope, hangs loose like a dislodged jaw. Inside, a pine tree car freshener swings from the rearview mirror when Anastasia slams the door, catches her coat there, reopens the door and pulls it closed again, folds her left knee up onto the seat and blows me a kiss while the car jerks into first gear, bumps over the curb, and a mound of dirty laundry tumbles to the floor in back and Evian bottles, bags, and books slide to the floor in front, and she's off. A beauty.

A beauty, her cheeks smoothed after a four-thousand-dollar cosmetic treatment, she walked around for days in bandages, her face a tomato-beet-apple hybrid of ruddy bloody reds. My Anastasia sometimes brings out the beast in me, and I hang my head in shame. Sometimes I snap at her for spacing out, for being late, for forgetting, for breaking chairs and plates and smearing butter and knocking over glasses of water on stacks of papers. My mother rides again. Sometimes I scold her about not taking care of herself, being sloppy, being inattentive. These are the times when I see my mother in Anastasia, the mother I cartooned with a frizzy head, cockeyed glasses, bulging out of clothes, beer bottle in one hand and cigarettes in the other, this cartoon that my mother carried with her everywhere, in her wallet, and would show to anyone to prove how much her daughter hated her. "Look what my daughter thinks of me," she'd say and cry. And I would scoff. Disgusted. Oh, that I could be as sweet as Anastasia, sweet and so much softer in the soul, a bubbly champagne night, no loner she, Anastasia teaches me and I try to battle my blackhearted demons as she does hers.

Hollywood?

I dreamed you naked with your back leaned up against a palm tree and your bronzed limbs languishing in the surf at Zuma. All washed in technicolor brilliance. A carnal shellac. You know, wanting to hump this dolphin, that beach babe, a surfer or two. Like, whatever came along, when the stars were all aligned correctly and in accordance with both the daily horoscope and the personal Psychic Friends Network tip, not forgetting 1-800-AVE-MARY who always has a prayer for you that bodes well for another bodacious orgiastic day in the California sun, where depression is outlawed (or heavily medicated) and sex is superficial, flagrant, and mondo delicto.

The Cow Jumped over the Moon

They found a cow on the roof of the Alexandria Hotel in downtown L.A. A dead cow. A dried-out skeleton of what used to be a cow.

They say a group of Satanists used to live in the penthouse. That the cow must have been a sacrifice. Nobody knows for sure.

Think about that cow, taking its first trip into the city from someplace like Chino Valley. Los Angeles used to be cow country. Where people from San Francisco came down and bought cattle for their ranches. People like Jack London. The cow wouldn't know that, but maybe she would.

Imagine what it was like for her, first setting those clackety hooves on the cracked sidewalk. Did she think she was the most civilized cow from her farm? The Chosen Cow. For those few minutes she high-stepped it on the poured concrete. There was a handicap ramp, that was dignified enough, a slow crescendo into the tiled lobby. Not much different from the hillocks she was used to back at the farm. She was all elegance in the lobby. Maybe thinking how glamorous it was to arrive at a hotel in the black belly of night. The lobby empty just for her. Those nice kids patting her haunches and gently tugging on her bridle. She was the lucky one, escaping farm drudgery and daily mechanical squeezing on her teats.

But when they led her to the elevator, that's when she got suspicious. That's when they had to force her trembling flanks into the tiny cube, a fraction the size of a milking stall. Her pink nostrils dilated and her eyes grew large and liquid. A long, lowing MOOOOOOOOOO escaped from her fleshy mouth. A curse if there ever was one. She had meant to say NOOOOOOOOOO. That's when one of the not-so-nice people shoved a rag in her mouth, his eyes darting around the lobby, but there was no one. A thick mass of cud slipped back down the cow's throat and practically choked her.

The elevator started with a jolt. The creaking nearly drove her mad. She tried to kick the person who held the bridle, but it was hard to maneuver. Numbers blinked. Finally she got him in the shin. He groaned and yanked her bridle. The door opened, then closed again and descended.

They waited, the boy and the Sacrificial Cow. She was quiet now, gathering strength in the fluorescent gloom of the hallway. For a moment she even enjoyed the way her hooves sank down in the carpet, and she thought of the fields in Chino Valley. She shook her head, trying to loosen the rag, but the boy shoved it back in her mouth, deeper. With that, she hung her head in despair.

The elevator door opened and the other people filed out. They were carrying lit candles, which frightened her. She danced back and hit the wall, bruising her rump. If Farmer Vandervort were here, he'd knock them all flat. Now the kids raised black hoods over their heads and she could barely see their eyes.

One of them opened a door to a staircase leading up to the roof. The cow knew this because there at the top was a piece of sky, city sky, but familiar all the same.

With a sudden burst of energy she rushed toward the elevator and butted the door. This made her dizzy, and stars wheeled all around the hallway.

"Keep it down out there!" yelled someone from behind a closed door. "Goddamn punks. Or I'll call the police."

"Just doin' some band practice on the roof."

One of the kids grabbed her bridle and pulled her roughly toward the staircase. Another plucked a handful of golden hay from a hidden fold. The cow's eyes gleamed. Maybe that was a farmer who yelled out to them and said what to do. Maybe city people just didn't know how to handle cows. Maybe up on the roof was the greatest, softest, lushest green field of all. With the golden hay glowing ahead and someone tugging on her bridle, she entered the stairwell.

The stairs were narrow. The cow's hooves clattered and slipped. People shoved from behind. The golden handful of hay bobbed just up ahead, and in the doorway the sky shone down, bright with city lights. She stumbled. Heard the snap of a bone. Hot trickle of sticky blood. They pushed harder, pulled harder, until finally the cow stumbled onto the roof.

"What a pain in the fuckin' ass, man. Better kill it first."

There was no grass, but right then the cow didn't mind. She knew she looked splendid in the moonlight, up there so high above it all, higher than any cow had ever been. The city lay beneath her, glittering with promises. Her coat shone white and the black splotches fairly swirled. She held her injured leg daintily on the tar paper and raised her magnificent head. As she did, there was a sharp stinging across her neck, and her eyes swam up to the moon.

The cow fell to her front knees, then back knees. Sharp smell of incense and burning candles made her nostrils quiver. The cow's belly hit the roof, mashing her udder. Scraped teats flared out beneath her crumpled body like bloated fingers. The tar paper was rough, there was gushing all around.

A sharper sting came from the side of her neck. She saw something silver flashing in the night. Drums were beating, they couldn't keep up with her heart, she vomited up the rag, the cud, closed and opened her eyes. There was another sting, her stomach flew up and out her throat and perched on her ears like a silly veil. The moon was clapping, the drums were pieces of her skin, every beat broke another bone, and she was something unnameable, something mysterious and overwhelming.

"How the fuck long does it take for a fuckin' shit cow to kick?"
"Gimme that knife."

The stingings came from everywhere. The sky was in her lap,

the greenest grasses lay heaped on glinting silver trays, the roar of the city poured splashing and shouting into the milk can, a thousand cowtails swatted away flies, a thousand cowslips brushed against her hide, and the nightshade from the beating-down Southern California sun was so delicious the cow thought she might just, maybe just, take a little nap.

But first, she rose to her hooves with a remarkable lightness and dignity, raised her immaculate white neck to the sky, and lowed out a clear and plangent NOOOOOOOOOOOOOOOOOOOOOOOOO.

Then the cow leaped over that big, beautiful dazzle of a moon.

On Not Becoming an Actress

"Are you an actress?"

"You sound just like Jodie Foster."

"You look like, what's her name in *Witness?* Kelly McGillis. Are you?"

"Hey look. It's Linda Hamilton pumping those weights."

"She looks like Shelley Winters. When she was young, I mean. She was pretty then."

I've been onstage as an actress twice: in sixth grade I played the Scarecrow in *The Wizard of Oz* and in ninth grade I played Gloria Upson in *Auntie Mame.* The first time, I wore my mother's clothes, she helped me stuff straw in the sleeves and legs, and I sang "If I Only Had a Brain." Afterward my mother told me my singing was so-so. She said my voice was thin.

Years later when I was living with another family, I got the part of Gloria Upson, a snotty uptight rich bitch with a mind as shallow as the surf of the Jersey shore. My big moment in the play was a rant about a Ping-Pong match. Each guffaw from the audience seemed to lift and buoy me above the stage. I didn't mind the boys' attention either.

I could feel the heat wafting up to me on the stage, under those hot white lights, feel the boys' eyes on me, my calves, my ass, my tits, my blond hair and lipsticked mouth, I knew they were hot for me and I loved it.

In Hollywood, they asked if I was an actress. "Me?" I'd say, shaking my head, waving my hand at their words like they were flies. But at night, at parties, at clubs, at dinners, at discos, I spoke different. With my clothes, my energy, I was making a hungry easy plea for attention. I was playing sexy with a sharp tongue, but all I wanted was to be loved, truly, deeply, and if not, then hotly desired because the initial sensation is almost the same, even though it doesn't last.

The truth is, my hair without weaving strands of gold and honey and ultrablond and winter wheat and ash blond in every six weeks or so is the color of old oatmeal, the kind of mush that's lain untouched in a bowl since six A.M. and now it's time for dinner. Pale and dull and flat and drained of all golden dreams, that is the real state of my locks.

The truth is, nobody escapes vanity here, or shallow dreams or basest desires. Nobody.

Things She Learned
in Therapy

After Rebecca's first abortion she went to a therapist. She chose the Feminist Women's Clinic because it was in a mini-mall, nestled between Flamin' Chicken and The Knitting Nook at the corner of Pico and Sepulveda—a twenty-minute drive from where she lived on South Detroit Street. BARBARA HART, M.F.C.C., INCEST AND ABUSE SPECIALIST was what the bronze placard nailed to the door read, and when Rebecca saw it she almost turned around and left.

Instead, the first thing Rebecca did was ask how low Barbara Hart could go on a sliding-scale fee. Rebecca said she hoped her case was arresting enough that it would be worth shaving some of the cost. In fact, this was something Rebecca was counting on. They agreed on thirty-five dollars an hour.

Rebecca told Barbara Hart her life story the way she'd told it so many times before—fast and funny, detached and tough. Same as always. In a way the story now bored Rebecca; it was too long and too complicated. In a way it excited her and she liked to see people's reactions. In a way it didn't seem like her story at all, but someone else's entirely. When she finished telling the story, she felt a mild relief, like after clipping her toenails, or getting a postcard from a friend. She also felt a mild disgust and impatience with the tediousness of the story, and the necessity to lay it out like a blueprint just to get the parameters down when she preferred to dwell on details; the short version offended her sense of storytelling.

It bothered Rebecca to bring up her mother with Barbara Hart who looked so bovine and maternal with her large bone structure, caftan-style dress, and limpid eyes.

Rebecca did go back and fill in one detail when she was done. She said her first memory was of sitting in a rocking chair in her mother's lap in the apartment on the Upper West Side in New York City when she was about three. They were back from Israel where Rebecca was born, the marriage was falling apart, and her father was "away" again. Rebecca asked her mother when Daddy was coming home. Her mother said she didn't know. Rebecca leaned forward and said, "Just as I was about to cry, my mother started crying. So I didn't. I told my mother, 'Mommy, don't cry.'"

Barbara Hart nodded as if she understood.

"That's why I fell in love with Isaac," Rebecca said. Everyone agreed he was the hottest guy on campus, but that wouldn't have been enough.

"I knew he was fucked-up," Rebecca said. When they met, he was studying French literature and acting. Though students praised his performances, chattered about them excitedly in the dining halls and under the Gothic stone arches, Isaac complained he didn't love acting, didn't care about it, didn't care about anything. Sometimes Rebecca would find Isaac, the night before he had a French lit paper due, sitting in his apartment, naked and cross-legged on the bed, staring vaguely out the window and blowing occasional squeaky notes on a harmonica.

She told him how talented he was, she discussed theater, tried to get him excited, poked and prodded to discover what interested him. Isaac told her he'd fallen for her smile long before he'd met her. "You're full of light," he said, and Rebecca glowed. Isaac was dark— the son of a former Black Panther turned real estate agent and a French model—and looked Puerto Rican with his black curls, brown eyes, and teakwood skin—but he was also dark of mind, tormented. "I'm so chill with you," Isaac would say to her—in bed, on the dance floor, in the library, on the street. She was able to make him happy.

"Does this make sense?" she asked Barbara Hart who nodded with a sad smile.

When Isaac moved in with her in L.A., he was listless. She would come home from work to find him fiddling with radio stations and eating Corn Pops. He wasn't able to make any calls to modeling agencies, job leads, or even friends. Rebecca had to make the calls or they never got done. The only person he saw was a gay out-of-work actor down the hall. They played KDAY, danced, smoked pot, and talked about Athol Fugard. The apartment manager called Rebecca at work to complain about noise Isaac made during the day. Once the manager came to the door to tell him to turn down the music and he opened it naked. Didn't even stop dancing. Women he met at supermarkets, diners, and used bookstores called the apartment looking for him and when Rebecca objected, Isaac refused to tell them to stop. Then he got a job waiting tables at Toi, an all-night Thai restaurant on Sunset. He worked the nightshift so he and Rebecca hardly saw each other anymore. She would come home from *ET*, drive him to work, he'd come back at six A.M. and be sleeping when she left for *ET* in the morning. After he got the job, he convinced Rebecca to buzz-cut her hair, complained about her weight, and asked her why she didn't wear lingerie like the women he saw at Toi. She wasn't a complainer. Rebecca never told him she faked the orgasms.

The possibility edged into Rebecca's mind that it didn't matter what she did. This idea was like a monkey wrench, tightening her love further down its spiraling thread until she couldn't imagine being apart from Isaac. Panic gripped her when Isaac complained about HelL.A., his name for the city, and mentioned wanting to visit his college friend in Tucson where the hippies still ranged. Then the diaphragm slipped and Rebecca got pregnant. With the first surge of nausea came an insight; Isaac wasn't in love with her. Rebecca kicked him out. She didn't tell Barbara Hart how that tortured her, nor did she tell that she had gotten pregnant right when a split between them was imminent. She certainly didn't tell Barbara Hart how much she had wanted to stay with Isaac and have their child. He was no good for her, but she knew she was good for him.

Barbara Hart was very pregnant herself. She told Rebecca she was due in a month and hoped that wouldn't be a problem. She talked about how she'd been an abused child too and how wonderful it was to be able to have a baby of her own after all that. Rebecca didn't say so, but she thought having a pregnant therapist who was happy about having a family was a positive sign, and that she should continue to see her.

At the end of the first meeting, Barbara Hart gave Rebecca a book for survivors of child abuse. On the cover was a black-and-white photo of a doll with ragged yarn hair, a limp arm, and one shattered glass eye. The doll was pictured at an angle so it seemed to be flying off the edge of the book cover. After looking momentarily at the cover, Rebecca handed the book back.

"I'm not interested in reading this," she said, thinking Barbara Hart hadn't paid close attention. "I don't consider myself a survivor of abuse, and I don't like the photo."

That week Rebecca went swimming at the YMCA every day after work, no matter how late. She checked the time on the wall clock, slipped off the concrete edge into the pool, and swam exactly eighty-eight laps for one mile. Arms like fan propellers, hands like grain scoops, she cut through the cool chlorinated blue, legs churning. Sometimes she imagined the yarn doll chasing behind and she swam even faster. The black rubber stripe at the bottom of the pool rooted her in the water. Without this marker, she didn't see well and would veer off and bump swimmers in other lanes. While she swam she heard Barbara Hart: "What we call this is emotional abuse." "Don't you see you're not your mother?" "You are a survivor." Only when she hit the tiled wall on her eighty-eighth lap, rose up out of the pool, and checked the clock did her mind finally bleach free.

Then there were the memories that sprouted like weeds at the strangest times. Once as she was removing a can of Hawaiian macadamia nuts from a pyramid SPECIAL! display at Trader Joe's, she heard again a phone call with her mother from years ago. When they weren't living together anymore, Rebecca had called to tell her mother she made honor roll in junior high and won a first-place ribbon at a diving meet. "That's nice," Rebecca's mother said, "but it's all external. Don't forget you're fucked-up inside." The clatter of the phone hitting the plastic cradle crashed in her ears at Trader Joe's, but then it turned into the rattle of wobbly shopping-cart wheels.

Another time she was lying on her futon missing Isaac. Light streamed in across her body, and she again saw Isaac's penis swelling in the sun on the mattress at Caltech where they'd stayed on his arrival in L.A., the splendor of his naked body, and his refusal to make love when she dropped a chain of kisses down his abdomen. "I'm just watching," he'd said, pointing at his solar-inspired erection.

The second meeting with Barbara Hart, Rebecca said, "I hate the way you look. I hate that you're pregnant. I'm afraid you're too soft and solicitous and weak to help me." She didn't tell Barbara Hart that her mother had been completely different. Rebecca's mother had looked like a bohemian cowgirl. She had muscled arms, she smoked Salems, drank cheap wine and beer, dressed her frizzy hair with Afro-sheen, wore Levi's jeans and Hanes T-shirts and old cowboy boots, and drove a pickup truck; she knew all about Italian Renaissance art, Martin Luther King, and Native American rights; she gave Rebecca *Playboy* to read as a kid and took her to see *Klute* at the drive-in before she was out of elementary school. Why should Rebecca listen to someone like Barbara Hart?

Halfway through the second session, Rebecca had to grab a Kleenex from the table between them and blot her eyes. She held the thin white wad of tissue in her fist, then buried it in her voluminous purse next to the Filofax and makeup bag and battered copy of *Day of the Locust*.

"You're sad," said Barbara Hart. "Why?"

"I'm not sad. I'm pissed I even have to go to a therapist," Rebecca said, balling her hands into fists and planting them on her thighs. "Isn't it enough I lived a fucked-up childhood? I hate spending time on this. If I'd had another family I wouldn't have to deal with all this bullshit."

Bullshit like seventh grade, when her mother stayed in bed all day drinking sixes of Miller, dozing, and flipping through Linda Goodman's *Sun Signs*. She didn't even get it together to take Rebecca to the bus so Rebecca kept missing school. "I can't be a mother right now," her mother said in a sober moment. "I need a break." Bullshit like her mother's side of the family refusing to take Rebecca in for being half Jewish and her father's side refusing because she was half Gentile. She finally got sent to New Jersey to her Orthodox Jewish father. After a few weeks with her there, he put an ad in the *Plainfield Ledger* newspaper:

WANTED: BOARDING SITUATION
FOR THIRTEEN-YR.-OLD GIRL
IN PLAINFIELD VICINITY

A kid in school came up with the newspaper open to the ad and showed it to her. "That you?"

Rebecca scanned it quickly. "Yeah," she said nonchalantly, rolling her eyes to suggest how ridiculous she thought the ad was, how embarrassing, yet how little it bothered her. She didn't let on it was the first she'd heard of the ad.

A family named the Jacksons answered the ad. There was a mother, a father, three children altogether, but only two kids still at home. Both were older than Rebecca. She went to live with them.

She told Barbara Hart: "I was called to the school office," said Rebecca. "I knew something was wrong. Not only did I rarely see him, I didn't have a dentist appointment." Rebecca got in her father's white Electra 225 that was parked in front of Orange Avenue Middle School on January 1, 1977. Before he could say a word, Rebecca knew: had a vision of her mother hanging from a rope, cracked cowboy boots sweeping the floor.

"That must have been hard for you."

"Yeah," said Rebecca. She didn't tell Barbara Hart that every New Year's Eve, she talked with her mother, tried to calm her uneasy spirit. Nor did she tell Barbara Hart that most of the time she was seeing her mother in the faces of random Los Angelenos.

That night after the second session, Rebecca couldn't stop pacing the tiny apartment on South Detroit Street. Something hot and fierce was beating against her forehead. It wasn't often that she cried in public, and she was humiliated about breaking down in front of Barbara Hart. She sat on the futon and stared at the black bowler hanging on the hat rack. She and Isaac had bought that hat together in an antique store in Providence before they'd left for California. Isaac had left the hat behind when he moved to Tucson. Isaac, the volatile son of a mixed marriage, the lit crit/thespian who called her Rio Ojos, and said she looked like a statue of a Polynesian princess. Isaac, the first man she ever told she loved; Isaac, the man who could have been father to their child. As she stared, the hat rose above the hat rack, hovered lower, and there was Isaac, standing tall grinning in his muscle shirt, suspenders, baggy pants, and bare feet.

His grin was a leer, a feral baring of teeth, a slow dissolving of flesh until all that was left was the bone-white hilarity of a grinning skull. Stripped of its fleshy red gate, the teeth and jaw were terrible. Isaac was terrible. Bones were mutinous. To kiss was a gesture in futility. A delay tactic. A falsehood. Rebecca's hands rose up; she pressed her cheekbones, palpating treacherous skin. It was like this, with her hands squeezed tight around her face, mashing the lips into a useless beak, that Rebecca closed her eyes and vowed not to go back to therapy.

Intruder

Beeep.

"Barrio Insaaaane West Side Temple Street Gaaaaang. We're wat ching you. We're wat ching you, we seeeee you, seeeee what you doooooo. We're the Insaane Chicanos from L.A., from the streets of L.A. We're baad motherfuckers, that's what we aaaare. They call me Cyclooone, 'cause sometimes I'm craaaazy. I'ma fuck you in the asssss . . . so you don't have babiesssss . . . bitch. 'Cause I'm a punk, I deliver, suck my big dick, my di negra."

When I got this phone message, it was one of the times I was glad Slim was a former Hell's Angel hanger-on, convicted felon, ex-junkie, alcoholic hothead. I wanted to think he'd know what to do.

Cyclone's words echoed. Paranoia set in. I was being watched. Marked for rape, murder, dismemberment. I listened to the message once, twice, thrice. Saw my heart blow up to monster size. Heard it pound out sound like those gargantuan Japanese drums that span twenty feet in diameter.

So you don't have babiessssss. Boom boom. Boom boom. Beat of heart, bullet time.

My apartment was no longer safe. I saw bullets whistling through my windows, through my door, through the walls. A great wind of bullets, a roar of rushing air bringing dead bodies on its back. I saw feet smashing through the door and footsteps falling falling on my fallen body. A cyclone winding circular round my body until I was surrounded. Ravaged. Dead. Somebody was out to get me.

I grabbed my bag, left the apartment, crashed at my friend Carla's. The next day Slim arrived in town for a week of gigs. Even in daylight, my apartment was nothing but a setting for death. One message had transformed it into a cursed place. Defiled. Invaded. Hostile.

Slim listened to the message. He scowled at me, as if I was a naïf and he was King of the Streets. I wanted to believe. I wanted a protector.

"He doesn't know you, got nothing specific. Showing off. How 'bout I go down there and kill him."

"Huh?"

"Easy. West Side Temple Street, Cyclone. Stupid motherfucker, leaving his street. I'll cut his throat. I'll cut his nuts off. Teach him a lesson, that fucker. Fuck with my woman."

"Really, it's okay. I'll just change my number."

Slim grumbled, but promised he wouldn't kill Cyclone if I didn't want him to. "I'll take care of it." He said the same thing when I got a parking ticket. Months later I found the ticket balled up in the back of my car. I had to pay a penalty on top of the fine.

Brutality of a Dead Bouquet

Yellow tulips, pink and white snap-dragons, sweet-smelling white nasturtiums, purple wildflowers, a hot-pink Gerber daisy wound with green wire to keep it straight. All dead now. The stems scummed and mucked with green rot.

To me there is enough brutality in folding a dead bouquet in half and stuffing it into the garbage. Rotten scent of decaying stems and moldering petals, leaves. Death of sentiments, transience of time and love. All the petals flake and fall from the once-yellow once-tulips.

To me, there is enough brutality here. The six o'clock news, chalk-marked outlines of bodies, and gruesome on-the-scene snap-shots put me over the edge, over the soft lip of hope and into the mouth of despair. Or terror. Or overwhelming nausea.

Yellow #3

At Pane E Vino, my young Australian philosopher friend Arthur discussed the topic of his dissertation while the two of us ate dinner.

"To say a color is dispositional is to say an object is colored solely in virtue of a disposition to bring about a color experience. For a postbox to be red or have redness, it gives us a red experience."

"You saying colors have moods?"

Arthur shakes his head mournfully and moves his fork toward my ravioli. I hit his hand away from the bowl. Arthur's one of those who sneaks bits of food off your plate if you're not careful, as if the food on his own plate is far inferior, even if it's the same dish.

"I knew I shouldn't bring up this philosophy stuff. It's in bad taste, huh? Boring."

"Come on, Arthur."

"That girl never called me. 'Single White Female, 30ish, tall and elegant. Hates Wile E. Coyote. Into saltwater taffy and late-night spooning. Sarcastic.'"

"It was the taffy. You didn't say you liked taffy."

"Wouldn't pay to get ruffled over rejections from ads in the paper, would it?"

"What color experience is that?" I say. I don't notice Arthur until he's already stabbed one of my raviolis.

"I just wanted to bonk," he said. "You need more."

Arthur pours me another glass of wine. A pale Chardonnay. He taps the glass with his finger so it pings.

"A glass is fragile, even if we don't drop it," he says. "That's disposition. Dispositional properties are not reduceable to light waves or molecular structure, they're different from size and shape. There's an underlying mysterious property. Aristotle said yellow-colored objects appeared to be gold."

"I *knew* it. The Hand of God, right?" Or Giorgio's Invisible Hand.

"You mean the soccer metaphor?"

"Huh?"

"When Maradona headed a spectacular goal, only they say he scored with his hand, not his head. Ref didn't see it, but reporters did. They said the Hand of God was with Maradona. Sad, huh? Great player, but no Pele."

"I didn't mean soccer."

Now the young philosopher was soaking up a rim of sauce with a bread crust. I batted his hand away again.

"There is a mystery, that's what attracted me to color in the first place. We have two perceptual systems, did you know that? Cones for color and daytime vision, and rods for achromatic nighttime vision. Chickens have only cones, that's why they go to sleep at night. And owls, they have the rod system."

"So are you saying owls can't see yellow, and since owls are known to be wise, then seeing yellow is connected to foolishness? Or owls are evil, witch familiars, and they can't see yellow because it's good."

Arthur shrugs his shoulders and leans back in his chair. The ravioli is gone. So is the sauce. There is only a white bowl in front of me. Wiped clean and without history.

"Not to worry," Arthur says with a smile. "The ravioli never existed."

Fontana Blues

I was hired because I liked fairy tales, and I was fired because I didn't have maternal instincts.

Stavros Papadakis was his name.

The job was to read his scripts, discuss them, prepare him for pitch meetings, help launch his green-lighted project at Angel's Flight Pictures, keep him organized, take care of phones, appointments, occasional groceries, and all-around general lackey work. Four hundred fifty a week. My life as a slave, continued.

"You're my assistant, you're supposed to be thinking so hard about me you read my mind," he hissed.

My life as a lowly disciple, part whatever.

At first I worked at Stavros's Studio City house. A skin of dead leaves covered the kidney-shaped pool. Inside, marijuana smoke suffused the air. Roaches littered the tables and carpet. Lots of candles, stuck in their own wax, twisty candelabras hung with crystals that winked in the smog-wrapped Valley sun. Chicken bones lying in greasy cardboard coffins. Empty Chinese food cartons.

Stavros never mentioned his mother. And I learned quickly not to mention anything about my own life.

Slave trade. Blank the eyes so they reflect the master. Beg occasional lashes so the blood keeps circulating near the surface. Ignore, deny, minimize the past that casts a pall over every movement. Obeisance. Concentrate on bruises, the way hurt radiates outward like a mandala carved in skin. Absorb angry words like a blood-soaked cloth. Mere drapery for other people's desires. Give up hope.

Early on he said the assistant before me tried to sue him for cheating her out of a co-writer credit on some script.

"You believe that? We were sleeping together and she got sore because I met Tanya. That's what really happened, she was trying to get back at me. Yeeeeaaaah. Teach me to trust people. No more writing partners."

"Don't worry," I said, "I don't mix business with personal." Stavros looked crestfallen and went back to scribbling and shredding paper.

Sometimes what the masters say they desire is not so. Read between the lines, behind the lips that lie. Often they want denial of consummation. Steadily feeding the possibility, stoking it with advances and retreats. In a muted state of arousal the dance takes place. It's all part of the bargain.

Stavros had a sneaky, manic voice; urgent, full of gravel and smoke.

When he spoke to impress or seduce he worked himself into a frenzy, like Yosemite Sam doing a story pitch. He mesmerized Bob Redford's development staff at Wildtime Studios. Otherwise Stavros's words came at you like Mack trucks thrumming on a narrow road, and you couldn't dodge them if you tried.

I went on location with Stavros to Fontana, where we were shooting *The Blond amd Naked Angel*. It was about a kid who's led around by his pecker like a mule chasing a carrot, and was based on Stavros's autobiography as a swashbuckling handsome Greek-American youth, the first biker Beat poet ever in Fontana. It was starring River Phoenix, who was on the verge of major stardom and still an innocent. Still alive.

Stavros took to carrying a mini-crystal in his pants pocket in Fontana. If he forgot or misplaced it, I caught Hell.

"I NEED THAT CRYSTAL. Don't you understand the creative needs of a director? You've got to read my mind. Concentrate."

Stavros was nervous enough to get superstitious. He hadn't directed a movie for over a decade, after being blacklisted for *Midnight Believers*. Enter the crystal.

He gave sixteen-year-old star River Phoenix a larger crystal, although I noticed it was more opaque than Stavros's. Outside the elevator they joked about the size of their crystals. Boys.

Monologue by Stavros at an Italian restaurant over soggy gnocchi with pesto sauce:

"Lemme tell you about Tanya. Tanya was beautiful from far away and not so beautiful from close up. In the beginning my consuming goal was to rinse the thick makeup from her face. She was either the sweetest hausfrau ever or a raging drunk. Drove me nuts. When I refused to marry her, she left and married someone else, a filthy rich guy, Jack Dupont. Then there was an accident. Jeep flipped over and her husband was killed. Tanya's teeth were mashed back into her head. Terrible. She arrived at my house the night she got out of the hospital in a diaphanous pink shimmering robe. She stepped out of a limo with a bottle of champagne, looking kind of like Frankenstein, but beautiful in that pink robe, and I kept thinking, she won't be able to eat with her teeth like that and in a few months she'll be the most beautiful, slender woman. We fucked. I was determined not to come but she felt so good and then she said, 'Jack is here, you feel just like Jack,' and I came (he snaps his fingers) like THAT, and I knew she was pregnant and Jack would be REBORN. Gee, I should be embarrassed telling this story, but I'm not. Am I?"

Right before shooting began, Stavros went to New York for the weekend. I was one month pregnant, by Carter Lang, a guy I'd met in Al's Bar. In the midst of all the smoke and small talk he was reading Don DeLillo's *White Noise*. No one reads at Al's Bar, or in Los

Angeles for that matter. "Whatcha reading?" I said. We began an affair and I found out he was recently divorced and raw. He used to say to me, "Those lips, those eyes, that nose," but I was never sure whether he meant me or the ex-wife-to-be. He also said this: "I can tell you've been hurt in your life. Badly." This observation struck me then as almost psychic, and as such was both appealing and repellent. My defensive armor was so thick I fooled myself, thinking no one could see what was plainly obvious. Even in my youthful confusion, I knew the Carter Lang affair was a bubble in the soap dish of life. I never told him I was pregnant.

But I was, and righteously nauseous. Stavros's slovenliness repulsed me more than ever. I was thrilled he was away. The job was different now, no more pitch meetings at Robert Redford's production company, no more casting sessions or brainstorming about story with Stavros. It was strictly groceries, housecleaning, and moral support. I was sick, disgusted, annoyed, and bored to tears.

I wandered around Fontana, set up an appointment for an abortion at the local Planned Parenthood, kept my pregnancy to myself. I was my own cycle of birth and destruction.

On Sunday night I was at Stavros's apartment when he returned. Fighting a wave of nausea I went to the door and opened it.

"How was New York?"

"Bad. Well, good and bad." He paused. "I'm ready to fire you, you know."

I just stared.

"When I got to New York, there were no check-in calls from you, my room was no good, I didn't have a limo to meet me, and I just suddenly felt this cold blast, y'know? A coldness, a lack of affection. EVEN IF I SENT A BICYCLE ACROSS COUNTRY, I'D CHECK IN TO SEE IF IT WAS ALL RIGHT."

"I thought you'd be fine," I said. "I thought I'd be bothering you. If I were going away I would have liked peace, and I did check in with you once . . ."

"Ah, but you didn't KEEP CHECKING. YOU HAVE TO

IMAGINE I AM THE PRODUCTION COMPANY! WHAT IF YOU LOST, MISPLACED, LOST CONTACT WITH THE WHOLE PRODUCTION COMPANY!"

I nodded, feeling queasy. Then he went on to tell me about a beautiful actress he knew, biblically, Ginger Vega, and SHE, right this very moment, was scrubbing the steps to the Krishna temple in Manhattan, and LOVING EVERY MINUTE OF IT, because she understood the power, the beauty of submission, because she BELIEVED in Krishna. "You've got to BELIEVE in me. Though we know that's not the real problem. You're out to get me. You've got a block against men and mothering."

Then, after a meaningful pause, he said, "I sense you do not have any maternal instincts. Maybe you're just too young, haven't lived with anyone, or maybe you just don't have a nurturing instinct, maybe you've NEVER had it." He reached in his pocket and dumped a shower of shredded paper onto the floor. Slow-mo confetti for the ugly showdown.

"See, if I came home for the weekend, my mother would fold my shirts, wash my clothes . . . I need a nurturing FORCE in this job, first and foremost. I've got to have my basic needs cared for."

I said, "Okay, Stavros. Sorry," and I left.

What I remember most about the abortion is the blue paper slippers. They made me put them on over my bare feet. That papery rustle, shuffle, toward the abortion room and back. Barefoot in the cold metal stirrups. Riding and bucking toward death, sucked empty. Put them back on. Blue paper slippers.

The day of my abortion, the day after I lost my job, the line producer took pity and switched me to on-set production assistant so I could stay for the shoot.

"Don't take it personal," the line producer said, taking me aside. "Stav's one crazy fucker."

Starting Over

"I don't know if I'll ever have a family," the woman said, twisting her hands.

Last night in a dream the woman gave birth to a girl who could speak right away. The girl was coal-haired and had stars for eyes. The girl was wickedly bright and trickily willful. The woman ached to give the girl her breast, but her child stayed only two days, then left because what the woman didn't know was that the girl didn't like the woman, or the girl didn't like the man the woman was with who was a gray shadow slipping up and down the walls, or the girl didn't trust the two of them together. She was gone. And when the girl left, the woman's body slipped away from her like a shadow. Darkness washed over the woman except for the aching bright white of her breasts.

Doin' Laundry with the Son of Gene Autry

"You mind watchin' this?"

A middle-aged man pulls a three-fourths full quart bottle of Christian Brothers brandy out of a white plastic bag to show an old man, then carefully slides it back in.

"My best buddy," the middle-aged man says. "I gotta get soap."

"Okay," the old man says, putting his clothes in a dryer.

Early afternoon dead zone in the Blue Ribbon Laundromat. As the middle-aged man walks by, the sweet smell of brandy and sour smell of sweat assault and linger. They mix with the powdery clean scent of water, detergent, fabric softener. When the middle-aged man exits, the old man snorts. Wipes his nose with his hand.

The old man has bushes sprouting out of his ears and nostrils. His old eyes, tired paunchy oysters sitting in hollowed shells, watch the dryer, watch the brandy, until the middle-aged man returns.

"Hey, thanks for watching. Want some?" The middle-aged man offers a plastic bag of teriyaki beef jerky, extends a pale white arm with a blue anchor on the bicep.

"No thanks," the old man says.

"I'm dying," the middle-aged man says, and laughs. "Yeah, but can't until I bury my three daughters. Already buried three sons."

The old man's eyes widen.

"Yep, yep, silk shirts, you can wash 'em all right," says the middle-aged man. "Nobody will help me. Not my mother. My sister says I'm mentally disturbed."

"The young generation," the old man says, "they don't like to iron anything."

"Not me, sir," says the young man in a strong voice. "I iron my clothes. I'm a Marine."

"Yes, they don't work for nothing, they don't *get* nothing. Kids."

"Thank you. Yes, sir, I'm with you, sir. I worked all my life, nobody never gave me nothing."

"Been here in Los Angeles now thirty odd years. How old do you think I am?" says the old man.

"Well, sir, you look good for your age. Mid-sixties?"

"What? Fifties?"

"Mid-sixties, sir?"

"Ha! I'm eighty. And I'm going dancing tonight. Going out dancing up on Cahuenga."

"Eighty. You look good, look good. How old you think I am?"

"You?"

"Want some beef jerky?"

"No, thanks." The old man gets up and leans on the orange laminated counter with his elbows on the middle-aged man's sheets.

"You're in your mid-thirties."

"No, sir, no. I'm forty-one."

"You look good."

The old man puts another quarter in the dryer. Sits back down.

The middle-aged man stares at the two shallow depressions the old man left in his pile of sheets. Pulls out his wallet and walks over to the old man. "This here's my father. Take a look."

"Gene Autry? Is that Gene Autry?"

"My father," says the middle-aged man proudly.

The old man starts laughing, a high wheezing bellow of a laugh that doesn't quit.

"It's my father." The middle-aged man retreats back to his side of the orange laminated counter.

"Gene Autry?" the old man says. "All you got there is a chopped-down postcard."

"Thank you, thank you," he says, giving the old man a mad dog look. "I never shoulda showed you. You don't believe me? Look at this book." He pulls out a dog-eared copy of *Lonesome Dove*. Waves it at the old man. "I went to college with him."

"Oh," the old man says, snickering. "In Texas. Right?"

"Yep, of course in Texas, because Howard Hughes was my god-father."

The old man pulls a wad of his clothes out of the dryer, tosses them quickly in a faded blue laundry bag, then hoists the bag over his shoulder. "You have a good night," he says, walking out the door.

"Lemme help you."

"No thanks, I don't need help. Tonight, I go dancing."

"Hey," the middle-aged man calls from the door. The old man's already unlocking his car. "Hey, lemme help you." The old man's already behind the wheel, turning the key in the ignition. The engine thrums.

"Hey, haven't I seen you here?" shouts the middle-aged man, a damp towel in his hand. "I have. You'll say hello to me next time, won't you?"

"Sure." The old man twists the steering wheel.

"That's all I want," says the middle-aged man.

Yellow

"You smell like yellow."

We are in bed. Two futons one on top of the other, both lumpy and flattened with age. Hardly thicker than quilts. Below a simple wood frame. Giorgio's head lies buried in my neck. Sniffing with that large Italian nose. Always sniffing. I've seen him stuff fresh basil plucked from a pot up his nostrils. Leave the leaves there, molting their green perfume for long minutes. Giorgio's greedy like that. I am greedy for him.

"Yellow?" I twist my body toward Giorgio. "Isn't that a color?"

My left tit flows down to the right. Each of my breasts is a little bigger than a handful, so the men say, but they're floppy when free. With them it's true I can create sculptures, rockets to the moon or rounded melons depending on the bra, but they are fickle things, never content with one form or another. Soft sculpture. Not frozen in pinup perfection the way I wish, the way I imagine men wish.

"No. What I mean by yellow is warm," Giorgio whispers in my ear. "Sunshine. Yeasty. Happy."

Happy. I look at the glow from the lit-up glass plate clock on the bookcase and imagine my aura as golden yellow. But it only makes me think of crystallized piss.

"So are you saying you like it?"

Giorgio grabs my left tit with one hand, raises it up, and fingers the nipple with his thumb.

"I love the way you smell," he says. Squeezing. Nuzzling my skin. "That's a good sign. People have to like each other's smell to stay together."

"So it's that simple," I say. Wishing.

Moonlight filters in through the thin white drapes. Mottles Giorgio's shoulder. Makes it look more distinct, a rounded spotted whale's hump rising out of the watery sheets. Crumpled waves. Soon to submerge again. Unattainable desire.

I place my hand on the back of Giorgio's head, mash it into my tit. He is the one I want.

He bites down. Hard. Wet mouth and sharp teeth on fleshy mound.

My tit embarrasses me. Squashed and spread now, it is a failure of male fantasy. A collapsed and trampled dream of conquered peaks and scaled heights. Maternal mountains slumped into mere hillocks. I speak foolishly.

"Tell me you won't leave," I say.

"Rebecca," he says. Pulling his mouth away. The moistness on my tit chills at contact with the air. At least the nipple stands at attention, but I am cold.

"Do we always have to talk about this?" says Giorgio, sighing. He turns on his side away from me. "You're going to ruin things if you keep it up."

"I'm sorry."

I stroke his dark curls and after a minute, an hour, a year, two years, then three of touching, he relaxes again, falls back onto my neck and then away. The mutiny of bliss. The betrayal of mothers.

It got so we were yelling I Love You from farther and farther away, and being together in bed, being together at all, became a fleeting thing, a rare happening, a memory.

Yellow: pissing your pants when you see Death coming.

Ode to the Black Dahlia: Everybody's Favorite Dead Girl

L.A. loves you, darling, dear, too ripe woman, upstart mama, promiscuous princess. The city swallowed you before you shed your widow-black. Starlet bound for screen fame, you lied through your legs so the city split you asunder. Cut your torso from your body and sliced an eternal smile from ear to ear. Did you really believe the city would let you be so bold? That's not how L.A. loves its darlings, dears. Black Dahlia, you were doomed to die. You struck the deepest chord of terror. All the bile vented on your perfect flesh. L.A. a city gone mad. You witnessed that. Your brutal death lingers like the imprint of a bomb, mushrooming pale and ominous against the skyline. Your severed body, tortured and bruised, maligned and desecrated, one who was never a mother, who loved womanhood too well, the desires it inspired, you could not last, not ever. You are the daughter, the sister, the lover lain low, the carnal female, ravaged and destroyed. Darling, dear, we love you now and forever. Forgive us our sins. Your black blooming flower encloses us all in hushed petals.

Girl on the Flying Trapeze

Esmeralda de la Cruz has just come from Malibu Castle, a miniature golf course in Van Nuys, not Malibu. Esmeralda wants ribs so she goes to Dr. Hogly-Wogly's Tyler Texas BBQ.

Esmeralda doesn't have a place setting so she nicks it from the big table next to her. They've got four extra settings. Skinny guys in cheap suits, dax in their hair. They don't notice.

The missing four guests come in when Esmeralda's got sparerib sauce on her fingers and meat between her teeth.

One is a man with a high pompadour and a primo hard body. Esmeralda licks her fingers. He is wearing a muscle shirt. Pinned over his left pec is a Mickey Mouse pin. Behind him are three women, pretty, stick-'em-up tits, zoned eyes, hot pants, asses like crystal globes. He ushers this bevy of spaced-out beauties in and sits at the place without a setting. He looks down at the empty spot.

"Yeah, it was me," Esmeralda says to him, her eye on Mickey. Brazen with her own secret.

Two minutes later he's sitting at her table.

"Amos Butane, maybe you hearda me," he says, shaking Esmeralda's hand. The women at the table don't even seem to notice he's gone, tits pointing at each other, vacancy signs in each motel.

Esmeralda hasn't heard of him.

"Amos Butane, porn king. *Fuck Train?*"

Esmeralda hasn't seen it.

"Where you from?" asks Esmeralda.

Nothing fazes Esmeralda. Under her gold quilted skirt she's sporting a hip-high fake leg. Lost her real one in a boating accident several years back. Luckily the doctor was good and left no painful bone stump, but the scar tissue is a constant source of discomfort. Fitted around the right side of her lower belly and right buttock is a shell of composite plastic—same kind they use for surfboards—that's held snugly in place by a leather belt and buckle. The bottom of the shell attaches to a titanium hip joint, then a bone of aluminum aircraft tubing, known for its strength and lightness. Molded around the entire skeletal form is the leg itself—polyethylene plastic that's air-injected to give it the softness and flexibility of foam so under stockings it looks convincing.

Esmeralda lost her virginity to Frank Zappa on his South American tour. Venezuela, land of multiple Miss Universes. Maybe she looked different then, otherwise she's lying. It's possible her teeth turned yellow from bulimia, or maybe she used to smoke. The white of her powder and the crimson of her lips only highlight those amber fangs. Everything she wears she chooses with care—her quilted skirts, her lingerie, her stockings, especially her shoes of the day— wild Spanish numbers specially designed for artificial feet, sloped platform sneakers with silver piping and suede, she's got them in lime green and hot pink, popsicle orange and aquamarine. She has obsessions. She is learning the twisting nature of her own shame.

"Hackensack," says Amos. "Used to play hockey, professional. Ever heara the Paramus Pitbulls?"

"I was born in Caracas but I lived once in Hackensack," says Esmeralda, thinking he must be tired of perfect bodies, golden proportions.

Amos closes his eyes. When he opens them they're off and running, him and Esmeralda. Reminiscing. Up close, Amos's muscles look kind of soft. Esmeralda thinks maybe porn does that to you.

Esmeralda's white powder is ghoulish, but it's the whole package that works. It's the mix that entices. Kind of a Gestalt thing. Parts equal more together than separate. Missing parts too have their place, exacting a power all their own. Commanding desire in certain men. Is he one of those?

A light film of perspiration coats Esmeralda's fingertips, underarms, and her skirted lower body, causing her skin to chafe against the plastic shell. It's as if her flesh wants to shed the artificial leg once and for all.

Amos and Esmeralda are nose to nose. Last steady man Esmeralda had was three years ago, an out-of-work botanist who used to grow rare strains of moss in champagne glasses all around the house before he left her. Since then it's been a string of devoted worshipers to the altar of absence, all brutal, all brief. None seeing beyond the ecstasy of disfigurement possessed and punished. Esmeralda checks the blush creeping up her neck. Hopefully Amos won't plant his hand on Esmeralda's thigh. At least her cane is hidden under the table. This one's decorated with a paisley motif. Brings out the paisley stitching in Esmeralda's thick quilted skirt and hides any sign of the plastic shell and belt. She wears such bulky fabric so if someone cops a feel they don't know. Not right away.

Suddenly Flatbush is trundled back into its ignominious grave. Two mouths chewing. Esmeralda mentions she works as an assistant to an agent. CAA.

"CAA?" Amos tightens his grip on the rib. "Oh, my God. Vanna White? Do you know Vanna White?"

Esmeralda laughs, shakes her glossy black hair. "Sure."

Amos lowers his eyes. Mickey Mouse turns flat in the glare from the rectangular fluorescent lights swinging up above. No emotion in those rodent eyes. Amos, though, Amos is lit.

"I'm in love with Vanna White," he whispers. "Those eyes," he says.

"I played a woman one time," Amos tells Esmeralda, his eyes moist. "*Some Like It Anal,* remake of *Some Like It Hot.* Brought out my feminine side. But I was fat. Looked funny in heels." Amos shakes his head sadly. "I didn't make a pretty woman."

Pretty women are for the unimaginative, thinks Esmeralda. She takes Amos's hand under the table, guides it under her skirt until it rests on the seam where plastic meets flesh. She smiles when his breath catches.

After that, Amos calls Esmeralda at work every day. Every day her platform sneakers get wilder and louder. She uses canes she's never brought out before: steel-tipped, Lucite, and polished oak. There is even color in those pallid cheeks of Esmeralda's. She's wearing no underwear at all. Thinking of Amos and his hands gripping her wasted hip and the wonders he works with canes.

At home alone, Esmeralda pops in a tape of *Fuck Train*. Traces red lipstick on her mouth, then the lips of her pussy. Touching herself, she watches video Amos get it up over and over and over. Put it in this way and that. The women's legs buck and flail. Flail and buck. She rubs herself furiously. The women's limbs are graceless, grasping tentacles. Cumbersome. She finds herself egging him on. Make them hurt, hate them. She hops to the TV, braces herself on the console, and smears red fingers over their stupid waving legs.

Amos calls Esmeralda at work. They talk a bit. Then Amos takes a breath. Asks for Vanna White's number. Esmeralda explains she's sorry, she can't give him Vanna White's number. Amos hangs up.

Esmeralda on the trapeze. It's what she does for exercise, her false leg wrapped carefully in silk, zipped up in a soft suitcase next to her gym bag. What a lightness. Esmeralda in a leotard, one-legged and lovely. Hands firm on the bar as she extends her leg up, wraps it around, gracefully drops her torso and swings. Black hair dangling down as she presses through the air, back arched, arms reaching. Push push push, get it up over and over and over and, nothing. Fly a bit and grab the tail of some wayward comet, then yank it down. Garters scratching, one thigh warm muscle, the other cold and plastic, the satiny drawers, the uplifting brassieres frilly and frothy. The secrets underneath. No shame in the flesh, in severed joints or truncated desires. When Esmeralda achieves a half-circle range from start to finish, she holds the bar again, lifts her leg with bent knee, somersaults her body, then releases the leg behind her in a flawlessly straight line punctuated by a pointed toe.

A Former Lover's Response to Trapeze Story

—A one-legged woman is sexy. You can stand her on the floor and spin her around until you choose where you want to enter her from. The best is a no-legged woman.

—Yes I have. She was the sexiest of all.

—Yashelka, from Yugoslavia, I met her in a bar. Two weeks before she was hit by a vegetable truck.

—No, I'm not lying. I was in Budapest selling art. You know how it is.

—Yes, I've been everywhere, and now I'm stuck in this horrible town. Up here in the Hollywood Hills surrounded by The View. The View of what? Thousands of cold, sparkling lights. Ugh. I'm sick of this city, sick of this house. I hope the whole thing slides down the hill in the next earthquake and takes me with it.

—Maybe you're the one who's sick in the soul.

—Yashelka again. You're jealous, how wonderful. When we made love she was all mine. I would pin her down on the floor and have my way with her. I could do anything I wanted, fuck her from any angle. Even the pus and blood oozing from her stumps drove me wild.

—I disgust you?

—You are so American. Everyone's a Puritan here, a hypocrite.

—No I'm not saying that. You don't need to have one or two legs missing. You are sexy the way you are. Really.

Infidelity

I had a brief job on a TV movie. I answered the phone, *"Infidelity, may I help you?"* *Infidelity* was the name of the movie. Guess what it was about. There was one man who called often, he worked at a sound-digitizing studio. After a few weeks, he confessed, he would call, then put my *"Infidelity, may I help you?"* on a speakerphone that was wired to an intercom. Everyone in the studio heard me in quadrophonic sound say, *"Infidelity, may I help you?"* And laughed.

Texas Bluesman

I met a bluesman named Slim in Little Rock.

She has her own blues to sing. Doesn't want to sing them. Wants to lose herself in her lover's blues.

He was playing in a dive called Club Handy that had sticky tables. Something to do after filming all day. Lots of amp reverb. Guy at the mike, blowing harp, looks Indian, wearing a thick red bandana wound around his head. Bass player using a beer bottle as a slide. Behind a rickety structure of drums, a man with his head down, hitting the drums just slightly off the beat, belly hanging over skinny black jeans. Guitar player grooves tight by the bass player, fringed shirt open to his waist exposing hairy chest, cigarette dangling from his knuckles as he plays. Guy singing, tall and lean, slightly bowlegged. Pocked face glistening with sweat under the garish blue and red and green houselights. Wet shirt stuck to his body as he sings, every so often cutting dirty looks at the drummer. Goofy grins at the guitar man. Sharp nods to the bass player who'd slide the bottle, then guzzle. And long stares at me, sitting nearby with the crew, cheap vodka in hand.

Desiring to be swallowed. In the belly of the whale, hunger. Deep closets. Desiring to be touched by one who needs her.

The band all wear scuffed cowboy boots. Some have tarnished

spurs, for looks. With cheap vodka number four in hand, I get up to dance with the best boy. Married, a pale band of skin on the finger where the ring should be. Smoke thick and stale.

End, ending, ended. Over and out. The way it feels to walk out a door and know you're shutting it for the last time.

Or not knowing. Never getting to say good-bye. Needing to.

At break. Singer's arms on mine. "I like the way you dance, let's go have some fun."

Lies. She lies to herself, pretends she's free. She is not free. She is her mother's daughter. Repeating.

At the entrance of the club I stumble, my right foot slips out of the vintage white fabric spike heel and twists on the asphalt. *Hit drag, hit drag.* Slim motions me behind a pickup. Backs me against the truck bed. *She didn't think of Maggie, even though Maggie was thinking of her.*

"You kiss serious," he says, pulling back and looking intently in my face. In my face. I don't even know him.

Hold out, hold on to what you fear. Little cabins built from tiny toothpicks, you built them, thinking sure, start small, plan perfection, this is the house that Rebecca built, one without a crash-bang family yet, a home for all seasons, a home to carry in a toothpick box, a home that doesn't overwhelm, a home meant to remain. There are smashing fists.

"I make most people nervous," says Slim.

"Not me," I say, grinning. Stupid with youth. Drunk. I look at this man, this stranger. His eyes brim over with pleading, twin gas tank holes, inside great upsurging liquid desperation that rises up, tops out in brown shiny orbs spilling HELP ME's all over. Never mind the wide smile, shuckjive stage show, the muscular notes wrenched from a ragpatch soul—Slim is a drowning man.

Pile into the car, me and the drunken band, Slim's bandana a bloodied bandage leaking from a charcoaled soul.

The lust of danger. Screaming orange caution tape ripped and fluttering free in her tearing hands, the ominous X's she stripes into stars, the skull she packs with flesh and flowers, the crossbones she uses to beat a standup rhythm.

Next morning, Slim snapped on a gospel station. Five Blind Boys of Alabama singing. "I'm not that way anymore."

I am.

Slim and the Sidewinders came down to Stuttgart, played for the wrap party. The filmmakers picked Stuttgart, Arkansas, because of the name. It reminded them of the Fatherland. Slim bunked in my Best Western room, the one littered with Arkansas swap meet finds like an entire collection of hats for ten bucks including one original Schiaparelli looking like a skinned baby leopard and an orange one built like the Guggenheim with a chin strap. Other finds included an art deco lamp with a base of three black balls stacked one on top of the other getting smaller and smaller as it rose and flowered into a green and yellow double-ringed Saturn black scribbled lampshade to beat the band, a thick brown Russian jacket with braid and buttons to keep away the cold that never hit L.A. All this and a bottle of Stolichnaya vodka pearly pure on top of the cheap varnished dresser.

"Te amo," he said, two days after I met him. *"Te amo te amo te amo."*

I poured us some more vodka into plastic bathroom cups.

"Don't ever lose me," Slim said before going home to Texas. We'd known each other four days.

He called me fifteen minutes later from a gas station on the outskirts of town.

"Remember, don't ever lose me."

He then commenced to cursing his band mates, the motherfucking drummer he had to clock, cursing the road, banging the receiver smack against the pay phone, cursing the bound-to-break-down van they called the Blues Goose, cursing, slamming the receiver against metal.

I never thought I'd see him again.

Until the letters. *She wrote nothing. Left nothing behind.*

They came daily. Scrawled on yellow legal-sized paper folded in three.

I wrote him letters, fewer and further between. I was cautious.

"*Mi Corazón.* Your letter is downtown being fingerprinted and registered as a lethal weapon," he said. *If words could kill. If they had that much power.*

He told me he loved me. "I love you I love you I love you." All I wanted was to hear those words on continuous loop, and still I wanted more. The carefully stitched gap inside me was ripping wider and wider, threatening to engulf us both. My hunger was Promethean. *Her lover isn't there. He is a stranger. A stranger in trouble who needs her.*

"I gotta photo of my mother down at the tattoo parlor. Gonna get it right on my chest, blown up big, so when I wear those transparent shirts on stage, my mother's face'll be smiling down on the crowd. Mama Querida. Ain't that hip? I want to see you."

I pick him up at the airport. Out of the Southwestern gate, Slim in long camel-colored gabardine coat (soon to be sold at a resale store), shiny aluminum harmonica case by his side, the DON'T MESS WITH TEXAS sticker prominent in the middle along with all the state stickers, Arkansas, Mississippi, Louisiana, Arizona, California, and his guitar (soon to be sold at a pawnshop).

One night in bed, his Trés Flores–oiled black hair fanned out on the pillow, my head on his hairless chest, he brought up the tattoo again. "I'm not sleeping with you and your mother," I said.

Slim told me he got sober. I didn't even know he was a drunk. Somehow, that had escaped me over the last long-distance year. *He drank the way she drank, she drank the way he drank.*

Hot sauce was on all his food. I didn't realize it was because smoke had so dulled his tastebuds, same way I didn't understand when he shook in cold wet chills in my bed that he wasn't fighting off road flu like he said, they were d.t.'s, pure and simple.

He'd spin me around, proud, *she is a spinning top,* introduce me to the boys. "Look at her legs," he'd say, eyes shining. *She is an object.* I wanted to look good for my man, to not think. *She doesn't have to do anything else. Girls don't count in this bluesclub world. Outside his need, she doesn't exist. His pain is her pain. Her pain can't be his 'cause she doesn't have any. She is numb. She is an object. She wants to look good. She feels nothing.*

Slim moved to L.A., but not with me, and got nasty. Gone all the time. Talking about other women. Busy. Too busy to see me. Gigging. Meetings. Screwing around. Hustling gigs and more gigs at two-bit joints. Scoring. Borrowing money. Even when we did see each other, he wasn't all there.

Toward the end, Slim mentioned her once. He said offhandedly, "Yeah, my friend Faye," in that new carefully adopted nonchalant manner of name-dropping I'd begun to notice in him soon after his arrival in Los Angeles.

"Faye who?"

"Faye Dunaway."

I turned to look at Slim, sure enough of the streets of my city to do so. My city.

"How do you know her?"

Slim told me, begrudgingly, how he just met her at a party. Some weaving older woman vomiting on the sidewalk.

I asked if she was beautiful.

"She was just some woman retching her guts out, some girl in jeans and a T-shirt."

Mother's Day

In the cemetery—chalky tombstones, clipped green grass, sunlight, silence.

Aunt Cookie taps the shiny, smooth wood of the coffin, and smiles. It's weathering properly.

Looks too new, says the daughter. They find the right one.

The coffin is partially upraised out of the grave for easy access. The cemetery is accommodating. Aunt Cookie taps the wood again. This time it is more worn, so worn the daughter sees a slit in the lid.

The daughter is curious and scared, scared that her mother will be decayed and rotted, but she looks in and sees only a white white hand, powdered Kabuki style. On one finger she sees an unfamiliar ring, gold inlaid with an enormous reddish stone.

The hand twitches. The daughter is thrilled, leans in farther and sees what looks like her mother's face. It is her mother, not decayed at all, only coated a rice-paper white. Her lips are full and painted red, yawning open as if she is sleeping unconcerned with appearance, a deep sleep of pure abandon. Her face moves and the daughter shrieks in horror and excitement.

She's alive, she screams at Aunt Cookie, who mutters polite inanities but the daughter pushes her out of the way, tears off the coffin lid, and pulls her mother out. The daughter holds her in her arms. The mother's limbs are weak, she sways back and forth, limply, flopping as if she were drowsy, or drunk.

Then the mother speaks. In a tired voice she tells her daughter she is an actress now. Her Death was a performance.

Yellow Doesn't Stop

I came here to California in part for the weather, the heat, the constant burning of a bright sun, the lemon trees, the yellow shafts that dance and bend around my floor.

I remember Faulkner's wind, the way it rushed about hither and thither and swirled around houses and played up a tree trunk and found me, a young girl seated in the branches, and I remember how that wind toyed and curled and blew and whistled right up into my skirts, I remember the way it moaned.

For me, the California sun was Faulkner's wind and the sun was yellow.

I remember sitting on a street curb with my feet planted on the ground, my head thrown back and my neck naked to the heat, and my legs spread apart so the hot-fisted sun could bake me and take me and fill me up with radiance.

This too was yellow.

If I with a vast cracked bowl did mix all these California yellows into one bright fire-sparking batter—painted shingles from the houses invaded by the Night Stalker and hot flaming tongues of Southern California light and the petals of a thousand yellow roses of Texas and that sweet and alluringly fleeting scent of yellow that one love found in my skin and soul and hot fresh human piss and a lock of my own woven-blondish hair and a half-dozen drugstore canaries for a bit of song and how about a City of Los Angeles parking ticket or two—what then?

Would I have created gold?

See Me Heal Me
Touch Me See Me

Sitting at the breakfast table, Giorgio stuck his foot in her lap. She cradled the foot in her left hand, spooned cereal with the right, talked, traced her fingers lightly around the foot's outline, sipped fresh orange juice, stroked the high arch, listened, talked, took the toes firmly in her peasant's hand and squeezed the top of the foot, kneaded the muscles, ran her thumb over the rounded pad of the ball of the foot, then down the arch, kept listening, kept talking, encircled each toe with her fingers, pressed and pulled, talked, spread her hand the width of the foot and squeezed, her hand a fleshy clamp that worked the length of Giorgio's foot until he made soft grunts in between words, bites. To have his foot in her lap, his restless eyes a silky calm green, this gave her immense pleasure. Whenever they were together, which wasn't often since they lived in different cities, Rebecca massaged him. For hours. Every night before they went to sleep. Even when she was tired. During the day.

What is love but a bridge spun of silver threads, tension spanning two opposite banks, suspended craving? In absentia, an uncontrollable desire to conjure up the lover with whatever means possible. There was so much space in which to sculpt The One, stitched with memory, pulsing with fantasy.

Giorgio's nervousness became hers. Stroking his head at night, scratching the scalp, burying her fingers in black curls, she imagined the mind of the man she loved. Inside, the curved walls of his skull pressed down, the sky was always falling. Everywhere, great glittering towers spired upward, but they were built on shifting sands and leaned in heavy winds, tilted, sagged; crowds of people of unknown nationality disguised in scarves scurried here, there, there, here; makeshift scaffolding swung against the gleaming towers, battered neck-stretched gargoyles, shattered windows, broken bricks; skeletons of other buildings groped spindly beams toward the sunshiny sky streaked with thunderclouds—sun and shadow were always chasing each other there. It was a brilliant city, unstable.

When Giorgio babbled words caught in the sluice between waking and sleep, she smiled; beneath her drifting hands she imagined she wove the buildings together with soft fleurs-de-lis of light; with each circular rubbing she erased the thunderclouds, brought the sun to bear, and didn't the towers pierce and prop the falling sky then? When his breath grew even she slowed the massaging, careful not to let her fingers retreat before his sleep was sure. This too was satisfying. More than that, necessary. Rebecca was driven to please him with her hands, her lips. He used to say, when she pressed her lips to his, "We must have kissed thousands of times by now and still I want to kiss you." Her voice chided, though, remonstrated, tweezed apart past glances, gestures, moments, absences, advances and retreats.

There was Adam and there was God, their fingers on the verge. The Invisible Hand. Nothing was more holy, more alive, more ruinous than the moment when she touched Giorgio. Even when the moment burgeoned into hours, always it was a moment about to happen, about to end.

More Things She Learned in Therapy

She went back.

At the beginning of her third meeting with Barbara Hart, the therapist said, "I dreamed about you last night. You were telling me what to do."

Rebecca was taken aback for a moment, but she was also proud she'd overpowered Barbara Hart. Now she didn't have to be scared. This gave her license to open up more, so Rebecca talked about how she was concerned there seemed to be a pattern in the men she chose, that they all failed her just like her parents had. How could she break out? Yes, she knew she was strong. Yes, and a survivor. But had she let a good thing slip by? "I'm so fucking tired of being alone," she told Barbara Hart. "Maybe I had the abortion so I could ruin things and hurt myself. Just like my mother." The fierceness in Rebecca's tone tasted like gun metal. Barbara Hart didn't have an answer.

After that third meeting, Rebecca was upset, confused. Had Barbara Hart breached some rule of therapy or was Rebecca overreacting? Her therapist's dream kept coming back to her. She didn't know who to ask, but Isaac called from Tucson and told Rebecca she had the sexiest voice he'd ever heard and he missed her. After the call she decided to clean the mini-fridge. She cut up a T-shirt Isaac had given her to use as a rag, but it seemed the more she wiped, the dirtier the old white enamel became. She retreated onto the futon. From the corner, the fridge gurgled like a huge ailing tooth.

At work, she transcribed three tapes from an interview with a young, attractive, educated actress who was also a political activist marching across the country with other actors and actresses as a protest against Soviet oppression. The tapes were long and tedious. Rebecca barely removed the headphones from her ears to eat lunch. She didn't care what the actress was saying as long as her voice bulldozed the others in her head. "I see you're back on a roll," Darlene Comer, her boss said, pleased with Rebecca's industry. "You'll be a star yet."

After work, she opened her gym bag and folded her Speedo into a corner, tossed in goggles, two caps—one nylon for comfort and one rubber for on top to protect her hair from the chlorine—a towel, shampoo, body lotion, and deodorant. The phone rang and her message machine picked up. Isaac's voice came on. Rebecca turned down the volume. There was no time. Tonight she had to swim.

When swimming wasn't enough, Rebecca started lifting weights before she swam. Abdominal crunches, leg lifts, squats, bench press, curls with the biceps and triceps. Each extra pound she lifted or pushed or raised gave her a tangible, steadying sense of power. Rebecca exercised so hard and slept so soundly, the voices and visions stopped.

Darlene gave her another raise. The fourth meeting came and went and then Barbara Hart went into labor.

During the month that Barbara Hart was recovering from the birth of a healthy nine-pound baby boy, Rebecca had many memories about her dead mother. In one, Rebecca's mother dropped her off at a new apartment they were moving into, and didn't come back until ten at night, drunk; when Rebecca complained, her mother threw a beer bottle at her and twisted Rebecca's arm behind her back until Rebecca's fingers scraped her neck. In another, her mother caught Rebecca dumping bottles of her mother's Almaden and Chianti down the sink and slapped her. These memories followed Rebecca to work where Darlene Comer gave her more and more responsibility. She supervised her first editing session alone, chose music for the Arnold Schwarzenegger stunts segment, wrote a script on an interview with Rosanna Arquette from *Desperately Seeking Susan*.

When Rebecca added ten pounds more on each side of the squat bar, she pulled a muscle in her lower back. Even this pain served to distract her. She didn't ease up on exercise. On good nights she had dates with Johnny the Rocker. When she did miss a day at the Y, something like a paralytic black cloud enveloped her and she could do nothing at home on South Detroit Street except stare at the rotting lemons on the tree outside her window and sip flat root beer.

A month passed, and Rebecca went for her fifth appointment.

"How are you?" Barbara Hart said, her eyes shining in a way that irritated Rebecca. In a billowing navy tunic, Barbara Hart looked almost as large as she had before having the baby. But she was back.

Rebecca said she met a new man but it wasn't serious. She still missed Isaac. Then Rebecca began to tell Barbara Hart about all the memories—the words came tumbling out in a glorious rinse cycle—when suddenly a baby's wail pierced the quiet office.

Barbara Hart leaned forward. "I'm sorry. I couldn't get a sitter—would you mind if I nursed him during the session?"

"Not at all. Go ahead."

Rebecca wanted to say NO, the words she had to speak about her troubles were damming up against her teeth and threatening to bust through and she needed all of Barbara's attention, but she could not say no. Rebecca talked about the time her mother slapped her face for not taking her brother outside to play when he hadn't wanted to go. The words flitted out of her mouth like glass shards. There was a glazed radiant look in Barbara Hart's unseeing eyes, and always, the stubborn wet sucking of the infant against his mother's naked breast.

Rebecca tried not to look. She talked about how her mother never believed her, no matter what she said. How she called Rebecca, Bitch. Rebecca glanced at Barbara, but her face was lowered, she was cooing softly. A faint warm milky scent, moist damp flesh, pink lotion and talcum, and something like slowly rotting potatoes. The baby's slurping was loud. Rebecca thought of deep-sea fishes with lumi-nous stalks for eyes and lantern jaws that hinged and unhinged, suck-ing and scissoring. Rebecca began again. Bitch, she called her. Now whenever she heard the word it was a carrot shredder on skin, a horse-fly sting. Rebecca looked at Barbara and was repulsed by the filmy eyes, like a cat's when the milk-white inner lid slides down. She didn't seem to be listening. Barbara Hart and the new baby were rapt. The curve of the mother's head, the swoop of her arm cradling the baby, the baby nestled at her breast, the mother's broad lap, these lines drawing them together were impenetrable, thick and unyielding as brush strokes. Rebecca's words sliced through her lips, pricked the air, yet cascaded over them in a gentle rain. Rebecca studied her heavily lined hands and told her about the time her mother challenged Re-becca to a wrestling match in front of Rebecca's friends and how she wrenched Rebecca's leg and bruised her back so she had to miss gym class for a week. The baby was ravenous. The baby was too noisy. Bitch, bitch, bitch, was the sound the baby made with its miniature pink grinding mouth. The baby pulled away to blast a raw cry, and the mother shushed it. "I don't remember my mother ever hugging me," said Rebecca, the words rushing together. "She used to buy me books on witchcraft. I was afraid of her. I think my mother hated me," she said. Barbara Hart nodded, murmured. Rebecca wanted to hold the baby. Babies were so fragile. Wanted to feel the squirm of breath and desire in her very own arms. If she did, though, she was afraid she might dent its tiny skull.

On Driving in the Valley

For my work on *Ghost Dancing*, an eight-hour documentary about Native Americans, I must often drive the desolate wide gray asphalt bands that lie like flattened elephants between the main streets in Canoga Park. Hell. This is truly hell. The interminable distances between errand destinations, those lagging flagging loose sluggard stretches that strain the bonds between people like taffy, hot and stifling in the chicken coop car, strain them so far that, alone in the car, behind the wheel, people disappear, people stop existing, there is only you and the car, and what does anything matter then? Life is a cheap flattened dream. Life is wheels spinning leaving oily tire tracks obliterated by other greasy tire tracks.

Frankie Lake, one of the AA dykes who works at the office and has suicidal tendencies, told me today about her Aunt Maggie, who cut off her head with a buzz saw. What? Well, not really my aunt. Aunt Maggie's brother married my aunt. A buzz saw? It was like a table saw. She was drunk, just set her head on the table and the saw sheared it off. Who found her? Her husband. Then he lost touch with my family. I didn't know what happened until a lot later. I was just a kid. Where? Riverside. Here in California.

At six o'clock I leave the office. When I reach the on-ramp for the 101 South, I remember my mother, whose name was Maggie, who's dead also by her own hand, singing to me when I was very young and she still had songs in her. She sang, "Down in the valley, the valley so low, hang your head over, hear the wind blow." And as I pass through the green light onto the freeway, I do, I hear that wind.

Fiona Molloy's Birthday Brunch

"It's Billy Idol's birthday today too."

"And Dick Clark. And June Pointer."

"And Fiona Molloy! Who was at your dinner party last night?"

"Let's see, Jeremy Steers, the man who accidentally killed Brandon Lee, was there, and Annie Flanagan and her boyfriend Vic the gaffer, Annie bared her ass for national TV on *Cops-O-Rama,* who else? Me, June, Pierre, Max, and Dana. Oh, and Larraine Newman and her husband Chad, he's in the Groundlings."

"Today's also the anniversary of the first meteorite known to strike a woman. 1954. Mrs. Hewlett Hodges. Sylacavga, Alabama."

"Wait . . . did you say Jeremy killed Brandon Lee?"

"Yeah. Said it ruined his life."

"Tell me you made that meteorite thing up."

They are all seated at a large round marble-topped table at Kahn's Pleasure Café in Malibu. Fiona, then there is June, Dana, Carmen, Penny—and Raul, Fiona's beau of one week. Behind them an indoor fountain bubbles. On a rock in the center of the fountain is seated a marble cherub dribbling water out of his plump lips. The fountain is surrounded by tall feathery ferns that give the illusion of a freshwater pond. It looks very new.

"I just read a story about a pro ballplayer who killed eleven fans with foul balls, all by accident of course," says Penny.

95

"What?" asks June, buttering a mini-muffin. Dressed in an A-line Simplicity pattern skirt, a blouse with a Peter Pan collar, and low-heeled white pumps, her unremarkable face bare of makeup, she is the plainest of all the women. "Why didn't he just quit?"

After reaching beneath the napkin for a mini-croissant, Carmen passes the basket to Dana, her press-on silver nails digging into the wicker.

"How's the auditioning going?" Carmen whispers to her.

"Don't ask," says Dana, taking two mini-muffins. "Haven't worked in months. I've got to switch agents. Hey, who highlights your hair? It's fab. I've got to get mine done."

"Did it ruin his life?" Raul asks Penny.

"I said it was a story," says Penny, rolling her eyes at June and Raul.

"I thought a real story," says Fiona, pouting. A tiny, curvy thing with cabaret beauty, she dramatizes the paleness of her skin and Tidy-Bowl blue of her eyes with black lipstick, a Fiona trademark.

"No, a short story. In *Harper's*. Jesus. Are we having a problem with fact and fiction here?"

Fiona closes her eyes. "Well, you would know. You're the successful screenwriter."

Penny flushes. "That's a low blow. I'm this close to an option."

"Have another muffin," June says to Fiona, handing her a fresh one from the basket. "Waiter?" she says, waving the basket, "can we have some more? Thank you."

"I feel like we're in Henry Jaglom's film *Eating,*" says Carmen, dabbing at her mouth with a cloth napkin. "Have you all seen that? I mean, is there a camera somewhere? I should write a pig-out scene for the sitcom. We haven't done that yet."

"Oh, God," says Dana, nodding. "Who can stick to a diet here? What a radical choice, Fifi. I never would have thought of this place. I didn't even know it was here."

"Thank you. Thank you, girls. I didn't finish telling about last night," says Fiona, glaring at Penny. "The worst thing happened. I was wearing, ah, this vintage black dress, a clear black—what was it,

June, crepe?—jacket, and a bustier, and all of a sudden I look down and my dress was in my LAP! The buttons had popped and the whole front of the dress fell over." Fiona slaps the table. "Can you bulleeve it?"

Raul makes an hourglass shape with his hands.

"Stop," says Fiona, tapping him lightly on the shoulder.

"Hold on. Was your bustier in place? I mean, what kind of exposure are we talking?" asks Penny. Fiona fixes a baleful stare on Penny.

"I need to meditate," says the Birthday Girl. "Excuse me. I'll be back in about ten."

"Would you anyway now or are we driving you to it?" asks Penny.

The Birthday Girl walks out into the courtyard.

"Well, to each his own," says Carmen. "Does anyone have an aspirin? That's what works for me."

"Penny, she doesn't mean anything bad. It's her birthday," says June. "You know how it is. Nobody wants to get older."

Penny kills her coffee and pours another cup. There's an empty seat next to Raul, who Fiona says is rich but she's worried he's not handsome enough. He's the son of a famous architect and a plastic surgeon to the stars, says Fiona. The women are all eager to hear him speak for himself. Raul tells them he can't meditate like Fiona, it takes him a while to get into it. But his mother can. She's a Buddhist. She just spent five months in a box, meditating.

"A Buddha box? Again, is this fact or fiction?" asks Penny.

"How big was it?" asks Dana.

"Six feet by four feet," says Raul.

"For four months? Were there ventilation holes? Windows? Portholes?" asks Penny.

"No, no, actually it was only enclosed on three sides," says Raul.

"Like a bus stop," Penny says. "Buddha's bus stop."

"Behave," says June.

"I need to make a phone call," says Dana. She gets up and heads toward the rest rooms past the dribbling cherub. A little breeze blows in, causing the huge blue-and-white crystal chandelier to tremble above their heads.

"Better hope there's not an earthquake," says Carmen, pointing up.

"My grandmother had a fit about it," says Raul. " 'You're gonna spend Thanksgiving and Christmas and New Year's in a box?' she said to my mother. She's Presbyterian."

Fiona comes back just in time for the main course: sloppy eggs Benedict with salmon and spinach and hollandaise sauce and rosemary potato wedges and orange juice and crunchy cranberry minimuffins and heartburn.

Here comes Max. "This is Jammin' June, Cutiepie Carmen . . ." says Fiona, pointing around the table, stopping at Penny.

"What are they, Hallmark wrestlers?" says Max.

"Eat, eat," says June, offering him the muffin basket.

"What I want to know, Max, is how could you leave New York? Don't tell me you actually like L.A.?" says Penny.

"Like L.A.? There was a cartoon in *The New Yorker*. A guy in a Hawaiian shirt and a briefcase says HAVE A NICE DAY to a guy in a Hawaiian shirt and a briefcase who's thinking in a bubble FUCK YOU. A guy in a three-piece suit and a briefcase says FUCK YOU to another guy in a three-piece suit who's thinking HAVE A NICE DAY in his head. I love L.A. People ask me why did I leave New York. I didn't leave New York. New York left me. It was fabulous in the sixties, hip in the seventies, and hell in the eighties. New York's in your face and L.A.'s in your lap. No, no, no muffins for me. Gotta go. Sasha, my darling, I just wanted to stop by and give you a kiss. Penny, is that your name? Next time I want to hear your song and dance. Don't I know you from somewhere?"

"Hey, where's Dana?" says June.

"She went to make a phone call," says Penny.

"She's been gone half an hour," says Carmen.

"Here she is," says June. "Your eggs are cold," she says to Dana who looks pale and bright-eyed.

Fiona's telling the story of how she got lost in Haight-Ashbury when she was a girl, and some man with an umbrella—it wasn't raining—and a tray of oranges led her to some hippies. They gave her a doll, a beatnik doll, just a rag with a tie-dye dress, but it spoke. The doll said two things. "Shoo boop de doo, don't bug me, baby," or "Don't bug me, Daddy-O." Fiona went around the house repeating the lines until her mother got rid of the doll. That's why Fiona is in therapy.

"Can you believe that? My mother," Fiona says. Another woman enters the café and heads for their table. "Kali, you made it."

Kali, a fit middle-aged woman wearing no makeup except for a bindi dot, dressed in a brown leather mini and yellow bodysuit, kisses Fiona on the lips. June makes room for her to sit.

"How did you meet Kali?" Penny asks. "Don't you both go way back?"

"Oh, that's a long story, I'm too tired," says Kali. "I just sang in a gospel choir for four hours this morning."

"I thought you were Hindu," says Carmen.

"In Bombay I am." Kali winks.

"I was wearing pink spandex," says Sasha, "when we met."

"And you?" Penny asks Kali.

"I was wearing saris."

"Don't you want to order some food?" asks June.

"No, no, I've eaten, thanks," says Kali.

"I was wearing pink spandex," continues Fiona. "I was nineteen years old, and about to be on the street. Kali's roommate was Blaine, the daughter of the guy who gave Timothy Leary THE MAYONNAISE JAR." She looks sultrily around the table.

"What mayonnaise jar?" says June.

"The one Aldous Huxley gave him in Switzerland," says Kali. "With LSD in it. Her dad's the one who turned Leary on, and the whole country."

"Blaine and I were friends," says Fiona. "She'd been given acid since she was four. When I met her she was anti-drug."

"She knew the whole *I Ching* book by heart," says Kali.

"So I moved into her loft and became the resident geisha."

"What'd you have to do?" Dana asks.

"I posed for sculptures and I made comet juice. My name was Venus Milo then."

"What's comet juice?" asks Raul quietly.

"Oh, she'd make it in this huge goblet—grape juice, orange juice, vodka, tequila, rum. It was good. It was different every time. You were the Unicorn Girl," says Kali.

"Projection from my Third Eye," says Fiona.

"You'd get up when I was sculpting and say, 'I'VE GOT IT. THIS IS HOW A UNICORN WALKS!' and you'd mambo around the room," says Kali.

"We used to make PURPLE JESUS down in South Carolina," says Carmen. "You take a thirty-gallon garbage can, put in sliced lemons and lime, cherries, fruit juices, grapes, then grain alcohol. Let it sit overnight and it would be purple. Was good for a week-long party. You'd keep it as a base and when it ran low, fill it up with more juices. We called it that 'cause when you woke up the next day, first thing you'd say was, 'Oh, Jesus.' "

Everyone ignores her.

"What were you doing in New York then?" Dana asks Fiona.

"She was a cigarette girl at Limelight. Had a tutu skirt, bustier. A regular sex bomb," says Kali.

"I was the Parachute Girl before that. Big blow-up ten-foot-high photos of me in the display windows. Ronnie made me a size one pair of parachute pants, I wore a flight vest and nothing else," says Fiona. "Everybody loved me," she says, fluttering her long lashes. Raul squeezes her hand.

"Buck sure did," says Kali.

"Buck?" June asks.

Kali turns to June and smiles brightly. "Yeah, Buck. My boyfriend at the time. He and Venus Flytrap would fuck every chance they got, whenever my back was turned." Kali looks at Fiona. "Isn't that right?"

Fiona gives a little snort. Her blue-black hair cascades into her eyes. "But we got over all that, didn't we, yeeeeears ago." She blows Kali a kiss. Kali's expression doesn't change.

"Girls, I've just written the best lyrics, and I want to sing them for you. Okay? Ahem." Fiona leans her head back, tosses her hair out, then brings her face back to the table and starts singing in a low, vampy voice:

> *"Why don't you kiss me, burn my lips*
> *Turn my insides all to drips*
> *Why don't you kiss me . . ."*

"What's the damage," interrupts Penny. "Gotta run."

The bill plus tip works out to fifty bucks a head. As always, whether it is her birthday or not, Fiona Molloy does not pay. That is the way it is with a girl who everybody loves.

Talk

In Los Angeles, because there's so much space, lines of conversation depart the mouth and become dismembered limbs, or chopped-in-half earthworms. They float, or they snake like trains, gliding furtively and leaving a track of liquid slime. These are the evil, biting lines:

You look tired.
I don't remember meeting you.
You're full of shit.
I want to take your head and slam it against this wall.

Then there are the ephemeral, empty voices. At parties, dinners, the lines like ticker-tape streamers. You catch and clutch, try to fathom, give up.

And those stolen in bed. Gifts of the evening. Guttural whisperings, naked and shining strips, they glow from the saturated heat. Radiator bliss, the steam hisses and the words draw you close, or they spurt out in great clouds of white water and your lover's face obscures.

You deposit these voices along with all the others, the strands of random conversation like so many discolored disfigured pearls, lasagna-shaped seaweed washed up on shore, some still chewy green and deep-sea moist, others dry and curly brittle. These lines. These phrases. Whirligigs in the black canvas of you. Neon pink stars, orange cubes, somersaulting, conical twists of black and blue.

Phrases. Snatches of conversation that dismembered, form their own branching body, even bible of one life. And always, the fulcrum is love, love as a burning through of skin to soul. Blending. What one does in aikido, a slow merging of energies so the aggressive energy bounds back on the aggressor.

You have a wonderful mouth, he said to you, a lover once upon a time. Thanks, you said. And he. When I compliment you, you mustn't say anything, just smile as if, perhaps, fifteen hundred men have said the same thing before. Lap it up like it was a small saucer of milk.

You lap up the talk you hear, the sirens, the ice cream truck trills, the children's shouts, the gunshots, the screams, the babbling of the homeless, the blipping at the blind crossing, the chatter of friends, the banter of lovers. You are fed. Finally. You snatch up sentences, phrases, stories, drape them over your body. You are clothed. Completely. A citizen conversant with the silent stretches between streetlights, between houses, between people.

La Brea Tar Pits Park

One week before I was to depart for Rome, I went to one of L.A.'s oases—a public park. Sunday afternoon, I was lying near a trickling stream, inhaling the gentle odor of tar.

Daring children leaped across the three-foot-wide bank, ignoring the clutter of slate rocks that earthbound picnickers use as stepping stones. A pipe jutted crooked out of the water, a periscope trained by a petrified saber-toothed tiger still looking for a way out of the morass. I had mine. An open return ticket to Italy, land of *la dolce vita*, Fellini, warmth, and *l'amore*.

A couple cuddling under a tree to my right sizzled a boundary around their patch of grass with lasered love, created their own immutable world and for once I wasn't even jealous. Where I was going people would embrace the whole whopping wide world, me included, not fire me like my film bosses had, three in a row and me only two years in Los Angeles. Nor would I continue living sad tales of the heart. In Italy I'd find a love that didn't falter.

Frisbees sailed in the green beyond the pathway and I imagined an Italian boy stooping gallantly to tuck a sprig of bougainvillea behind my ear and brushing the lobe lightly with his wine-smooth mouth, not knowing and not caring that the alluring American object of his affections had been bumped out of one entertainment job after another, roundly and soundly. Not to mention the failed affairs.

A street person walked by an empty bench, growled ferociously, and flipped it over. Sun danced on its shiny green slats, its black legs helpless in the air. The Italian boy fizzled away like the effervescence of a glorious orange soda gone flat.

If I stopped and stripped away the veils for good, gave in to the lonely savagery of bench-beating and stopped dreaming of tempestuous Italian family dinners, then I was a dead girl.

Behind me a father and son played a noisy game of tag (mother missing). Every few minutes the father yelled, "FREEZE!" and his son screamed a shattering ululating scream, but stopped moving, made his body immobile. It was all there in that boy's madly bobbling Adam's apple, the seed of something strange.

I didn't know then that yelling "freeze" seven years later could mean anything besides a cop yelling at a criminal. In those early years in L.A. I could still focus on the boy's throat, and think instead about how I impressed a grade-school teacher once by knowing that "wattle" was the name of a rooster's wobbly neck flesh, a word I'd come across in the dictionary and instantly adopted in my daily vocabulary. I have always wanted to be set apart, known and admired.

Careful and considered reading can lead to fame of a quiet kind. My father is a Pura Obstinate Reader Award winner, the only one in the United States. He pored over some obscure book and read every footnote until he got to footnote two hundred and seven, which said for him to please send his name and address to the book publishers. He did. In return he got a special Pura Obstinate Reader Award certificate. There were seven winners in the world, four in Israel, one in Germany, one in England, and one, Mr. Abraham Roth, in the United States of America. My father.

I did have a father, but having one did not add up to family. Early on he taught me, "You can choose your friends, but you can't choose your relatives." I learned you also couldn't decide when they came or went. He left when I was four. In his absence, I did a little tinkering with Dad's Own Adage. Ever since then I have been choosing my friends and making them family. Why not cast the parts in Italy?

The cuddling lovers across from me kissed, not hiding the soft sucking noise of lips on skin. I was restless for Rome.

A man came up to me and said, "I'm sorry to bother you, but you have a great figure, are you interested in modeling?"

I laughed, still with a shred of amusement and a fragment of ingested flattery even though I knew I did not in the slightest have a model's physique.

"You've got to be kidding. Try that line on someone else."

I thought myself so sophisticated, when the true sophisticate wouldn't have spoken. He looked hurt.

"No, I'm serious," he said, handing me his card that I stuffed in my back pocket and opened Luigi Barzini's *The Italians,* ignoring him until he left.

I was using the slip from the security deposit return from my vacated South Detroit Street apartment as a bookmark. My mind slid over obelisks and Vestal Virgins, golden church domes and pigeon-flocked piazzas, and got stuck on the image of my landlord, Jim Tandy, with his cigar-stained teeth, slipshod toupee, and beady, close-set eyes. When I'd met with him to get my security deposit back, I'd had to hear his story about a recent robbing in one of the apartments where the thieves slashed all the couches and curtains for no reason. I also heard about an eviction he'd had to enforce on this would-be-drummer junkie, his divorce from the greedy Brentwood Bitch, and losing his job writing copy for the Soupy Sales radio show. But, he went on, still wrote chatter for Charo, he said, and best of all he was a free man. Tandy said to drop him a postcard from Rome. "And when you get back I'll check your body for handprints," he said.

Men are pigs, I thought, but I didn't tell Jim Tandy to fuck off the way I would learn to in Italy, yelling "Fuck off" in American, or even, with the really tough cases, spitting in their faces or at their feet. That worked every time. When Tandy threw out that line about the handprints, I smiled because I was going to a place where a guy like Tandy couldn't exist. Italian men were angels. Italian men spoke winged words, moved with grace and style, loved their women swooningly.

The architecture, art, the oranges, the sunlight, the dark-eyed boys, the cloud-blooming sky, the courtyards. There would be no tar pits in Italy, no toupees, no slimy film producers, no cheesy Charo, no slashing thieves, no bench-flipping transients. Everything would be beautiful.

LA LA LA LA LA

L.A. repeated over and over is a trill, a silly child's song, a light leaping laughing updown pitter-patter.

Repeat a word enough times and it loses all meaning. Sing a city enough times and the rhythm falls flat. The lyrics get ugly. The song goes tuneless.

Stick on something that happened in the past, repeat it, recycle it, rerun it through the life, and something gets ugly, and tuneless, and flat.

Rrrrrriottown, Before and After

L.A., city of mine, you are a woman full of mystery. I embrace you, shattered lovely, all your brood scattered and fighting on your fair body. The men, though, they see you as the Grand Betrayer. You seduced them, then you filled their lives with riot. You promised golden dreams and success and sweetness and big boobs and thin waists and round asses and fucking and loving and scoring and big lights. Then you turned around and ripped them apart. Showed them what was underneath your shiny veneer. Foolish men. The Haves and Have Nots, up in arms, up in flames. L.A. burning. L.A. rioting. What did I do during the riots? I fucked Giorgio's brains out on the couch. Sucking in the smoke, we timed our moves to the choppers' blades cutting through the hazy sky, while a nearby burning gun store in the corner mini-mall bathed his body in a red-gold glow and I fucked him hard. I imagined gunshots piercing the window, the secondhand couch where we fucked and how I wouldn't even care, this was how I wanted to go, with him inside me, with him in my arms and us drenched in fire glow with smoke blurring our edges together.

At first Giorgio gathered all the local papers, thinking he would write a story. But he never cut them out. He said later he thought this would give him an angle on L.A., but instead there was no political thrust, there was no rhyme or reason, there was no clearing of the smoke. The city was revealed for what it was. A betraying bitch of a place. Strip her golden promises away, her red neon lipstick, and she's a lying, cheating whore, dirty and gray, a cement soul, an asphalt jungle, a vagina dentata.

Giorgio left. I didn't understand. I thought it was me. It was. It wasn't. It was the City, L.A. Woman. He abandoned you, Los Angeles, and me, but we both betrayed you. Left you naked and vulnerable and stripped of all illusion. Men can't stand that. Then every Angelyne, every Black Dahlia, must be stripped and struck down, mutilated, raped, murdered. Subdued. Annihilated. Humiliated. Deserted.

Women, link hands and pray, and sing, and ring around the rosy of your one and only city, mysterious and sprawling as you are, phoenix rise again, I love you, Los Angeles, you spiteful woman you, I see myself in your gasoline-soaked puddles, in your shattered shop windows, in the way you wear your hair all tangled with street signs and telephone poles and ribbons of freeway. You are mine.

Me and Larry

Hollywood meetings! Thrusting that foot in the door! Whew, naive youthful exuberance, wide-open optimism, tiring just to REMEMBER how I saw the world like a big bad coconut and me with my cornerstore hardware hammer in hand, how I was going to crack that baby open, chew snow-white coconut meat 'til my baby belly was full, bathe in the sweet white mother's milk spray of it all because LIFE WAS GOOD AND IF YOU WANTED SOMETHING, REALLY WANTED SOMETHING, WELL HOT DAMN, YOU'D GET IT AND IT WOULD BE GOOD.

I called the few names I'd gathered of people who worked in film, vague connections at best, had some lackluster meetings that always ended with the courteous and mock-concerned mildly doubtful, "Good luck, sorry I can't help you," and then the suddenly animated, "By the way, you went to Brown? Hey, you know Larry Pitts?" And was I confused then.

Larry Pitts dated Brooke Shields twice and made sure people knew. When his name was actually mentioned in an article on Brooke in *People* magazine, Larry beamed a smile strong enough to cut London fog. From then on he took to dashing in late to Film Society screenings, his black trench coat flapping behind him like soggy moth wings beating a path into the air from sheer willpower. He hardly spoke to anyone anymore, like he just had to conserve the precious commodity of his speech for some mysterious and exalted purpose. If he did speak, he'd say, "What's your name?" even if he knew. Back then I thought he was becoming a parody of a pompous ass, but now I know he was a producer-in-training.

Larry lied his way into the Buckingham Club, an exclusive, pretentious group where members first had to prove there was royalty pumping in their veins and then sat around behind closed doors smoking expensive cigars, sipping cognac, gossiping, and stroking each other's egos like they were caviar-fed cats. Larry, who we called "Tweety" around campus for his bright yellow curls and noisome habit of matching the colors of his sweaters and trousers AND SOCKS, claimed he was descended from English kings. English kings! Everyone knew he was the son of a CPA in Carbondale, Illinois. Didn't the Buckinghammers ever hear of fact-checking?

When people in Hollywood asked me about Larry, they said things like this: "That guy's sure got chutzpah. Came out here with his blond hair and year-round tan, dropping Brooke's name left and right, driving a spiffy black Porsche 911 Turbo. Had the balls to take over his boss's office when he left town. Went right for the Rolodex." They'd shake their heads with feigned disdain and then proudly announce, "Yeah, had a meeting with him at the Polo Lounge last week."

Back then, in the beginning of my L.A. odyssey, I thought there was no way a guy like Larry Pitts could make it. At least not for long. They'd call his bluff, those auteurs, those visionary studio heads, and if you wanted to draw a graph, starting right then, well, Larry Pitts would start out strong, shooting up with a nice bold stroke of black—for his Porsche—while I would inch along (shocking pink would be the color of my line, for the girl thing and for the shock appeal my later success would have on all the Pitts patsies). I would then creep steadily up up up until shocking pink ruled the graphic roost and Larry's black line like a fresh-tarred freeway diminished to a skinny black line from the height of my exultant pink jet plane.

From then on, I resolved that Larry Pitts would be my own personal tracer, so I could measure how far and how fast and how steadily I rose to my rightful position (as what, I didn't know) in the wonderful world.

Unwanted: Windshield Washer

We are on the corner of Western and Pico when a man leaps on our windshield and starts rubbing it furiously with a dry paper towel. I watch the layer of soot, smog, and dirt form whorls, and I think of the hair on the head of a fetal child. Those same hopeful spirals. The Ancient Minoans used them everywhere in their lush murals. I think of an unquenchable thirst coming in waves. I think of the Pacific, where dreams expire in the crashing surf. Swirls. I think of women bending. So I do, when the windshield washer's face bobs at my window, I crank it down and offer him a dollar. He thrusts his hand inside my window, each finger segmented like chocolate Tootsie Rolls when he curls them tight around the bill. Then his clenched hand is gone and we are driving again. One of my passengers asks, "Why'd you give him any money?" The other says, "Isn't that dangerous? What were you thinking?" I say, "He washed my windshield with a dry paper towel."

Girl Whose Head Is So Large Because It Is Filled with Stars

Not the kind of stars you think.

"I whipped a prince once," says Anastasia. We're at a cheap Mexican restaurant with friends of friends, Fred and Lucy, a couple. Not for long with Anastasia around.

"Whipped him 'til he came all over his wop heirloom comforter, did you?" This is Fred. Somehow he doesn't seem to notice the ominous looks Lucy is shooting him.

"That's right," says Anastasia with a wink. It is an old story, a true story Anastasia tells to titillate men she meets. And it works.

Anastasia curls her rubber-flex vavoom body up on a restaurant booth seat, her black bra poking through a stained and tattered black vest that's missing a button, babbling lovely as a backwoods brook released from the fetters of a makeshift dam, boldly racing from Kant to cryogenics to Lorena Bobbit's trial, all the images sparkling like skybound drops of water shining with exuberant randomness and rapture, and as she rambles she doodles on the tablecloth, a balloon-bursting head, tiny dot eyes and mouth. She then fills in the frame of the skull with a million stars.

"This is my head," she says, and I realize it is the first time I've seen her draw one.

Fred's tongue is literally hanging out of his mouth, and I can hear panting. Lucy kicks him under the table so hard I hear the thump. Still no effect. He's gone for Anastasia.

"Where do you live?" says Lucy. "Beverly Hills? Malibu? With connections like yours . . ."

Anastasia blushes. She takes a quick gulp of her margarita. A few grains of salt cling to her lips.

"Panorama City," she whispers.

"Panorama City?" says Lucy. "Panorama City? I've never even heard of that." She takes a long sip of her margarita. Fred's eyes are glued to Anastasia's cleavage. "You got a fancy condo out there? Mansion or something with a dominatrix basement?"

"I live, actually, just for a little while, y'know, a week or two, with my parents out there. I'm kind of in between things."

"I see," says Lucy, looking triumphantly at Fred, who doesn't notice. He's had a chip in his hand for the last ten minutes.

Anastasia scribbles over the head she drew until nothing is left but an inky black mess.

Who Loves You, Baby?

L.A., my fearsome master, rough-tugging at those silvery strings of mine, you teach me well. With your telescope turned first this way and then that, you show me life's galaxy in all its shabby glory. One moment it's magnified into a fabulous solar blur, the next diminished into blackest mud shot through with delicate traceries of starlight.

L.A., my love, my crazy lady, hold me in your night-dark arms. I am small, yes, terribly small. Shrinking.

Puppetmaster

There were five puppets in the movie: Ms. Leech, a vampire lady who spat bloodsucking leeches out of her crimson mouth; Tunneler, whose head was a death drill; The Jester, whose tiered head spun around in Jekyll and Hyde style; Blade, whose knife did lots of flesh slashing; and Pinhead, a burly-bodied puppet with a teeny bullet bald head who pounded the bones of his victims to pulp.

Today they hired Sally, a middle-aged midget, to do Pinhead stunts.

I had never met a midget before. A miniature being. A substandard adult. A failure of genetics and perhaps willpower. A freak of nature. I recalled the years of my youth when I collected miniatures with a passion:

Miniature toasters, miniature mandolins, miniature china cabinets, miniature scissors, and miniature flower vases. I was greedy. Obsessed with microscopic perfection. I begged, borrowed, cajoled my mother. I spent all the money I had. I sought and bought miniatures with a fierce proprietary desire. I proudly displayed these miniatures in a glass case bordered with brass tubing. Kept it locked, and wiped clean, and dusted. Every time I moved I wrapped each miniature carefully in Kleenex and then placed all of them in a nest of floaty white toilet tissue. FRAGILE! I wrote on the boxes in big black marker. DELICATE! TAKE CARE!

The miniatures were always the first things I set up in our new apartments, new houses. I was devastated when I found any piece broken, and ecstatic when a case was first properly cleaned and then filled with the miniatures. But when I hit my teens I grew sick of them. I thought miniatures childish and precious and queer and ineffectual. Enlarging my personality, my anger and muscles would serve me better. So I wrapped them up haphazardly and put them away for good. Since then, the thought of anything miniature, short, or delicate has always conjured up a deep disgust.

Sally arrived a few minutes before her call time. I went downstairs to greet her. She was a ruddy-faced brunette in jeans and a T-shirt who reached to my mid-thigh. I had a strong urge to pat her on the head.

"Hi," she said, smiling cheerfully, as I searched her eyes for shame or awkwardness. There was none. Her face was sort of squished, her nose squat, but scrubbed fresh and clean. Butterflies, moths, and hummingbirds beat their frantic wings against my belly. She looked abnormally normal. Miniature, yes, but sturdy.

"Why don't we take you over to Wardrobe?" I said.

"Sure, sure, let's get a move on, don't want to keep the director waiting." She winked. I was appalled.

I slowed my gait, but she pumped her stubby legs speedily across the street. When we reached the Wardrobe trailer, I reached out to lift Sally up to the doorway, but she navigated the metal stairs with great fortitude, one step at a time. "I heard it was a killer schedule," she said over her shoulder.

Thirty minutes later Sally was ready and I escorted her to the elevator. She was dressed in a bulky puce sweater and black pants, just like Pinhead. Except her head was enormous.

"I make some Pinhead," she said, laughing. "My husband will really get turned on when he sees this flick."

"Your husband?" I said. Sally looked up at me and cocked her head.

"Yeah, how old do you think I am?" she said. "Sweetheart, I'm thirty-eight. Been married ten years. My husband Ted's an actor too. You married?"

I raised my eyebrows. "I'm not sure I even have a boyfriend," I said. "I met some guy in Arkansas, a blues musician. Name's Slim. I think I'm in love."

"Slim!" said Sally. "Does he live up to his profession?"

"He's a rough lover," I said, and Sally laughed.

"You remind me of me when I was your age," she said.

And then, right around floor four, the most peculiar thing happened. It was like I had eaten the cake in Wonderland and shrunk down to beetle size, and Sally had drunk from the bottle in Wonderland and shot up to giant size. She stood towering over me, her head hunched to avoid the ceiling of the elevator and her eyes swimming gently down on my head. I was small, my shoes dime-sized, but strangely enough I had no fear at all. Sally's clean brown hair hung down like a radiant curtain over me and I was safe.

The elevator door slid open and we stepped onto the top floor. Sally reached to mid-thigh again as she stepped into the hallway and I followed, thinking maybe I needed some black coffee to clear my head.

We picked our way through the jungle of light stands and lights and sandbags and cables, apple boxes and discarded coffee cups and candy wrappers. The walkie-talkie swung mightily from my hip and my legs were marvels of graceful musculature.

"Over here, over here," shouted Vlad, the First A.D., from the end of the hallway. "Pinhead's up next."

We arrived and Vlad gave Sally a quick glance. "Okay, she looks good, fine. Rebecca, stick with her on this end because we need someone to lock up the back rooms."

"Vlad, this is Sally," I said. "You didn't say hello."

"Right, right, you got it?" A squawk came over the walkie and Vlad strode off.

"I'm sorry," I whispered, kneeling down.

Sally's eyes flashed. "Don't be silly. Stand up, stupid. Get me some coffee, black, with three scoops of sugar, real sugar, and a tablespoon of half-and-half. Fast."

I took my sweet time. Maybe that's what midgets were all about. Pretending to be normal, pretending to be nice, and underneath they were all daggers and prickles and sourness. Waiting for the chance to strike. One big boulder-sized chip on the shoulder, ready to roll off and crush anyone who got close. Huh. Telling me I reminded her of her when she was young. Dream on. I was normal and I wasn't going to let her drag me down to size. I got back just before the first take so Sally didn't have time to drink the coffee. It would be cold when she finished.

"Okay, Pinhead?" said Vlad. "This is gonna be a close-up of you punching. Can you throw a good left-right?"

Sally shot her fists out expertly. "I'm a black belt," she said. And I knew she was saying it for my benefit.

"Great, great, okay, we're ready to roll."

So Sally punched and trotted down the hall, and pushed open doors, and spun around and punched some more and pounded an extra's shins, snapped a fake leg over a bedstead. I stood at the end of the hallway watching, thinking how each shot framed just her body, or her fists, or her torso, and always cut off her head. I wondered how she felt playing a murdering puppet, a Pinhead. And how she met her husband. And whether he was a midget. And what kind of sex they had. And whether they lived in a normal apartment, or one scaled to size, and whether those existed. And whether they always bought kid-size furniture. Or even miniatures, like the ones I used to collect. And where they lived, and where all the other midgets lived. Was there a Midget Village somewhere I didn't know about? I thought about all this, while I was locking up the end of the hallway, shushing the crew members, and holding back foot traffic until Sally's scenes were wrapped and I escorted her back downstairs.

On the way, Dirk the cute grip popped out from the depths of a black shellacked coffin.

"Midnight! Frightwig time!" He'd mussed his long hair so it stood out in a black spiky halo around his head. "This is what happens on low-budge flicks when we don't get treated right. Late hours, bad grub, no dough. Right, 'Becca?"

"You're stepping on the satin. Propmaster'll kill you," I said.

Dirk waved me off. "See, you're flipped too. Good night, Little Lady," he said to Sally, bowing low, muscles in his back rippling. She laughed pleasantly. I said nothing more, walking by briskly so Sally had to trot. I could not believe how thin and tall and stretched Dirk looked.

This time the elevator ride was silent.

In the foyer we met one of the actresses, Ida Surprise. She insisted it was her real name too, with a studied sweep of her hennaed hair she wore wrapped in a scarf, silver moons hanging from her ears. Ida played the fortune-teller in the film. Only those forecasting powers didn't prevent Pinhead from snapping her leg over the bedstead, and Tunneler finishing the job in the dark hotel hallway. This was her first movie. For some reason, she'd taken it into her head that I was on the fast boat to Producer Land.

"Hi, Rebecca," she said with a bright, fake smile and a quick nod at Sally. "Some high-class production, huh?" she said in Sally's direction, then turned eagerly to me. "Just wait 'til we get on a real set, right, Rebecca? In a real studio. We'll show these guys how to make a movie. A regular blockbuster."

"That's right," I said, for a moment believing Ida's dream for me. Sure, why not, maybe I would be a hotshot producer, maybe Ida was picking up on a natural talent, a destiny scribbled on my face. Not the one my mother wrote there. Sally tapped her foot impatiently. I said see ya later to Ida and we walked out of the castle into a Hollywood night.

It was cool. No stars were visible.

Sally turned on her tiny heels and swung her clean brown hair as she walked pistonlike across the street, but not before turning back to look at me.

"See ya in the big time," she said.

Hollywood Riff: A Warning

Hollywood's a lecherous lizard sporting star-spangled scales and a tail that curves as easily around Midwestern girls' pliant waists as around country boys' buttocks, long-stem wineglasses, leather-wrapped Benz wheels, and sleek-shining handguns.

A horny little town, Hollywood's in heat year-round.

The Door at Luna Park

"Get him drunk so you can take advantage of him," winked the waiter.

I looked at Gene.

"I don't need to get him drunk for that," I said. "Bring on the ahi tuna."

"Ahi means tuna in Japanese. So ahi tuna is redundant," said the waiter.

"Thank you," I said. "Bring it all the same."

We were inside Luna Park, looking forward to a Hollywood evening where we would indulge in major amounts of attitude, bullshit, insincerity, and self-involved hallucinations. I needed a hallucination. I was bored. Instead of leather booths, I saw slides made of green cheese, each booth a reproduction of a lunar mare. A definite improvement. I slipped my elbow into a gentle crater. Above hung a righteous round chunk of moon star, spreading its milky shine over our heads like halos. We sat on a swing. We got a rhythm so our bodies would brush to and fro and we could take syncopated forkfuls. In the center of the park was a grand set of monkey bars, and on the very tippy top was a little girl walking boldly across the parallel bars, her arms stretched out to either side for balance. The little girl was me. I clapped my hands.

"Look at that, would you look at that," I said to Gene, and toed the floor with my moonball platforms so the swing would stop. I try and dress for occasions. "It's me. Me me me. A hologram sprung from my mind. Look, sweetheart. My planetary munchkin. It's me as a kid."

"It's always you," said Gene, grumbling. "And anyway, this ahi is dry as Death."

I pinched Gene deftly on the left buttock. I knew the sting would be heightened from the air that stirred around us, simulated lunar winds that blew and eddied gently round the room. These savvy owners spared no expense. Of course Luna Park was the new happening place to be in a city where the communal attention span was a fraction of a second. We all wanted OUT of our town, while remaining put. The Luna Park owners knew.

"We Angelenos are an impressionable lot, don't you think?" I asked Gene sweetly, thinking to soothe his furrowed brow.

"Me, I'm an Angeleno. Born and raised here. You're just another chickenshit infiltrator."

The little girl stumbled on the bars and nearly slipped, but she regained her balance and even smiled at me.

"Take away all the infiltrators, darling, and the city would collapse like a great big sinkhole."

The little girl slipped and landed on her crotch on an unforgiving bar. The playground crumbled. Luna Park became clear then. A neatly lowlit Hollywood club, nothing more and something less, no moon but the covered-up ones we all carried around, no trees but the ones that were sawed down into planks that held up another club's wet dream walls.

I took Gene's hand in mine and dug my nails into his palm. He liked that. If he couldn't get love, abuse was second best. If I couldn't get the man I wanted, then abusing one I could get was second best.

Just then, Ray Manzarek himself with about-town poetess/ chanteuse/housecleaner Lena Slovena stopped by. And with him he brought the trees. And in her hair a beam of moonlight was caught. Everything was the usual bullshit.

"May we sit?" Ray asked. I raised my eyebrow at Gene. It's like that, getting to know people. There's always something new and surprising and only when all the pieces fall together do you know whether they're boring or not. How did Gene know Ray Manzarek? They sat. Lena across from Gene and Ray next to me. A horseshoe curve of conversation. No swings, just solid black-bolstered booth for our booties. After all, we're simple folk. Me, sitting at a booth with the keyboardist extraordinaire of The Doors. Sure. Of course. Once again, I was reminded I was in L.A. Where larger-than-life figures mingled with lowlifes. Or were the lowlifes larger-than-life? The confusion was part of it. In the end, though, we were all a bunch of cockroaches.

"Oh, well," said Ray. "I've just come from a drive up to San Luis Obispo. My wife and I watched Mexicans pick row after row after row after row after row of strawberries. Did you know," he spoke to me because Lena was giving Gene the big mascara-weighted eye flutter, "that they could use all that dirt for compost?"

"Did you tell them?" I asked, thinking about Giorgio (the man I wanted) who'd once spent a whole day searching for the perfect strawberry. When he found it, he squirreled it away in a jacket pocket where it squooshed and left a permanent red blot.

"I'm a white man," Ray Manzarek said. I noticed he'd set his martini down in a crater and it was wobbling. That meant he fancied his life a dangerous one, despite his talk about compost.

"It was all green up there," Ray Manzarek told me affably. "Bottlebrush and bunch grass and eucalyptus, columbine and choat."

I was impressed. "You know the names of all the indigenous plants?" I was a sucker for men with lots of trivial knowledge.

"I'm a man. I rape and pillage. I don't know the names of plants, my wife does. Do you?"

"Oh, no," I said, knowing the reference to "wife" was a come-on. "I prefer to rape and pillage myself."

"I like that," Ray Manzarek said, sipping his martini. "You seen the latest Polanski film? It's S&M to feed the heart."

"Perhaps I should have brought my whip. If you like, I'll order one flambé from the waiter."

"I would like that," Ray Manzarek said. The tree he brought

with him was hiding in his pants, afraid to face the artificial light. More along the dimensional lines of bonsai rather than redwood.

"I," said Lena Slovena, wiping sun-dried tomato paste onto a thin slice of focaccia, "was driving down the freeway the other day when I thought a tornado hit. The wind smacked against the car and tugged and whooshed. I found that I liked that, very much." She glanced meaningfully at Gene.

Lena was a lusty wench, with a marvelous gap between her front teeth, and I wanted to kill her right then because she was running her hammer-toed slippery nylon foot up and down Gene's shin. Only I knew it would turn him on later, the fool man, thinking he'd finally gotten me jealous. Meanwhile, Ray Manzarek and I hadn't even touched but we had already advanced past post-coital cuddling and were each smoking cigarettes. That's how above it all we thought we were.

"Have you been playing with Gus Manzoni?" Gene asked Ray Manzarek. Gene knows everything about music, from baroque harpsichord sonatas to West Coast jazz to El Salvadoran cumbia, all in minute and useless detail.

"We just got back from Mexico. You remember Woodstock? Well we played a Mexican Woodstock. They loved us. The Doors down there are still big. They hear, 'I want to fuck my mother, I want to kill my father,' and they go, 'Ahhhh.' On top of that we all wear leather. They're beside themselves. Two Doors is enough to give every one of them an entrance into rock heaven."

"Wild, man," said Gene. "I'm a little rusty on my history, but did you guys play Woodstock?"

Ray Manzarek blew a sweet cloud of smoke in my ear. "They invited us. Some outdoor festival in New York. Central Park, we asked? No, no. Upstate. Some place called Woodstock. So we declined. The Doors didn't sound good outside. We needed a space, a concert hall. Outdoor concerts were always a disaster. All we had was the moon to bounce our music off. That's why we never made it to Woodstock."

Lena winked at me then. She winked at me, Lena did, and the

moonbeam slipped out from behind her ear where she'd tucked it along with her wild chanteuse hair, and that moonbeam slid across the thick linen tablecloth, up over the bread crusts and pot of sundried tomato paste and ash, over my glass and right around my hand in a cool, knowing grasp.

The moon, the moon, the moon. A star for Women Only. Not that I was fooled. I knew this was merely a brief moment of recognition masquerading as a mild come-on. One L.A. Woman to another. It didn't mean a goddamn thing. Even if I wanted it to, hallucinated the Hallowed Virgin/Whore's arms thrown warmly around my neck, it just didn't materialize. I was left, alone in a crowd, with my elbow stuck in a crater.

Carla

Carla is the same height as I am, and we have the exact same size shoe with our long narrow eight and a half double As, but then her waist is a mere twenty-two inches to my twenty-eight, twenty-nine . . . it's still the "waist that can't wait." I remember Carla's undershirts coming out of the dryer doll-size at college, and me laughing as I held them up in the air, What is this? Around her, I became an ogre—heavy-footed, ravenous, clumsy and brutal, plain and coarse—and she was a perfect punk black Barbie.

"Goddammit, Carla."

We are like quarreling squirrelly sisters after a dozen years of friendship. She was my freshman roommate. I still remember seeing the slip of paper with her name, Carla Desmond from Hollywood, and my expectation of a starlet. The startling truth of Carla with her mohawked Afro, miniskirts made out of oilcloth tablecloths, witchy pointy buckled boots, quadruply pierced ears, her X and Blasters records and talk of '56 Chevies, rubber chickens, the Whiskey A-Go-Go, Pink's, her prom date Che who wore a mohawk with each strand stuck with a different country's flag and a kilt. Since then our lives have diverged, overlapped, crisscrossed, and run parallel. We don't have as much in common anymore, but the years have forged a chinkalink bond.

Carla designed Dee-dee's wedding hat, took pictures at the wedding, and catered the whole affair. Carla is a former costumer for *In Living Color* and now a feature film still photographer, but on the side she makes hats, tiles bathrooms, shoots documentary photographs, sews her own dresses, etches gold and silver sheets, cooks gourmet meals. Creativity lurks in every pore of this woman. It runs in her family. Her uncle, a neon artist, invented the car bra, a piece of fabric that stretches over the headlights and front bumper of the car to protect from road dings. The headlights peep through the fabric like electric nipples. Isn't that like men to see breasts everywhere.

"Rebecca, you're not listening," Carla scolds me as she scrapes her ice cream parlor chair's wire legs. The conversation's not over. Chihuahua eyes—loose and straining bulbous at the sockets, skin stretched tight as a tarp. This means she's talking about the real rats. Men who don't call, men who can't pay for dinner, men who break promises, men who disappear. Carla is prowling for love, prying for love, vying, spying, trying. Do I remind her how her gaze goes honey-glazed when a man's around? How she turns deaf to the sounds of other women? Do I tell her a woman deaf to women is a dead woman and that's why we run parallel or crisscross but never ever blend as one warm burst of joyous laughter? This is what I say.

"Uh huh."

When I say Carla's name, I mimic her voice. Operatic high-pitched shrill trilling double-syllabic roller-coaster ride of a name. When I say Carla, I linger on the final L.A. and know that the city breathes through her. Sometimes the sound is mournful as a foghorn. Listen.

Ode to Fellini's Cinecittá

Ah, Fellini! This is where you shot all your greatest films, you merry prankster, with your big-breasted dreams and carnival wonder. The snake charmers and belly dancers and bosomy women wearing only scarves, the harlequins and sunglassed Sicilian beauties, the Roman playboys in cream-white linen suits, cigarette smoke pluming out of sensuous chattering mouths, any minute they will spill out of a building and parade forth. The wide fat world, Fellini's juicy tomato with plump cheeks to bite. Tears of sadness and colored streamers in the wind after the players have left town. Fellini, you're the whistle on a dark and dusty village road, the daisies in a whore's hair, the first taste of waves on a man's tired foot. You are the ache of life. The song. The dance. The cacophonous traffic jam I long to be stuck in.

Ripeness Is All

In Rome, I find myself dreaming, dreaming L.A. What once gave me a sense that I belonged is now revealed for what it is: I can stroll the piazzas as if they were my private grounds, can perambulate where I like, but I am not Roman. I walk everywhere; one day and I can cover the whole town, and yet this does not mean the city is mine. I can live in the midst of shouting families and mothers who hang the laundry on lines outside their windows, but I am not one of them. Tolerance doesn't equal acceptance. Hospitality is not tantamount to a familial embrace. The Romans are amused by me, but I cannot escape the label "Americana," or worse, *"straniera."* Stranger. Some desire my mystery. Some strike up affairs, even declare their undying love, but always I am a foreigner. I begin to trip and stumble on the cobblestones I used to cherish, and I find myself longing for the vulgar stretch of six-lane freeways.

I remember what a rush it was to round that curve in Santa Monica where the PCH spills off Ocean Avenue into the glory of the Pacific Coast, that feeling that everything was mine for the taking. I can almost feel the measured sweep of my car as it hugs the incline, can almost see the striking blue of the water and the coast stretching upward like the scintillant arc of my desires. In my car I was armored and potent, a heroine loosed on the freeways and surface streets of the city.

In Rome, I am off track. Stuck. Circumscribed. Peripheral. Eternally orbiting the eternal city, but never landing. Never penetrating. Whereas in L.A., so many countries and beliefs and backgrounds are represented that there's a slot for everyone. L.A.'s an amusement park ride, The Grand Tilt, one of those spinning, lilting circular jobs rotating on a twisted axis. Got a ticket? Hop aboard. Welcome to the city of sunshine and blotted-out pasts.

In Rome, everything's the past. At first I was breathless standing before ancient crumbling walls, sun-dappled noseless statues and passersby with classical Roman faces; but now, the weight of history oppresses me. The past too is a kind of smog.

So I am dreaming L.A., imagining the city opening its sooty arms to me, welcoming the Prodigal Daughter back home, ready to forgive all mistakes and failures I've made and yet, something nags me. I cannot leave Rome without trying one more thing. If film is what I love, and this is the city that created Fellini, then before I return I must work at the studio where Fellini worked. Maybe that is the missing ingredient; maybe Cinecittà will engender the magic of my transformation into a true, impassioned Italian, a being completely disconnected from my past. Perhaps there's still a chance.

Siesta time in Rome. Church bells ring in the distance as wind clatters a garbage-can lid to the ground of the courtyard. On schedule, a dog begins his frenzied barking and faces appear at the windows. *"Ogni giorno, ogni giorno!"* one woman screams, paddling the air with a dirty spoon. More people appear, some nod vigorously. An old man waves his bony fist and the dog barks louder. "You, Dog Woman, show your face. Stronsa, one day I kill your dog, kill it dead," shouts the woman with the spoon. But no one appears at the window of the apartment where the dog lives.

Fat pigeons promenade on the gutter outside the window where I lean over the courtyard, watching, listening. Soon the dog stops barking and faces withdraw. There is a moment of silence that promises eternity and I close my eyes. Then someone blows his nose twice. A handful of change crashes onto a dresser and a girl sings a made-up song as she reels in bedsheets.

I pick up today's *La Repubblica*. So far the only newspaper stories I can fully grasp are the Mafia ones. I read about a twelve-year-old boy from Naples who worked several jobs to help support his family, jobs that took him all around Naples at odd hours. One early morning the boy saw and heard too much. He received a *"colpa di grazia nella bocca,"* which meant the Mafia shot him dead through the mouth to make sure he didn't talk. The last line of the article departs from factual report and urges readers to mind their own business if they want to live long. Although the story disturbs me, I feel safer in Rome—the Mafia seems preferable to American violence, somehow more controlled and even stylish, with principles and rules that you can follow. They know what they want.

Soon after arrival: by my own admission, I am a nervous person, at least back in the States. I attribute my current lethargy to the high concentration of art, carbon monoxide, cream sauces, a sagging bed, loneliness.

My American friends told me, my Italian friends tell me, the only way to learn the language is to get an Italian boyfriend. While I talk to Italian men and boys, even making appointments, I usually break them. Either forget or don't care or change my mind. Or spin them out for an evening, sometimes even a night, but never more. Without regrets. Until I remember I'm alone, in a new country, thousands of miles from home. Unloved in a romantic city. Yet there is something less harsh about the lemon light that suffuses the air in Rome, compared to the sepia sky of L.A. Luckily for me Roman time flows on despite my stillness.

So I straighten my back and remind myself I came to learn the language, to live abroad, to work, not to find a lover. Which comforts me only briefly. Rome is a city that encourages love as a way to defy the haunting decay and ruin, a way to celebrate life in a place full of ghosts. Love stretches moments into timelessness and makes the weight of history bearable. When you deny the city, you suffer a sweet-tasting despair. Yet something holds me back from heeding the whispered words of Rome, something I cannot put my finger on. I feel curiously empty, a hollow shell floating alone in a sea of vibrant fish.

For one month I lived like an American heiress, which I am not, camping in a penthouse room of a *pensione* in the Ghetto that gave me a view of the mud-red terracotta roofs and flowering *terrazzas*. I purchased lace-patterned hose that fit snugly round my thighs, Italian books about things like bisexuality and biocosmic energy, quarter-size pastels from artists in Piazza Navona, gelato every night, cappuccinos daily in the most picturesque and costly cafés where I studied Italian grammar and gossiped with other foreign students.

One day during this time, I met Gregory Corso of Beat Generation fame wandering the narrow streets stumbling drunk, mumbling lines of his poetry, and pointing toward street names. "See?" he said to me triumphantly. "They've named them all after me . . . Corso Vittorio, Corso Venezia. Italians love me." He winked and smiled a sly toothless smile. "Want to be my future ex-girlfriend?"

That got me wondering about my life direction, and whether I really knew why I had come to Rome. It was also the day I realized I'd run out of lire, the rainbow-colored bills spent so freely because they looked and felt like Monopoly money.

The language intensive class is over now, and so is life as a dilettante. For the next month in Rome, I am broke.

One of my classmates, a Swedish actor named Lars who was staying around for the summer, offered me a room in his apartment because another roommate was traveling. So that is where I am. In my own room with a floor like a drained swimming pool, aqua-blue tile cool to the foot, the same color as Lars's eyes.

At first, other students nudged me, "So, you and Lars?" which set my heart pumping. His mouth was very fine. If not an Italian, then why not a Scandinavian? Aren't they foreigners too? Until the evening we had espresso and Lars held my hand and told me how much he liked me, how much he trusted me. His eyes were shining as he sipped his espresso. Then he told me about his lover Lucio.

Next door I can hear Lars and Lucio arguing about something, the way Lars overcooks pasta perhaps. Only last year Lucio was a Calabrian Don Juan, until he wandered into the Magnani Disco and met Lars. Lucio has a shock of jet-black hair and a curling mouth, and like all Calabrians he loves to fight. Their voices float out the window and into the courtyard along with the other noises. Someone slams their shutters and lets out a horrific wail.

My first job in Rome is to help a man translate an instruction manual for a machine that tests blood samples. I do not tell him I would not understand such a text in English, let alone Italian. His name is Pietro Limone, which literally means Stone Lemon. He is an acquaintance of my father's remedial Talmud student, and runs his own translation company.

Pietro's workroom is dominated by an enormous antique table covered with flaking geodes, piles of dusty dictionaries, and a jar of pistachio nuts from Turkey. Because the windows are streaked with dirt, the room is poorly lit. While we work, Angelo glances repeatedly at his watch, sighs, and pushes his chair closer to me.

"You have not been here long, I know this," he says. "Your Italian, it's not so good." He offers me a nut and a resigned smile. There is a web of perspiration on his middle-aged forehead. From frustration at the pace of the work or at his ineffectual sexual gestures, I do not know, as I furrow my brow in mock concentration and shift my leg to the other side. I am not that lonely.

After one hour of work, the Mama shuffles in the room, holding her hip and shouting at Pietro. "Help me!" she yells. Then there is a stream of words I do not understand, and Pietro gets up from the worktable and leads his mama into the other room for some minutes while I crack pistachio nuts. Most of them are shriveled and bitter. I wonder how many years they've been sitting on the table.

When we finish the translation, Pietro engages me in a lively discussion about Woody Allen, "He is my favorite, very European," and says thank you many times, but does not call me again. Maybe the Mama disapproves. I earn enough money for groceries that week.

In the late afternoon I run in Villa Doria Pamphili, a former papal family estate that is now open to the public. I run past gurgling fountains, headless, armless statues, and the Italians stare and shake their heads as they stroll along graveled paths. I run over bullfrogs that appear at dusk, past mottled ocher walls, empty recesses that once held statues, past dark-haired children kicking soccer balls in ancient gardens. The memory of starting guns and races round circular school tracks rigidly chalked into lanes strikes me as ludicrous, and I erase the memory by concentrating on the parasol pines that line the paths of the Villa Pamphili, their foliage pluming like luxurious puffs of green smoke against the darkening sky.

One early morning in Campo dei Fiori, the open-air market, by the statue of Giordano Bruno who was burned at the stake for heresy, I meet a Romanian actress named Magda who hennas her hair and wears only leopard-print clothing, including her shoes. Magda is buying blood oranges.

Magda invites me up for tea and a joint, and tells how she edited the first collection of women's sexual fantasies, but Nancy Friday had a better publicist so she got the credit because in those days Magda cared more about nature and world peace than fame and money. Now she's approaching fifty and she's changed her mind, but it's too late. (Once she was lying on the beach in the Bahamas, wind passing over her baking body took the form of a Russian man who spoke in his language that she didn't know but understood and he offered her a wish. She said, I want to know how people make money. She had a vision of people stepping on other people's faces, thighs, and tailbones on a mad stampede toward a glinting gold sign. Before she could take back the wish, the vision was gone.)

Each wall of Magda's living room is a different color—orange, lilac, green, lemon-yellow. The cushions we sit on do not match. I am not sure I like this woman.

Magda has a son named Leopold and a daughter named Nadia. She knows R.D. Laing and Lina Wertmuller and Bernardo Bertolucci and Dacha Maraini. She is afraid of menopause and of losing her beauty. She has a lover who is an Italian prince, who has an apartment overlooking Piazza Navona and at night the reflections from Bernini's Fountain of the Four Rivers ripple on the ceilings and it is the most wonderful sight. The sex is fantastic, he also has a wife, but Magda is the favorite. "Better to be the mistress, right?"

I tell Magda that I am looking for work. I do not ask her why the sex is fantastic.

"It just so happens," says Magda in her Italian-Rumanian-British accent, "that I have a wonderful part in a movie soon, where I play a blind courtesan, a great acting challenge, and I get to sing too, Bernardo heard me sing at a concert and rewrote the part for me, so I am giving up a funny little job I have. You're welcome to try, but it's kind of bizarre."

"That's fine," I say. "What do I have to do?"

This job requires a long bus ride to the suburbs, which in Italian is called the Periphery. That's where Father Morlion lives, a ninety-year-old priest who writes and edits a quarterly newsletter called *United Peoples* that urges World Peace. Unlike Magda, he has not changed his mind since his youth as a political activist in Amsterdam.

"Hello, hello," he says to me when he answers the door dressed only in a stained blue bathrobe. Even bent-backed he is a tall man. Father Morlion offers his hand, which feels dry and callused as a bunion.

"My body is the body of a ninety-year-old, my brain"—he taps his head—"my brain is the brain of a twenty-year-old, that's what the doctor tells me. There is much work, however, so I must keep working while I can. Come in, come in."

For ten thousand lire an hour, roughly equivalent to ten dollars an hour, I sit on a metal stool before an ancient Olivetti and type the *United Peoples* articles in English while Father Morlion dictates them from the red leather chair behind me. The hours are flexible, which means when I can stand it no longer, I tell Father Morlion I have to leave.

Father Morlion smokes stogies to activate his brain, says he got the idea from Jefferson. "Jefferson, and as he was a genius I believe him, said unsophisticated Virginian tobacco, no perfumes, is the only tobacco. Purely to awaken my mind, eh? This is the most powerful way of getting new ideas. There would have been no Declaration of Independence without it."

So Father Morlion smokes. There are shreds of tobacco scattered on the floor and piles of papers on the tiles.

"Type this in capital letters. 'PERSONAL. URGENT. TO THE POLITICAL LEADERS AND THE WIELDERS OF MASS MEDIA.' Yes, mmhmm, here we are, now I give you a letter. 'Dear Friend, I write to you personally as a friend because I am sure we tend to the same aim: to develop mutual understanding and esteem between the civil and religious authorities of the 152 countries of the world, not only the democratic West and Third World but also the nine communist countries.' "

I check my watch with a sigh and tense my buttock muscles on the hard stool. The keys of the Olivetti frequently stick and I have to pound them.

On the bus ride home I try to read all the billboards. I am startled when a sturdy old woman knuckle-jabs me in the kidneys because I did not move aside, which gives me the sudden insight that I am always looking but not seeing.

When I arrive home, Lars and Lucio have pasta with capers and a bottle of warm wine waiting. Lars nods suggestively at the bowls. "Lucio's night," he says. "How did he do?" Before Lucio can speak, I tell them the pasta is perfect. And it is. I am sure I will never tire of pasta, which curls warmly inside my stomach and fills every hungry part.

On good days, Father Morlion dictates clearly and with only minor pauses. On those days, I can stand up to four hours.

"Don't you ever take vacations?" I venture one good day.

"My head will not let me. There is work to do. If I cut off my head, I could take a vacation. Remember I have twenty-year-old arteries bringing blood to my head, you, yours are probably twenty-five!" This irritates me, I am only twenty-four and not interested in getting older, but I say nothing.

When I do respond with a contradictory statement, Father Morlion always shakes his head and says, "No no no no no no no—no no no no no," in an energetic burst.

But on bad days, Death is there, palpable and sticky. Father Morlion's bathrobe gapes open, bares his swollen stomach, chest hair littered with bits of tobacco. The pauses between his words get so long I bring a book. While Father Morlion says, "Half a minute, half a minute," mouth opening and closing like a guppy's, I read lightning fast, as if I am in a race, sometimes finishing a chapter before he starts up again. Then the odor of urine is strong, mingled with tobacco, and muffled farts rise from the red leather chair with no antimacassars.

On those days I keep my back turned, hold my breath, and dare myself to stay longer, reminding myself I need money. On those days I keep my bottle of acqua minerale capped so dust and decay won't pollute the water. Everything in Father Morlion's house is sticky. He never asks for help.

A friend calls Lars about a short-term job coaching an Italian actress with American dialogue. Lars suggests me. The actress's name is Fiammetta Grizi, and she is twenty-eight years old. She will play an Argentinian private detective who also looks good in a G-string bikini, and Fiammetta must be able to dub her dialogue with an American accent for the U.S. market. That's where I come in.

The job will allow me to alternate between Father Morlion and Fiammetta.

Walking to Fiammetta's that Monday afternoon, I see a monkey seated on a window ledge. I wave at the creature, which promptly turns its back and disappears into the apartment. I realize with embarrassment that the monkey's snub irritates me, and I walk through the narrow cobbled streets at a fast pace until sweat dampens my back.

Fiammetta is an actress against her parents' wishes. They wanted her to join the Parliament. Fiammetta owns a dress shop around the corner. She and her sister live together in an apartment that their parents bought for them, right near Piazza Del Popolo, which is the most prestigious neighborhood of Rome. The opposite of the Periphery where Father Morlion lives.

At Fiammetta's, we always begin the twice-weekly lesson after she's brought me a glass of water laced with Lampare, a sweet pink syrup that swirls to the bottom of my glass like hair unwinding underwater. Fiammetta watches my every gesture, every expression, which makes me both amused and uncomfortable.

Fiammetta is always sniffing my dark musk oil, pulling off her sunglasses, poking down my shirt. "Do you wear a bra?" she asks me. "Are your eyes bad? What is that perfume? Do you have this drink in America? Do you have a boyfriend?" I don't answer all her questions. When I do, invariably I lie, which pleases Fiammetta no end. Fiammetta is used to being entertained.

I tape Fiammetta's lessons. Bring in script pages that I've broken down phonetically. Since Fiammetta has a video camera, we also use that. Fiammetta insists that I demonstrate the correct way to read the lines. "Let me direct you!" says Fiammetta eagerly. I refuse until the final lesson. I have never liked getting my picture taken, let alone acting in a video.

Saturday is my twenty-fifth birthday. To celebrate, Lars and Lucio and I dress up and go to a new club called Brazil. I wear a blue minidress and sparkly tights.

The club is down an alley behind an ancient palazzo that's been under restoration for years, and there is a strong scent of rotting oranges. I walk between Lars and Lucio, and feel proud to have them on either side as I enter the club.

Inside, the music pounds, steel drums and skin drums and guitars and flying hands. The club is narrow and tightly packed, and everything is bathed in purple light from thin strips of neon that crisscross the ceiling. Although the music is strange to me, I feel the old nervous energy again. The drummer, a bullet of a man with dark black skin and a sweat-glistening bald head, points to me and the crowd moves aside, azure-eyed *ragazzi* whose collective gaze follows me, their lithe-bodied girls by their sides, clad in body-tight scraps of stretch fabric, mouths pouting, dark hair cascading round their faces. I close my eyes and gyrate, each section of my body hoolahooping in its own orbit, feet shifting lightly, inspired by the primal rhythm and the drummer. If not an Italian, then why not a Brazilian? Gold chains lie heavy over the drummer's sculpted chest, but when the song is over, he flashes me a gold-toothed smile and points to another girl. So my roommates and I dance, close and tight, and Lucio holds me by the waist. Then it is over, and we three walk home, through cobblestoned streets, past mumbling fountains. I am almost happy.

Halfway back, a tiny black man with large eyes emerges from a shadow and offers us a bottle. "It's African wine, from Africa," he slurs repeatedly, thrusting the bottle of muddy liquid at our chests. When we, giddy, laugh and say, "No thank you," he becomes furious. His eyes grow larger and he holds the bottle high, then swoops it down near our heads saying, "I know what you're thinking. Don't think of me like that." Which leaves us speechless as the man staggers away.

Lucio breaks the silence. He tells us two years ago there were no Africans in Rome, only Italians, Gypsies, and tourists, the occasional short-term foreigner. "Now there are many Africans, and soon there will be trouble." Lucio nods at me, and I know that he means the black-white conflicts in America.

"You look beautiful tonight," Lars says to me, and squeezes my arm. "Yes you do," says Lucio, and pulls me closer. "A real woman."

His lips brush my neck. Though the warmth is fleeting and incomplete, it heats even the aqua-blue tiles for that night.

The last session Fiammetta and I have, we are sitting on a bed, which is covered in a silky peach fabric, and watching the video. The second I appear, Fiammetta screams with almost perfect American enunciation, "You should be an actress!" I smile distractedly, do not tell Fiammetta I am thinking of my birthday. I think of Father Morlion, and wonder how old my brain is relative to my body. I think of Magda, and worry whether I too at fifty will change my mind about how I chose my life.

That night walking home from Fiammetta's, I pass a fat woman moonbathing. She is sitting against an ancient wall near Campo Dei Fiori dressed in a bathing suit, slathering herself with suntan lotion, slapping great gobs on arms and chest. Oblivious to passersby. To me, the woman seems boldly content.

A hot day. I am already on my second bottle of acqua minerale. On the way to Father Morlion's for the last time, a fire engine with a blue light speeds past one way, then, apparently with the wrong address, speeds past in the opposite direction.

Father Morlion invites me for lunch. Thinking first of saved money, I accept, then wonder whether I should have. I have never been in the kitchen. Even more so than the den, every surface in the kitchen is slick, dirty, dusty. In the sink is a pan of congealed yogurt and other unidentified elements. All the bottles are sticky. There is a signed color photo of the Pope above the table.

Father Morlion offers me lukewarm orange soda, then turns his back. I watch him add a shot of brandy to his own soda, slide the bottle into hiding, then pull out a dish from the refrigerator that his cook prepared. He serves me a bowl with badly shaking hands. Seeing all this makes me feel pity at first, then discomfort. As if I have seen more than I should, or can.

The seafood pasta waits nightmarish in the plastic bowl. My head whirls. Rubbery purple squid curls and wrinkled peas in noodles. I do not eat. Father Morlion doesn't notice. He is cheerful, fortified.

He tells me how the Pope was almost assassinated and how the secret Vatican police came after him, as a prime suspect! All due to the rumors started by a jealous rival of his who does not believe in politicians being life-bearers instead of death-dealers. Who does not believe that the time has come to pass from nationalistic policies to normal human relations.

"Our hope lies with the U.S. and the Soviet Union," he shouts. "We must convince Reagan." He looks into my face searchingly. "He is not as smart, not as brave as Gorbachev." Father Morlion's eyes spark behind thick lenses, his brows bristle with emphasis, but his skin betrays him. His face drags downward and his chin and neck sag like flesh leaking out of a torn bag. More than I can bear. I thank him for the lunch and say I must go, I have an appointment I forgot, but thank you so much, for everything. At the door I tell him I hope Perestroika succeeds, and mean it.

On the crowded sweaty bus ride home, the world becomes pelvic level, swollen organs on all sides, brushing my hips, bumping my buttocks, all ready to explode. It seems I am the only woman on the bus and all the men are one grinning creature. I wedge myself behind a metal rail for protection.

That night a man I met once in a café on Viale Trastevere, the director of a documentary about teenage girl pyromaniacs, stops by. His name is Pepe. He is tall and wiry, has a mop of soft Caravaggian curls that fall coquettishly into manic eyes. He has a wife and two little girls with long dark braids. There is no living room in the apartment. I let him in my bedroom. I am wearing a green shirt.

"Do you feel green in your head?" he asks, standing near the door.

"What do you mean?" I say.

"What I really want to know is how you're feeling," he says. "What color."

"I don't know. What about you?"

"I feel red and white. Red because I feel something." He stares at me. "White because I don't know how to live my life. I respect Angelica and her lovers and she respects mine. Let's play a game."

Pepe shuts the door, the windows, paces back and forth.

"You were scared when I shut the windows," he whispers.

"Angelica," I ask.

"Don't worry, I just want to caress you." He sits next to me on the thin-mattressed bed.

"*Bellissima.* I know you have many lovers." He kisses my neck. "I want you I want you I want you," he says, sliding us down onto the mattress. "How do you say, travel, I want to travel in you."

"You want a vacation?" I say, each word a post in a temporary fence I erect between us the closer he gets.

He tells me I am an ocean and he wants to swim in the blue, do I understand? He unbuttons my shirt. Pulls off his sweater. Jeans. Then we are both S's curled into each other, he is holding me, and he whispers he wants me to touch myself, yes, with him inside. "When you come," he says, "on the one night you are alone each week, when you touch yourself, I want you to think of me. Think of me until I'm the only one. Then I'll be back." I want to tell him I don't have lovers every other night of the week. I want to tell him I'm lonely, but I don't. He goes away on his motorcycle. Soon after he moves to Milan. I never see him again, but I see his wife and two girls around Trastevere now and then.

I get work on a monster film at Cinecittá. I fill condoms with stage blood, tie them off, and load them in hollow plastic hands. I slather Leviathan's tentacles, claws, scaly belly, and tyrannosaurus jaw with K-Y jelly and Ultraslime to make him glisten and drip for the camera. I puppeteer a rubber latex tentacle. Find real hanks of human hair to match the actors' for use on mutated dummies. Make little pointed teeth and glue them into monster slugs' mouths.

What makes the work bearable is a P.A. named Paolo. He's got headphones and a walkie-talkie and wires all over his soccer player's body. Wide forehead, light dusting of freckles over high cheeks, petulant red lips. Paolo is half American, half Italian. He's a younger version of Christopher Lambert. All feral virility in khakis and a polo shirt.

On lunch break, I disappear to a solitary spot on the steps near the Cinecittá Sculpture Shop. As I pick bits of "plankton" off the hairs of my arm, the smell of wet fiberglass drifts out from the windows and flavors my tomato and mozzarella panino. An exact replica of Michelangelo's *David* lies prone before me, face curved toward a tangle of vines. Munching, I study an ant marching across his perfect thigh until it disappears over his hip. Think of Paolo.

Later that day, as I'm leaving the stage, a voice comes from behind me.

"Hurry up, Rebecca."

"Paolo," I say with surprise.

"What," he says gruffly. "What's taking you so long? The rest of Effects is long gone."

"Think you can give me a lift?" I say quickly. "It's so late I've missed the last train."

"If I have to," he says.

Paolo speeds down the narrow Italian streets, barely avoiding parked cars and people walking, until he gets to Santa Maria in Trastevere. I am tired; I don't mind silence. I know this game of not talking hides the terrible need he has for me. Perhaps underneath the bravado he is shy.

"This is my apartment building," I say, pointing to the right.

Paolo brakes his car. Turns off the engine and sits there with his face straight ahead, drumming on the steering wheel. He looks better than Christopher Lambert in the flickering shadows from the streetlights. Suddenly he leans over to kiss me, pinning me to the back of the seat. The kissing is feverish, as if we fought something and now we've given in and all the tamped fires are raging. Before I know it, I'm in his lap, straddling him, and our backs are damp with sweat.

"Let's go upstairs," he says hoarsely, pushing me off him.

Paolo leaves the Fiat double-parked. He doesn't touch me or talk as we walk up to the dark building.

I slide the brass elevator cage door to the left and yank open the heavy inner door with the tiny vertical slit of a window and we get in. Before the door snaps shut he is on me, claiming lips, hair, throat, breasts. The brass mesh clanks and the pulleys creak with our heavy movements as the elevator shakes upward. Paolo has me in the back of the elevator that is barely big enough for both of us. A crackling old bulb spills harsh yellow light down on us. He's got his hand up under my shirt, pinching my nipple, then his mouth is a warm wet circle, suckling. He reaches out a hand and stops the elevator between the third and fourth floor. They call "floor" *piano* in Italian; he is running his fingers up and down the keys, a mad stringendo that kicks up orphic dust, striking chthonic chords. There is a single plum tomato on the floor of the elevator. He kicks it and it splits against the dirty yellow tile. I want to suck him. With a firm hand he turns me around and tugs my pants down; immediately his finger is probing my wetness and I hear him unzip his pants, scooping up the tomato pulp and smearing my flesh with it as he rubs against me. All there is, is breathing and the creak of the ancient elevator. Him rigid against me, still and hungry, but I am hungrier, my body crying out to be stolen, consumed. Then he is inside me, and I am climbing the walls, my legs, my feet, palms and heels pressed to all sides, holding, straining, I am a monkey aloft in its cage, airborne and flying, my primate fur in flames. All is breathing, sighs, and groans. We are rutting wildebeests, the floor beneath us a thicket dense with burrs, alive with whirring flies and shiny green beetles. I am a bound golden calf, my hide sleek and gleaming for the knife. The air is my altar. Eat me with wild mint after the flames have licked me clean. The elevator rattles. Someone bangs on the metal chute farther up.

"Ascensore!" they cry. Elevator. Paolo lets go of me. I slide slowly back to the ground, first one foot, then the other, yanking my underwear and jeans up with stinging hands and tucking in my shirt. On

147

my palms a maze of red lines. Hair damp and tangled. Only me, a lustful human. When Paolo presses five, he is already zipped and buttoned back to normalcy. We pass a woman on four who stares at us through the tiny vertical window with suspicious eyes. Paolo gets out on five with me.

"Well, come on in," I say, my voice a thick whisper, clutching at his khakis. He stands a moment with my hand there, shakes his head at me.

"No reason now," he says, laughs, then turns and runs down the stairs.

I finish out the one month remaining on *Leviathan*. Amid the acrid smell of liquid wood and fiberglass resin, mechanically blown sea anemones, the slowly rising dust, I dream of dark-haired airbrushed babes on gold-trimmed lowriders, of chainsaw-juggling Sikhs walking the Venice boardwalk, of skateboards and carne asada burritos and Korean BBQ and freeway onramps and friends. Who's to say but that Rome was what I needed to shave, comb, and cheek-smack clean my vision of the city that summons me.

I call Father Morlion before I leave Italy to see how he is, but can't get through. After some hours, I get a connection, hear a strangled gargling, then a click. I immediately call Magda, who calls his cook and caretaker. "Everything's fine," Magda calls back to tell me, "he's just had a bad period." Then says the film she just finished will probably be nominated for an Oscar for foreign film, shouldn't she go? It might be her big chance, Hollywood and all, if she could just master that damn ugly American accent. I thank her for the job with Father Morlion, but I do not call him back.

Some days later Magda calls to tell me Father Morlion died. The funeral will be held on Sunday. My ticket is for Saturday. I ask Magda if Father Morlion had great pain, but myself feel nothing but nausea and a melancholy relief. Magda says she does not know, she did not ask.

Fiammetta calls to tell me she is featured in *Blitz,* which is a semi-porn magazine. She is not naked, she says triumphantly. It is a silly magazine, but she is featured and that is important. I wonder what is important. I think of Father Morlion, who seemed to know what was important, to him. "Good luck in America!" Fiammetta says. "Find a rich boyfriend since you haven't had luck here! At least there is lots of work there. That is why I am learning how to speak American!"

The day of my departure, Lars and Lucio present me with an armful of fresh-cut anemones and a cookbook. "You know, we have a confession to make," says Lucio, flashing his black eyes. "Since the night we went to Brazil, we have been dreaming about you, and also when we have sex." Lars's ears flush but Lucio only smiles more broadly and continues. "Anyway, you must keep in touch with us, it has been wonderful. Rome will always be here for you, waiting!" "Write to me," says Lars. I kiss them fast and roughly, run as if I'm late though I am not.

Already memories of American time have resurfaced, and I race through the streets, now surefooted on the cobblestones. The thought that I may never see Lars or Lucio or Magda or any of the people again does not slow my steps. The city is harder to leave.

In Campo Dei Fiori, I pass Bruno one last time before reaching the taxi stand, and take a moment to touch the blackened metal curve of his cloak that is warmed from the afternoon sun. Bruno somehow is simpler than the rest. Steady, unflinching, Bruno welcomes all without judgment.

The garbage truck arrives and several men flood the piazza with water. Piles of trampled celery stalks, bruised fruits, and chicken heads left over from the morning market rush by my feet. A grizzled man in a sailor's cap pulls his three-wheeled cart down a narrow street, and a waiter sweeps radicchio leaves off his patio. I kiss my hand and touch it once more to Bruno's cloak.

Hollywood Dream

Hollywood:

I dreamed you sullen and sweet, a mango shake pulped with overripe fruit that I'd sip, slowly, craving more on a Sunday in the center of Farmers' Market, mindless of the Japanese tourists and their telephoto eyes seeking my febrile surrender.

They want this: an American girl captured, crushed to two dimensions. Facsimile of vulgar foreign girl. Drained of blood and mango pulp. Masturbatory travel snapshots.

I want this: sensual obliteration. Me disappearing into the city's sodium vapor and neon lights. Evaporating along with spilled and wasted juices. Gone.

In the Los Angeles hills coyotes still roam. Snap the necks of house cats. Rip the throats of domesticated yard dogs. Feast on garbage, drifters, lost souls.

Remember red ghosts and the coyotes. Keep your howls to yourself.

Day 'N Nite

Kate met Tommy at the Day 'N Nite parking lot. Tommy was leaning against the plate-glass storefront with one leg propped up behind him, squinting at her, when she got out of her Range Rover. Bare-chested, he had a banana-yellow La-coste shirt tied around his waist, tight Calvins, and filthy white Pumas a few sizes too big. A street person, his skin was burned a reddish brown by the sun, his teeth were attractively crooked, his hair greasy with natural oils from not bathing. He smelled of sweat and cheap suntan lotion. There was a white scar in the shape of a parenthesis on the side of his left eye. Kate looked at him, appraising. He whistled as she walked by.

"Sexy mama," he said. He couldn't have been more than twenty-five. Kate's age exactly.

She came back out with a pack of Marlboros and hesitated. A punchy orange-ish frame of light radiated around Tommy—was it the glare from polluted sun on car metal bouncing into her shades? The smog? Standing close, Kate felt an energy around him, some-thing bobbing and weaving with her own tingling nerves.

"Cig?" he asked. Kate slowly peeled the gold thread tab, shucked the cellophane onto the ground where it lay glittering in the light, folded back the triangular flaps of silver foil, and tapped the pack smartly on her palm. The cigarettes glided out the top. She handed one to Tommy and took one for herself. Before she could get her lighter he lit them with a silver Zippo, then bowed. The gesture touched her. They stood in the sun, the thick haze, smoked, talked, and sucked the burning fire into their bodies. Tommy didn't have a place to live so she took him home to Venice.

Kate was a successful screenwriter. She wrote about troubled girls from broken homes, drunkards, dope fiends, night lifers, psychics, child abuse prosecutors, and Marines. Even though none of her films had made it to the screen yet, they had all been bought for good prices. She was always working. With the money she made she rented a large bungalow on the canal, had two Siberian huskies, and bought expensive clothes she stored in boxes under her bed, in the closet, in drawers, and never wore.

Kate was always bored, bored, bored. She was also shy. Ask her on a date and she would mutter incoherently, or agree and then not answer the phone until the person gave up. Industry men she considered no more men than pipe cleaners. Once she answered personal ads, but the men who said they were attractive invariably were missing an arm or a leg or were deformed in some other way when she met them for coffee at Denny's. She gave up and concentrated on her writing. Until Tommy.

When they were driving, Tommy would point at men crossing the street and say, I did him. This didn't bother Kate because she was in love. He needed help and she could give it. She knew he was a street hustler, so what? It was a job. Also she'd never had such good sex before as she did with Tommy. It was his unpredictability that kept her hot.

Sometimes Tommy would only say the words "I love you, Kate" the whole entire day, even when she asked him questions or when friends called him. Then, he often needed to fuck her seven or so times in a row. Other times he would sit in the den with the shades drawn and drink Maker's Mark rum.

You're the devil, he'd say. It's your fault the sun is always on. Cunt. Witch. Admit you control the weather. HAH!

He would throw her against a wall, laugh hysterically, then re-treat back into the den whimpering with another bottle she kept in supply. Or he would fuck her in the ass, grind out his cigarette in her hair as it lay fanned out on the rug—the smell would tease her for days. She glued patches of fabric in matching color over the rug holes. Kate let him do whatever he needed to, anything to calm him down. Then there were the times Tommy would go for coffee and not come back for a week, two weeks. But he would always come back, his chapped hands gripping Birds of Paradise snapped from neighbors' yards, or pockets full of rubber bones and pretzels and spiny plastic balls with bells inside for the dogs.

"You don't get it," she said to her father when he ordered Kate to get rid of Tommy.

Once a friend of his stopped by when Tommy and Kate were out. The friend grew impatient so he busted the living room win-dow, made off with Kate's jewelry, and let the dogs escape. Tommy apologized. Said his friend just got out of prison, he was frustrated, he'd just kicked a bad heroin habit, y'know. Kate did. She rounded up the dogs, gave them rubdowns and cooked them real calves' liver, got the window fixed, and replaced some of the jewelry, which she put in the boxes under her bed. Then she took Tommy out for sushi and afterward they made love on the beach at Zuma. The sand made them both raw.

Kate was at a script meeting at Universal. She was late and Tommy couldn't wait. Tommy opened the boxes under the bed. Silky trousers, velour jackets, gauzy flowered dresses, and cotton jersey shifts. He tied the clothes in knots to each other and coiled them around the house. Looked like a magician's trick scarf—first one, then another, then another and another and another. Tommy used rum to soak the clothes, then gasoline from the garage. The silver Zippo was long gone, probably the cops snatched it, the cocksuck-ers. He used a matchbook, lit the whole thing, sizzle, and dropped it on the clothes. Orange fingers leaped up, groped along the clothes, circled the bungalow. Ducks squawked in the canal, beat their wings against the brackish water. Tommy flicked his tongue in and out as the flames licked the sides of the bungalow. Jungle heat. It was Tommy who controlled the weather now. The dogs howled inside, but he had chained them to the pipes under the sink, a big yellow bowl of water nearby with all their toys in a pile. Tommy rubbed slowly, the flames swelled, a window bulged out then burst in a miracle of jagged hard rain.

Waiting for him to get out of jail, Kate sent photos. Racy ones. Her staring soulfully into the camera, buck naked, ash smeared over her nipples and cunt and around her eyes in black, hollow circles. She had coffee with a friend and showed her the photos. Wanted to make sure she looked sexy enough. In most of them, she was lounging on a red felt pool table. Survived the fire because it was covered with a tarp in the garage. That's where she slept now, on the pool table in the garage.

The burnt smell was everywhere.

There Are Cars and Then There Are Cadillacs

My Great-aunt Susie, eighty-eight years old and chipper as a white-capped chickadee, drives a Ford Thunderbird. She still tools around the Boston suburb where she lives, going from environmental meeting to market to newsstand to environmental meeting. Narcoleptic, she does take care, though, to attach a special no-sleep gear to her head when she drives; there is a foam-padded headband that fits snugly on her skull. From either side of this band dangle clusters of brass bells with thick brass tongues. If and when my Great-aunt Susie nods off to one side or the other, these bells *ting-a-ling ting-a-ling* so she doesn't go crashing into a guardrail.

The car my Great-aunt Susie drives is economical. Protestant. On the other side of the family, my Jewish grandparents swear by their silver Cadillac with the burgundy interior, the one with the massive doors that always clip the shin and bruise the elbow. My mother drove a green Ford pickup that she repeatedly damaged in accidents. My father drove a white Electra 225 with rust stains and dents until it stopped running one day. Then he walked. I drive a Toyota, but I dream '56 Cadillacs—soft sinking leather upholstery, chrome fenders, sleek metallic stretch.

My car is cramped. In the back is a suspicious mustard stain that never came out. I keep it covered with a batik bedspread that faded in the bright SoCal sun. From the rearview mirror dangles a *comboloi,* sky-blue beads strung on leather. *Comboloi* means "pray words" in Greek. When you finger the beads and speak, each word flies right up to the sky. Sometimes at a stoplight I bat them to and fro. I don't suppose that has any effect on the heavens.

Once I left my car unlocked. The next morning the right visor was hanging from its metal bone, tattered blue plastic and bits of urine-yellow foam. The radio was still there but the face was ripped off and the plastic all around was chipped and chewed. The radio wires sprayed from below the radio's belly like copper arteries coated in colored plastic. A faceless radio. Deformed and defaced. Anonymous intrusion. Car as tin can. Driver as canned sweet pea, wrinkled and pale green in a syrup of water and sugar, vulnerable, edible. Stick shift the axis of the mobile world.

When my friends commented on the radio, I said I'd had theft-proofing. Some neighborhood kids helped me out.

At night, one of the radio wires with a miniature bulb on the end spreads a tiny circle of shine onto the worn blue carpet. All around, the streetlamps spill their wobbly arcs of light, chiaroscuro slashing shadows and illumination, secrets of the city, and above them the choppers with their Nightsuns cut through the air, swooping great swaths of hurting white brightness, and the gala spotlights spread a fan of white rays against neon, tempting, come one come all, here is happiness, here is excitement, here is what you've been looking for you saps.

L.A.: Città Chiusa

You're walking in L.A., not far, because it's not cool to walk in L.A., just from the Blue Ribbon Coin-Op Laundromat in the Lucky Plaza to L.A. Conversation for a cappuccino and a scone, except they're out of scones because yesterday was New Year's Day and people bought more than the bakery expected, but you remember expectations are planned disappointments so you don't lose it, you calmly order a sugary almond croissant instead and guess that you were meant to indulge in a sugar high, and you note even the Sunday *New York Times* today said fewer Americans than ever made New Year's resolutions to quit smoking or eat better, finally fed up with the healthy, ascetic, fitness-crazed life they've been trying vainly to follow for the last decade and it's just made most of them madder than ever because nothing changed for them. Didn't you just see a bumper sticker this morning that said: EAT HEALTHY, GET FIT, AND STILL DIE? So you, wanting to be a good American, wanting to be hip, wanting to be part of the pulse, wanting to be part of, and wanting an excuse to indulge anyway, order that sugary almond croissant and a regular double cappuccino, and you try not to think about your four loads of laundry tumbling in the washers a block away echoing your own internal misgivings about the New Year and life in general because, dammit, you've got those holiday blues, and you're wondering what the hell the point of it all is anyway, and why every time the holidays roll around you're not happy or festive or light at all, ever. The holidays are a big happy hand pressing down on your head making you want to disappear into the ground, but then you're walking back to the Blue Ribbon and you notice on your left something hanging from a clothesline stretched between the traffic light on the corner and a tree; it's not a pair of shoes, like you see tossed over phone lines to advertise a drug deal rendezvous, no, it's smaller, and on closer inspection—because you veer off from the crosswalk and approach the clothesline—you see it's a tiny wooden cross, and lo, behold that tree on the right is wrapped round with three strands of tinsel—blue and gold and silver—looking a little ragged like tinsel with mange, and there's a flattened-out card of half a Santa face (the other half's torn off), but the greeting "Merry Christmas" is still intact, all this taped onto the trunk; and there's more: set up on the balding grass below at the base of the tree is a tiny gift-wrapped box, open-ended on both sides, and next to it a flattened-out box that reads: 7-PC. POLYSTONE NATIVITY SET, YUSHA COLLECTION, MADE IN CHINA, SI-1001, ETERNAL FAITH, ETERNAL HOPE, ETERNAL LOVE, but the gift-wrapped box that is shaped like a manger is empty of the Nativity scene, hollow and dark, and there's a pile of dog shit nearby that you avoid even though in Italy stepping on dog shit is good luck and there they have spontaneous shrines on the streets, with tiny soda bottles of carefully arranged flowers, gilded framed icons hung or leaned just so, burnt candles waxing nostalgic over the ancient stone shelves. So you kneel down in front of this shabby urban shrine, this American antidote to anomie and apathy, this open-air answer to Macy's Christmas windows, all the more charming because it's not announced, it's not streamlined. This street-corner makeshift Christmas shrine is the gritty, grimy, soil-stained, garbage-gilded Hand of the Urban God right here in front of you, and before you even know it, before your canny clever eyes-peeled urban self even gets a bead on your own brain, despite you and all your holiday funk and family junk and clankety cynicism that's weighing you down, yes, hallelujah, before you can even STOP it . . . you're praying for the city and all its people down there on your knees in the dirt.

158

Revolving Door

Faye Dunaway and I almost met once when I was working at *ET.*

I had just valeted Darlene Comer's white Benz and was about to enter the posh Beverly Wilshire Hotel to join Darlene in the bookstore where we would interview Irving Arbuckle. This was an interview I looked forward to. Something less glitzy, more grounded, concerned with words and not just whirl.

But before I could enter or even step away from the revolving door, a slender blur of pale yellow silk, white linen, blond hair, and big dark shades burst through and jostled me without so much as a sideways glance. She was a hurricane windwhipped lemon chiffon pie of a woman who was all angles, angles, angles and anger, anger, anger arrowing ahead. Though she was a vision of cheekboned cream and lemon loveliness, in that brief brush of bodies, I sensed the lemon was sour to the taste.

Only when she leaped into a waiting cab did I realize who she was. It was Bonnie in the car, making a fast getaway. As a kid I'd loved Bonnie's style, her rebelliousness, her romanticism. When she and Clyde perished in a hail of bullets at the end of the film, I used up half a tissue box to wipe away the tears I shed—for gutsy love and female fearlessness, for world-class beauty and for outlaws.

I never dreamed she'd reappear in my L.A. life the way she did. Years later, after a painful split with a bluesman named Slim Vargas,

I learned through the papers that the reason for our breakup was none other than Faye Dunaway, who at that point was just turning fifty. I wasn't able to then, but now I can only applaud her for stealing away a man twenty years younger than she. Bonnie all the way. Would that I could do the same at fifty. And if I ever do meet Faye, I will thank her for taking Slim off my hands.

So Faye whizzed off in the cab and I headed to the hotel's bookstore where Arbuckle was supposed to meet us. He appeared on time, but drunk. Brown hair disheveled and spiky as a matted thistle. Stinking of cheap cocktails. Ranting about the appalling state of illiteracy and saying it was places like Hollywood and people like Darlene that shoveled dirt in the grave of America and why even bother with an interview, did she really think he believed she'd put him on TV, some ugly middle-aged fuming academic? And if she did, what the hell difference would it make? The whole thing was a farce. He was going back to the hotel bar, why didn't she quote that.

Star-Fucking

Wedging the jimmy right in there between the shiny points.

How Frankie Spent Her Five Thousand Four Hundred

On October 28, 1995, Frankie Lake won the jackpot at the Normandie Club, a seedy card club in Gardena.

"Rough night?" I said to a bleary-eyed Frankie the next morning at work on *Ghost Dancing*.

Frankie pulled a thick wad of bills out of her jeans jacket pocket.

"I won this last night," she said in that shy, Louisiana bayou voice.

Frankie fanned her wad. Hundred-dollar bill after hundred-dollar bill flashed by, like crisp green breakers crashing against the palm of her seawall hand. When I asked her why she looked so tired, she told me she got home and didn't know what to do. Only thing that came to mind she said was to clap. So she sat on her bed, clapping, for herself, all night.

At work, I secretly watched Frankie's every move: outside smoking cigarette after cigarette in the overgrown courtyard, chewing both-sides-buttered morning toast, copying hundreds of copies of Native American artifacts at the copy machine, bent over her computer charting more artifacts, her slick pompadour falling into fallen lime-green eyes, she was a lipstick dyke, but wore boyish buttondowns, ripped baggy jeans revealing boxers, Doc Martens. Stomach flat as the feet she stood on, long lean torso. I liked the rough lunar skin of her cheeks that were pocked and pale. I liked the rural purr of her voice, the murmur of her mouth that held a map of other mouths, her shyness didn't hide this knowing, not to me.

Later that morning Joan Red Thunder, the only Native American in the office, snatched the bills away from Frankie. "Downpayment on the land you stole." Frankie smiled softly, so softly even Joan Red Thunder relented and gave back the cash.

This is how Frankie spent her fortune.

Five Thousand Four Hundred Dollars

$15.00 × 7 ($105.00)—To each of the seven players at the table.

$100.00—To the dealer (who will probably lose her job now after dealing three jackpots in only two months).

$20.00—To the floorman.

$10.00—To security man Manny.

$100.00—To her friend Sigrid Gustaffson because she drove there to the Normandie Card Club and because she wasn't a winner.

$5.16—Cream cheese and tomatoes; and $6.50—Two dozen bagels. Breakfast for the Kokopeli Productions crew the day after she won.

$52.63—A bottle of Single Islay Lagavulin Scotch for Brett Fay, the production coordinator on the Native American documentary Frankie's working on as an archival photo assistant. Brett's straight and has told Frankie repeatedly she is not interested in Frankie or any woman for that matter. Brett refused an offer for dinner from Frankie that night to celebrate Frankie's win at the restaurant of Brett's choice. But Brett took the Scotch.

$140.00—Owed to Kokopeli for fixing her Jeep's transmission.

$500.00—Gift to her only sibling Rich who's unemployed.

$100.00—Old tax debt.

$93.48—Old business phone bill from when she had her own computer parts exchange business, which was also when she lived with her lover Leanne in a big house in West Hollywood and they had two foster boys, Tray and Eric. Eric's an AIDS baby who wears leg braces and uses crutches. They're both six years old, but Eric is much smaller than Tray.

$172.00 and $99.57—Wrangler Jeep repairs: wheel alignment, new EGR valve, oil lube and filter, new headlight, smog check.

$200.00—To Leanne for her car payment. Leanne left Frankie one year ago, after which Frankie lost her business because she couldn't keep it up and take care of the boys. Then Frankie lost the boys because she didn't have the money to take care of them anymore. Now they're back with their AIDS-stricken mother.

$38.00—Thrifty's for thyroid pills. Frankie doesn't have a thyroid because she had Graves' disease—hyperthyroid-ism—and had to drink this stuff that radiated iodine and disintegrated her thyroid. Now she has to take these pills because they regulate her metabolism. Otherwise her heart would stop.

$116.89—GapKids. Frankie got both Tray and Eric a pair of dark blue corduroy pants and Ben a pair of olive-green ones. Frankie's friend Jeffrey came too, and he kept trying to get Eric to put on a velvet dress. Eric said, "Yuck." Eric thought Jeffrey was crazy. Jeffrey is Frankie's best friend at work. He has long black hair and a shelf butt from dancing. He likes to wear velvet shirts to work and flirt with the straight men there.

$142.88—FAO Schwarz. They went there after GapKids. Tray rode this little red bike around most of the many hours they were there. When it was time to choose, he said, "I won't fall off this bike, but I fall off every other one." Frankie bought the bike. Then she asked Eric what he wanted. He looked dazed leaning on his crutches, but he said, "I want a sword." So he got a plastic sword, helmet, shield, and a suit of plastic armor. He said, "When the bad guys come I will kill them with this sword."

$43.30—A bottle of Paloma Picasso perfume.

$102.30—The Gap. A pair of corduroy pants, one pair of jeans, a pair of plaid boxers, and two pairs of white socks.

$40.00—On Friday night she took her friends Jacqueline, Shiho, and Missy to dinner at Tango before they went to see the play *Cloud Nine*. The whole time Frankie and her three friends ogled the female singer who was silhouetted behind the curtain. She wore a skintight dress, had sky-high legs, and a tangled mane of blond hair. She looked like Ellen Barkin. Maybe she was Ellen Barkin.

$483.00—Late registration and a stack of parking tickets that Fred racked up.

$76.53—Frankie's baby picture restored and framed. Her mom had the picture in her cedar chest for years. Rich had been threatening to frame it for Frankie for fifteen years so she finally did it herself. It was taken in Pittsburgh at a department-store studio right before her father died in a car wreck at the age of twenty-six.

$16.24—For Calvin Klein boxers, extra long and with buttons in front, not a flap.

$100.00—To horse races. Saturday was Hawaiian Day at the Santa Anita track. Frankie went with Jeffrey's entire family. She had a list of horses Brett chose in her pocket. Every horse Brett picked crawled across the finish line so Frankie lost all her money. Frankie decided to go to the races instead of getting a gynecological exam. (Frankie has a history of bad pap smears, and has already had a frozen cervical scrape operation done twice. She had a bad pap smear test two years ago and hasn't been to the gynecologist since.)

Total: $2,863.48

$2,500.00 saved away for taxes and just to put away

Grand Total: $5,363.48.

Missing: $36.52. An error in accounting, lost receipts, stolen?

Celebrity Scientology Castle

"Maybe you'd be interested in taking a personality test," the Scientologist says, bobbing his Kleenex-white face close to mine. Scientologists don't fucking quit. They're as persistent as Hare Krishnas, without the benefit of catchy chants and drums and those gauzy tangerine togas. They all wear dark blue suits, modeled after Navy uniforms. The Blue Zombies plant recruiters everywhere to waylay visitors such as myself. They play on fears.

"Does it test whether I have a personality? Or give me one?" I say. Not my mother's. Any one but that.

"No," says the Scientologist. He is thin, with a Cro-Magnon brow and neat black circles like gazelle hoofmarks under his eyes. The kind of guy who probably never went to science class. The white button-down shirt and cut-rate blue suit hang loosely on his gaunt Ichabod Crane frame. Definitely an ex-junkie rocker. The Scientologists pluck most of their recruits from ex-junkies. His eyes, pale blue, give me the creeps.

The Celebrity Scientology Castle is a Gothic structure built in a lush garden right off Franklin Avenue and just down from the celebrated and celebrity-strewn Hollywood Hills. The top floor is rented out to our production company. I heard John Travolta and Lisa Marie Presley hang out here, but I haven't seen one celebrity yet. My mother was a crazy woman, unable to cope, to deal. That is not the case with me.

"You've got problems," he says slowly, like he's absorbing mine along with his right there in the elevator. He even slumps heavily against the wall. I imagine a platoon of meaty hands pressing his shoulders. "Frustration. Despair. Anxiety. The personality test zeroes in on those issues and lets you see the truth." What is he getting at? My genes have rearranged themselves into an entirely new pattern. Fuck him.

"The one I've got right now is simple: Should I accept another low-paying, thankless, second second assistant directing slave gig on a shit film I'll be ashamed to admit I worked on, or should I give up movies? Got an answer, hotshot?" Strike out. Fists always in combat readiness.

The guy doesn't even flinch.

"Remember, the personality test is free," he says, pushing away from the wall with great effort. "It's a way to get clear. Maybe start new. Room 317, all day, all night," he says, and slouches off the elevator. Clear of her ghost.

I tap my foot to each creak of the cables and roll my eyes to the ceiling. Adopt an attitude of bored indifference.

I'm surprised when my body shudders and doubt seizes my brain in a nasty chokehold. And even more surprised when I get the swift kick idea maybe I'm not as tough as I think. Still, tougher than my mother, surely. Tougher than that.

Could be hunger, could be exhaustion. I don't buy into cults and religions. Not me. I'm thinking I just brushed up against a cyborg masquerading as a human, and he's out to snatch my personality, my soul. Invasion of the Soul Snatchers. And I'm trapped. In a creaky wooden cage. He's probably out there on a metal ledge sawing away at the cables right now. Or sending subliminal messages through the lit-up floor buttons. Or slowly drawing out the oxygen so I get dizzy and the elevator will open on three and he'll drag me off to the dreaded Room 317. My mother's trailing me. She'll be there, in Room 317. She'll prove our personalities are identical. Our fates bound up, inevitable. That I am doomed.

By the time the elevator reaches the top floor, I am clear. Clear why film is for me. How I fit into the pell-mell world of film production, how suited I am to its high-intensity short-term shoots, those frenetic camps for adults where you give all you got to a goddamn movie, which you live and breathe and forget there ever was anything or anyone else, forget there ever was a lunatic mother, everyone on the crew's your darling, your family you'd fight for to the end, until the last shot's over, and then the whole thing disappears, most every person you met on the production loses contact, fades away, and all that's left is a battered script inked "PUPPETMASTER" you file on your shelf, the whole silly grown-up camp's sweaty longhoured heroic effort funneled into one two-hour flick you'll probably never see.

On the ride down, everything gets even more clear. It's just like the life you've always known. Chopped-up chaos. Always new vistas and new dreams. That bubbling-up starting-over energy you've got foaming on perpetual tap. Bumping from this place and that, meeting this girl and that boy, making friends, losing friends, meeting boys, leaving boys, shaking the dice of your life in the cup until you get a crazy juiced-up spots-swirling headache high just thinking about it. Give it all you got. Film's the only world for you. Hollywood's the only town around moving fast enough to keep you from upchucking, where you can play master to your own past's killing puppets, the Kiddieland toyjoy demons that haunt you, girl on the go-go move, ROLL ON. Roll on past, roll over the past, roll over her.

MAAAAAAAAAAAAAAAAAAAAAAAA

I'd yell from the bathtub. But she wouldn't come. Too busy swimming in a bottle of Miller's. I guess. Chugalug brown bug, my skin would be prune-wrinkled and pale by the time I hauled myself out of the dirty water. Throat hoarse. All the plastic beads pop-joined in a loud plastic link of joyous toys, I hung those around the hot-spitting faucet. Even at age three or four, I liked my water hot. I knew what I wanted.

An example.

I would have liked my mother this way. Tall, willowy, blond hair to her waist, slightly tilted green eyes, slender and feminine, draped in silky material. I told her so once. On top of looking like a fairy princess worthy of the Grimms' ink plate, I wanted her to play with me.

She never did. Unless you count when she was drunk and did the Ouija solo, and made me watch. "Why is my daughter a bitch?" she'd ask. Glare at me as her hands raced over the board, curling and swerving, stopping and spelling.

When I think Ma, I hear the step. Hit and drag. Hit and drag. Years ago she'd busted an ankle riding horses and it never quite mended. Hit, drag. Tiny floating bones. Up the stairs, down. Every step she took hurt, and this knowledge burst in my mind like tiny floating bones.

They're there now. She's not.

Ma is gone. I suppose because she chose to go I can't complain. Don't we live in the land of the free, home of the brave? In France they pound stakes through the hearts of suicides. Me, I wanted to erect the biggest, tallest monument for her in the whole fucking graveyard. When they told me only the head of the family gets that, and the rest of the members in the family plot have to get flat-lying plaques, I said I wanted Ma disinterred. I wanted her to have her own plot, her own towering monument, a blazing angel, a sky-piercing obelisk. No one would be allowed to forget my mother. But at four-teen I barely scraped enough together to buy her a stone. So she stayed and got a flat-in-the-ground grave marker, rose quartz, tough like she wasn't.

Yellow

When I first came to L.A. the Night Stalker was striking terror into the city's inhabitants. There was a steady accumulation of clues, but the one that got me was the Stalker's penchant for yellow houses. Preferably yellow houses near the freeways, and preferably with their windows open or doors unlocked.

Why yellow? Was his despised mother a blonde? Did some pissed-off boss dump a bucket of yellow paint over his head when he fucked off on a job years ago? Did an uncle who wore loud yellow shoes molest him as a child? Maybe yellow was the butter shoved down his throat when he spoke dirty at the dinner table.

The man I was living with at the time, Isaac, bore an uncanny resemblance to the Night Stalker. Each day there would be another police sketch rendering of the Stalker, sometimes closer to Isaac and sometimes further.

"Maybe I'm him," he would say, pulling me down onto the bed. I'd struggle to get away.

"Not funny," I'd say. But Isaac was a handsome man and I'd stop struggling, even when his kisses tasted darker. "Look at your eyes glittering, Jesus."

"Hah," he'd say. Rip my clothes off. I wonder if part of me didn't secretly wish Isaac were the Stalker, and that he would destroy me once and for all.

Our relationship disintegrated. Isaac became a stranger. The Stalker kept on killing, marking yellow houses for hits, until, one day, a whole neighborhood caught him, one neighbor shouting, another tripping the Stalker, another beating him, still another calling the cops.

Not long after they caught the Stalker, Isaac and I split up and he left town. I kept thinking about quiet yellow houses, placidly painted and shingled, windows wide open like innocent eyes, bolted firmly and hopefully to the shifting California ground.

Crossroads of the World

Los Angeles, intersection of the world. Come one, come all. Crazy spread-out city, thumbing your nose at the European chunk of land they call continent and you call anachronism. Who needs concentric circles spinning out from a city core when cores (you as a young fiendish city understand this well) are poof! gone AWOL, no more. Spread your thighs and welcome the displaced urban dwellers landlocked in their new Chinatowns and ghettos, barrios and Polish quarters rubbing elbows sideswiping hips like in the old days. Don't despair. Ethno-intersections are a natural phenomenon, and the world of Lost Angels branches.

A Linda Blair Experience, or Rebecca Speaks with Her Head Turned Backward

—Me? I came here to see films. I mean, work in them.

—I mean everything from painting clear skies on backdrops, to serving crew coffee with a steaming smile, to banging on the honeywagon doors routing the actors GET YOUR GODDAMN BOOTIES off their toilets, to walking the actors to the sets, to telling them what to do, how to sit, and what to say how to move when to cry, yeah, I mean I came here to direct films.

—No, I'm not asking for a handout. I'm telling the truth. You wanna hear more or not? I'll take a cup of coffee. That's what I did. Except I kept getting fired. Not that it was my fault or anything, you know, but this town is so fulla phonies. It wasn't my fault I didn't like any of the scripts they gave me over at Taft-Barish. They sucked. I didn't study English Literature for nothing. Why shouldn't the story of Emma Goldman be a blockbuster? And was it my fault Wanda Chang and Speedy Cohen let me go after *Infidelity* just because I didn't like the script Cohen wrote? Why didn't he put his name on it then if he was so proud? And hey, I wasn't the only assistant fired by Stavros Papadakis, doesn't that tell you who's the nutty one? Who in their right mind would want to keep working in film, y'know?

—You work in film? All right, well, that's different. How about movies, let's call it movies, 'cause when you say movies it's popcorn and dark theaters and kissy smooch and thigh strokes and bucks bucks

bucks, don't think I don't know. Movies is entertainment, pure and all-American.

—But film is art. I want ART. Where was the ART?

—Damn straight. Where *is* it? I could put more art into one frame of a whole reel of movie footage, boys and girls of Tinseltown, only, hah, sure they wouldn't give me a chance because the whole town's a labyrinth, pay your dues, PAY YOUR DUES. No thanks, pardner. Hell, I could take a big pair of snips, long daggered scissors, and cut up a whole movie, pick and choose, frame here frame there everywhere a frame frame. And make a real film. Something to jog the senses, sure. Who needs to run it through a projector so fast nobody gets a chance to engage the brain, the heart, the loins. The whole goddamn town is moving too fast. Always in motion, flying down the freeways, floating through life, grabbing at the money trees, shaking down the poor bastard working-class moviegoers, getting away, always getting away. I'd slow it down.

—Thanks. Good luck to you too. Hey, thanks for the coffee. See ya around.

THAT'S what I'll do.

I'll pour beautiful blond honey all over the whole heap of snarled, chopped-up movie frames. I'll pick, I'll choose, I'll juxtapose, I'll cruise through images and signs and smells and symbols and chase scenes and screen kisses and lay them edge to edge, or overlap, or underlap.

That's what I'll do. I'll make a collage. Los Angeles AFTER the Big One, AFTER the Last Picture Show, AFTER Math, AFTER Madness. Year 1 A.B. AFTER BLADERUNNER. Yeah. And I'll call it, I'll call it SUN-DOWN CITY for the way the sun plunges down into the Pacific in that splinter of a second when light fades to dark JUST LIKE A KLIEG LIGHT you bastards you.

The Italian

He was Italian.

Italians have families. They laugh and sing and eat and fuck.

He had a family. A big family.

They laugh and sing and eat and fuck. Not each other. But they are a family. They pull each other's hair, rub each other's shoulders, they joke, they cook and clean and scream.

He was kind. He was generous. He said I was *bellissima*. He called me *bellissima*. He believed I was. I knew he was. He was nothing like Hawk. Nothing like my mother.

He would let me in his family. I could be part of his family. Families are together. Families don't leave each other. Not in Italy.

He wouldn't leave me.

Even if he did leave me, I would always be part of the family, part of his family.

Families had fun. They drank, not that much. They cared. They fought. They laughed with each other. They stuck it out.

His name was Giorgio. His name was Giorgio and he was the son of the Italian Minister of Culture. Giorgio knew how to make people feel good. To smile, to charm, to captivate.

Giorgio captivated me. Even though ordinarily I didn't go for economists. But. I met him on a film set. I was bored when he appeared. His stare demanded immediate attention. What was he doing on a film set? In town, visiting a friend, an actor. Not so different from politics, show biz. Besides, he was tall. Spoke about bell curves. And handsome. Spoke about the Invisible Hand. And had a sweet jump shot. And pigeon toes.

There were problems, though.

One, he didn't live in Los Angeles. Not only did he not live in Los Angeles, he lived in New York City, which was a world apart from Los Angeles.

But he loved me.

Two, he had a girlfriend he lived with. Not that he was still going out with her, not that he was even remotely in love with her, just that, things like that took time to unravel. It was over, not to worry. We'd be together soon. To prove it, he mailed many boxes of stuff to Los Angeles with his name scribbled all over. Giorgio.

He loved me so much he would fly out to visit on weekends at the last minute, because he couldn't stand being away. He'd fiddle with the boxes. Didn't unpack them. Not yet.

But he was away, most of the time.

I loved him. I told him I loved him. Why did that hurt. He went away. He came back. He was the son of a minister of culture. Of course, he had bigger things to deal with, inevitable things, *matters of importance,* matters involving a country, the country he loved, the country I loved (the country my mother loved).

He was an economist. He saw things in graphs, saturation points, balanced economies, GNPs. We negotiated a deal. (A silent one.) I would see him when he chose. And I would be grateful for every moment with him, because we were family. I was part of his family, part of him. After all, he was Italian, wasn't he?

He came. He went. He came and he went. He went.

Of course he went. Of course he left. I wasn't good enough. Not nearly. I wasn't enough. Not even close. And he deigned to love *me.* The son of culture. The son of Italy. The son. He *had* to go.

My love remained. My love grew tortuous and my heart twisted in my chest. Bled. This seemed altogether right.

Never unpacked the boxes.

He said I put pressure on him. I expected him to be father,

mother, sister and brother and lover. He said this was too much. My demands were too much. I was too much. I was too American.

I couldn't stop loving him. Not for a very long time.

What else was love if not pain, if not absence, if not this?

The Sweetest Hand
I Never Held

When I was seven, and far from California, a little boy slammed a door on the ring finger of my left hand.

"Open the door," I said.

I held my finger in my right hand, the tip hanging off by a thin strip of flesh, and walked upstairs to the mother of the house.

"Look," I said to her, holding out the bloody finger in my palm like an offering.

When we got to the emergency room, I insisted on watching the doctor sew the tip back on my finger.

That night was feverish, spent in bed with my mother where I tossed and turned and sensed her annoyance even through the blur of pain. The world was my finger. A throbbing, tortured thing. I don't remember my mother hugging me, or holding my uninjured hand.

I considered myself courageous. Nothing was too much for me.

An Educational Film

"Ever worked on an educational film?" Gina asked. She was this friend of an acquaintance whose family summered in the same teeny town on Cape Cod as my family.

I was hired as production coordinator on *Frame*. It was a story of a stressed-out teenager who tries to kill herself, but reaffirms her hold on life through painting. I guess this was to boost the art class enrollments in high schools across the nation. The producer BZ wanted to make something good for the community, give a little back . . . help the kids.

BZ lived in this stately white house on the edge of Los Feliz, a ritzy middle-brow neighborhood on the east side of Los Angeles. Two growling plaster lions guarded the front door. From what, I didn't know. One of them had a chipped mane that lent him more ferocity than the other, like he'd been in a bang-up fight.

When I first met BZ I thought he was Gene Wilder. Unkempt halo of brownish curls, darting blue eyes, bobcat pacing, and frenetic bird-flapping gestures. "Where's my belt? Anyone seen my belt?" he shouted. Then, "Hi, there," in a sultry voice to me. He was not what I'd imagined a man with community in mind to look or act like.

I worked with Gina, the line producer, and Barbie, the production manager. Together we made up production, generally the hardest-working, least-appreciated, and drabbest folks around on a film. Production carried clipboards, dressed conservatively, sharpened pencils, wrote up call sheets, enforced call times and meal penalties. We were the organizers, the solid hub of the film's wheel, while the other crew members were the creative spokes spinning around in a blur—the art department, camera, props, actors. These were the ones I admired, the ones I lusted for.

After a week, BZ decided we'd break every day at eleven-thirty for yoga with his friend Yetunde. Yetunde would come strutting in telling stories about those crazy times with Andy (Warhol, that is) and clapping her hands together to liven us up. No way could we get as lively as her. She was middle-aged but full of juice, a woman with a killer body, high-flying buttocks, and a close-cropped Afro. We stretched and posed, balanced and bent, and didn't know the pain until later. I perused the art department boys with their paint-stained hands, doing the Natarajasana, Flying Pose.

Then it was lunch, cooked up by Billy Saint, also a former Warholite. He was an actor, best known for playing Pan. Gap-toothed like Chaucer's Woman of Bath, sign of lusty appetites, but he looked and seemed more like the Cowardly Lion. His mouth was wreathed in smiles, his body stout and round, his face creased and shiny like a well-worn shoe. He would serve up sloppy stews and regale us with stories about the Factory. A heap of salad and a tale of Aqua Velva, the knockout woman he took back to his room, quickly stripped and found that in place of a vagina, there was only a sealed pouch. Another dollop of potato lyonnaise? He was telling us she hadn't finished her sex change operation, and would he front her the money?

I thought these guys on *Frame* knew how to have fun. I thought Hollywood was onto something. A looser, wilder way to work.

I did think it was weird when the art director Willard Booth, sixth-generation descendant of John Wilkes Booth, ran by naked on the roof one day, waving and puckering his mouth against the windows like a grotesque guppy gone berserk in an aquarium. He didn't look like Booth at all.

Willard had a soft pink body, a tuft of white-blond hair on his peaked head, and looked like a tadpole. He would always tell people, "I used to be adorable, I don't know what happened, wasn't I, Tod?" Tod was his brother, who was cute, and straight. Willard was a flamer.

Tod painted sets. I had a crush on him, only he wouldn't talk to me because he didn't think I was cool enough. Even when I brought in a Joy Division tape, he thought I got the idea from him.

A fashion designer, Willard was famous in Japan but not in Los Angeles. He designed those clear plastic liquid-infused bikinis with the plastic fish inside. They got picked up by Gaultier, but he designed them. He was friends with the actress Susan Tyrell and convinced her to work on the film. She was a sparrow with a bleached blond shag and a chain-smoker. I was fascinated by the tattoo of tears that snaked out from her scalp and down the nape of her neck. She told me they were for someone in prison. I remembered she played Stacy Keach's drunk girlfriend in John Huston's *Fat City,* and I wondered if she'd had hard knocks.

Years later I found out the truth, slowly, of what *Frame* had really been all about, and what the plaster lions were guarding. BZ was a major coke dealer out on probation who was mandated to do something good for the community. Or they'd haul him back in. And the Los Feliz house was a notorious drug hang, with a reputation for fabulously reckless parties. I didn't realize until years later that lots of the crew were alcoholics or addicts. I'd only been in L.A. one year, so I didn't get that some of the crew were shooting up heroin and hammering back booze. I didn't even know about tying-off then. That's why BZ was always missing his belt.

BZ is now clean and sober, and looking to produce karaoke videos. Willard Booth is red-hot with men's fashion in Los Angeles, with a line of body-hugging, boldly bright clothes. I ran into Tod dressed in a suit, looking pale and pudgy, pushing art at a gallery, no paint stains on him anywhere. Another art dog I had a crush on got sober and made amends to me years later for being a heel during the shoot. It took me a while before I remembered what he'd done. Besides spurning my advances, he'd said I looked like Olivia Newton-John.

Pas de Deux

It is late Sunday afternoon in the La Brea Tar Pits Park. The shadow of leaves on the grass is so many grasping hands.

I fled my South Detroit Street apartment in search of peace. A DJ next door was spinning monotonous funk for a high school birthday party in the apartment parking lot. Sickening smell of grilled meat, sweet warmish ketchup. A herd of kids, jabberjaws and jeans. I had to leave. I had to buy a wedge of fruit cheesecake from Canter's Delicatessen to sweeten the disruption.

I'm sitting on the grass at the park, a green mansion for the masses. The place is blessedly empty. The earth is cool on my ass. With cheesecake in one hand and *The New York Times* in the other, I read an article about Laura Dern in the movie *Smoothtalk,* and think of Treat Williams pressing his body against the locked screen door, whispering sweet stabbing nothings through the buckled wire mesh, the words squeeze through. I think of Laura Dern cringing against the wall inside, fighting the inevitability of male intrusion in a woman's life. The violence of lost innocence. Where is the goddess Diana when you need her?

Such thoughts in this L.A. oasis. Green trees in an asphalt jungle. Bubbling primeval tar mocks the modern dilemma. Isolate or connect. Retreat or join. Everything is quiet.

I notice a man walk by out of the corner of my eye. Hispanic.

No shirt, a swelling stomach and belted khakis. I wish I hadn't looked. I forgot my city etiquette in a darkening park. My knee is draped in shade. I shift my foot to the left.

The tiny black newsprint begins to irritate me. Each letter a prick of vision. His eyes were empty-seeing. Pig eyes.

Perhaps I'm prejudiced. Against men. Against Hispanics. Against men without shirts and overhang stomachs. Against such eyes.

I look up again. He's standing fifty feet away, stopped.

Probably the thud thud of funk summoned this bout of paranoia. There's nothing amiss. Just don't stare. Everyone's got a right to the parks. Instead I study the photo of Laura Dern. She's one of those actresses who's not classically pretty but she's compelling. She gives women hope. The sun is delirious up there in her late afternoon prime. I stretch my right leg out and scratch my thigh.

Suddenly I look up. He's closer, close, fifteen feet, and something's different. Wait. The khakis are down. Blurry flesh. Fondle and tweak. Fondle and tweak. A let-loose mouse in his hand. Frantic. I look. I look at his face, looking askance with the empty-seeing eyes. Eyes of an animal. He's making guttural noises. One foot moves closer.

My heart becomes a panicked beast and pounds against the screen of ribs.

Then everything simply slows way down and I am in a ballet. Grass is graceful, each bending blade a dancer's back. Tar murmurs liquid pirouettes and leaps. The trees stop breathing. Mesmerized. I calmly gather my things, each movement precise and smooth. No rough edges. With a delicate touch I pull out a tiny jackknife from my bag, open the blade, hold it in the palm of my hand. I get up and walk away deliberately, not looking back, I point each toe as I go, I have never been so conscious of the muscles in my legs, the cords and tendons stretching and contracting, they are music, I am a ballerina.

When I pass the last row of trees before the sidewalk on Sixth Street, I turn with studied nonchalance and profound sadness toward my abandoned partner. No one's there. The verdant stage is empty. I get in my car and lock the door. Drive.

Daddy-O

O-No. Daddy-O. Cheerio and away he go.

Daddy-O wasn't around a whole lot. They split when I was four and I stayed with Ma. After that it was articles clipped from *The New York Times* with words I didn't know sealed up and sent to me in white envelopes and yearly visits to Jersey. I remember taking a lot of baths there. For years my father would pick me up in the tub, wrap me in a towel, and carry me out. One year that just stopped. I didn't understand. I thought he hated me then. I remember my father wincing at the ring I left around the tub. And I, mortified. No, it's not dirt. Dad, it's skin, my dry skin. Sure, he'd say. Your (squinched disgusted look) mother doesn't even keep you clean (squinched disgusted look).

When I spilled things, every stain was a sign of my mother's negligence. A splurt of ketchup, a drip of oil. I could do no right.

He bought me clothes. Velvet vests, psychedelic socks, striped bell-bottoms. He took me to plays, operas, movies, shows.

When I came out of the dressing room at Macy's in a red corduroy gaucho and vest outfit once, he grinned and told me I looked like a "mensch." I didn't like that.

Later on, he told me stories about women he'd had affairs with, and about the nonkosher food he ate. These were things he couldn't tell his wife, and I thought he loved me.

One day he confessed he both loved me and hated me.

Long ago and far away we spent time together. Before I was four. Years later we spent two weeks together in Israel. We visited the Wailing Wall and he bought me a Bedouin necklace. I got him a portrait of Rabbi Kook, a cheap pointillist rendition, except the points were actually hundreds of tiny Hebrew words.

Flowers

There once was a pygmy goat named Flowers. Flowers would jump straight in the air. Like a pogo stick. Or jump with head arched one way and legs thrust out the other. A Scottish jig position, frozen. Flowers was a virgin. Flowers lived in Echo Park. The owners took her to get freshened. Freshened is a euphemism for breeding. Sometimes, with no warning, when Flowers stood still she would shoot a string of black pearls from her rear end. Tiny black beads. When Flowers was young, she was not clearly anything. She didn't have a goat shape yet. She didn't look like a dog, she didn't look like a cat, she didn't look like a goat.

Her identity was unclear.

The Blacklite

Gene thinks I need another drink.
He pulls up in front of The Blacklite. A sign on the storefront next to the bar reads, USED FURNITURE, GOOD AND BAD. We just had dinner at El Cholo Mexican Restaurant where Gene told me it was over, that I needed to clean it up with the other guy, The Italian. I didn't tell him that wasn't so simple. The way I saw my situation, I was lingering in a lukewarm bath—wanting to get out of the tub and stay put at the same time, dreading the stinging slap of cold air that would greet me if I let go, lamenting the tepid water that didn't warm me anymore but held memories of luxurious steamy heat, the kind that exfoliates the heart, stripping everything down to such a pureness it seems love will never happen again.

That's what I was thinking about over yellow, blue, and red tortilla chips, enchiladas suizas and margaritas, even though I was chattering brightly. At one point, there was silence. Gene took my wrist in his hand, arranged the three Mexican silver bracelets in equidistant lines, then gently turned my arm so they glinted in the candlelight. I couldn't help it, I thought of Giorgio's touch, about the comfort and thrill it always gave me. With Gene's gesture I felt more annoyance and pity, a bit of flattery, vague unlocated sadness. Was it possible Giorgio didn't experience my touch like I did his? Did that explain his absence? Gene and I sat that way for a while, me thinking about Giorgio, about what he was doing right now, why I couldn't be with Gene, was I making a mistake, until I loudly crunched a mouthful of tortilla chips, which got us both laughing again. I withdrew my arm, finished cleaning my plate with a tortilla; Gene sent his back with a barely nibbled garbage burrito. After dinner he said, "Let's have one last hurrah."

Gene still calls me the girl-next-door even though he says he thought she didn't exist. We met two months ago at the Villa Ardmore in the driveway one rainy night when his car was blocking mine. He gave me his card. There was a red maple leaf on it. Eugene Nerval. Band promoter. It probably would've been better if we hadn't met.

Gene walks up behind me and puts his arm around my waist. I am a sunflower shooting up through the cracked sidewalk. I am the long stem of a margarita glass. I had four margaritas at dinner after he told me it was over. Usually half a glass makes me tipsy.

"They shot a film in there." Gene points at the furniture store. "Lashed all the chairs to the ceiling."

The chairs are still there. I think about how when I was a kid, I used to stare up at the ceiling and imagine it was the floor, imagine how I'd sidestep the chandelier once I was there, right side up. In my fantasy, the furniture I took with me I coated with rubber cement so it would stick, drew designs with tempera paint so the ceiling looked like a Day-Glo Turkish rug, wound green crepe paper around the chandelier to give the place a patio effect, lugged my books up there and attached them to the table with yarn hair ribbons, stashed a box of Cap'n Crunch and a few bananas in the stapled-down laundry hamper, taped the lid—I thought of everything. Up there I was self-sufficient, away from bickering parents—a father who kept skipping town, a hard-drinking mother—free. I used to spend a lot of time as a kid imagining anything to get out of my life. Make it look different. I don't tell this story to Gene.

"I'm Buddy Greco tonight." He slouches in his trench coat, leans against the dark furniture store window.

On an album cover Gene once showed me, Greco looked tweaked, with greased dark hair and a cigarette ash inches long about to fall from his fingertip. A real washout. A too-smooth, sleazy, heart-less Sinatra I wouldn't even play in a supermarket.

"They call me The Loveless," Gene says.

Greco disappears. The thought of someone being loveless, think-ing they're loveless, gets me every time. I rub Gene's head affec-tionately before I remember I shouldn't, that's how drunk I am. Hand with short-term memory. He keeps his on my waist. Propels me to the bar. Bye-bye chairs in the air. My feet are hitting the splintered sidewalk hard. I wouldn't move if Gene weren't leading me. I am an unwilling horse, a dapple gray, and my hooves are shod with heavy stone.

Bruised-black and candy-pink neon hisses at me as I walk un-derneath the bar sign. First thing I see inside The Blacklite is two transvestites up against the back wall seated at a table, staring at me. The one on the left is in a body-hugging red number with a purple sequin bodice that shows off her dusky skin, eyes done Egyptian style and wig in a glossy black flip bob. She's big as a quarterback. The one on the right's closer in size to an overweight ump and looks twenty years older. Like her face was chewed up and spat out, then smoothed into some kind of lopsided egg shape. She's got a perox-ide blond wig that's stiff as fiberglass, a silver bustier, and a cheesy black mini. They've both got their black heels hooked around the rungs of the bar stools. As soon as I see them I imagine I have big-time loser in love scrawled all over my brow. There's a sadness etched in both their faces, visible beneath heavy makeup, familiar. No won-der they can see mine.

"Don't stare," says Gene. "Stoli?" I nod fast.

I watch him go, short and beefy with his Downey bebop, be-bad hop walk, his soft black trench coattail swings with style. I see each foot hit the ground solid, rooted like his soul. Gene's black hair is a perfect wave frozen forever in high, proud silhouette. He's a former warehouseman, former punkrocker, a true Los Angeleno born and raised in Downey in spite of the maple leaf. A grown man. I am just the girl-next-door. Only I don't think girls-next-door are supposed to have any complications, doubts, or worries. Fresh-faced virgins with squeaky-clean hearts and clean simple minds are more like it. So maybe he's right after all—they don't exist anymore. Or at least, I'm not one.

As soon as Gene leaves, I steady myself on the bar stool at the table, find a piece of gum underneath, and stick my finger to it. Red chili pepper lights strung behind the bar wink like mad dogs' eyes flashing in the dark. There's a whole row of Central Americans sitting at the bar. One wiry young man in a striped cotton shirt and knee-length shorts, black Pumas, runs his chestnut-brown hand down the spine and ass crack of a Central American's back and butt. He's wearing white jeans, a white net shirt over a white T-shirt, and he giggles. I know it's at me. He's guessing I'm a transvestite.

I think about Gene, how he's got a raging temper he's trying so hard to hide. The transvestite with Egyptian eyes stretches back like she's tired and the fabric slips up over her muscular thighs to reveal black hose and garters. Seeing her (his) legs makes me think how much Giorgio excites me, with his muscular body and smooth, urgent lovemaking. Gene's got a soft, almost womanly chest and his body, though solid, is unathletic and slack. Not my style at all. When we fool around, it's always him who starts things.

We'd come back from an evening out, say, eating Thai and seeing Cassavetes's *Killing of a Chinese Bookie,* I'd say, "Thanks," he'd say, "Tea?" "Well," I'd stall. "Come on," he'd say. Next thing I'd know I'd be in his apartment, sitting on his green Naugahyde and steel couch from JC Penney's, two cups of untouched Stash's Ruby Mist tea steeping on the coffee table, while he's holding my hand, moving closer, kissing my neck, breathing hard, murmuring my name, I'm squeezing my eyes shut, and slowly, if I banished Giorgio from my mind, concentrated on hair follicles, square inches of skin, nerve endings, the gradual stirring below, I'd let it happen.

"Here," says Gene. He sets down the drink and sits next to me. Tonight, unlike other nights, the mere heat from his body makes me desirous, just knowing it's not mine anymore. Sure it's only been a couple of months, the two of us. But already the language is lost. Altered. Used to be Gene said, "Here," and inclined his face toward mine for a kiss. I look down at his hands holding the glass. They look strangely simian. So he's not my physical ideal. So I'm not in love. On the other hand, Gene is a man. Knows what he wants. Said he could see marrying me. And marrying is what I want. Two years and Giorgio hasn't said shit. Besides, we don't even live in the same city.

Gene sips his Sharp's non-alcoholic beer. He's a French-Canadian who can't drink and doesn't. Except during earthquakes. Gene catches me staring at the transvestites again.

"You watch," says Gene. "I know men. Someone's going home with those two tonight. Central Americans fuck anything."

"Yeah?" I say with great deliberation, sipping on the Stoli. I'm in complete control. I pull my finger from the gum and wipe it discreetly on the damp cocktail napkin. I am disgusted with Gene's harshness, his intimacy with the seedy side of L.A. Giorgio would never take me to a place like this. How could I even consider giving him up? I've already given him my heart. But what if he doesn't love me? If he did, wouldn't he be here? Love the one you're with, that's what they say.

"Wouldn't be surprised if the Wackmaster had calluses on it," Gene's saying, his lips misshapen with spite. It's that rage leaking out.

"Who?" I ask casually.

"That roommate I had," says Gene, peering into my face. "In Inglewood. One day he made twenty-seven calls." He kisses me on the cheek. Lips soft again. Not to be trusted.

I take a long gulp of white liquid fire; I'm burning from the inside out.

"Good-looking cat, but got hooked on whores. Then phone sex. Owed me three thousand for old phone bills when we split up. I don't like when motherfuckers don't pay me back. I work hard for my dough."

The nasty edge in his voice gets drowned out by tinny jingling, *ping ping ping,* muted sirens, bells and trills. I tap the side of my head.

"What's that noise?"

"Pinball," says Gene, jerking his thumb behind me, studied and full of authority. I follow his thumb. There in the corner is the machine. The headboard's alive. Pure, aggressive desire. It's Devil-woman in a slick red bodysuit, rocket cones, a white-toothed sneer. Rocket flares flash, stars explode behind her. PIN-BOT in flaming red letters. Then the bed itself beneath her. A mattress of moving flippers and pads and blinking lights and whirlpool neon. Silver balls blowing around aimlessly.

The bed we never fucked on. And now it's over.

I can't stop looking. She is what I was, what I became around Giorgio, what I am no longer. She is what I want to be again.

Gene pulls out some quarters for the jukebox. "Any last requests?"

"You pick," I say. "You're the aficionado." Having managed to get that word out in one piece, I know he'll leave me for a few minutes, so I can visit Pinball Land.

I turn my back on the transvestites. Drop in a quarter and embrace the metal waist of the machine. My finger on the trigger, I shoot that silver ball into airtight space. Devil-woman's eyes follow my moves. Though I will the silver ball to stay high and bouncing, it dribbles dribbles down until it drops back into the belly, a sad tinkling of bells and harsh tinny pops following it like a techno-dirge.

From the jukebox comes what sounds vaguely like Frank Sinatra. Silk tones tap me on the back. I shrug them off. Devil-woman's leering. She points at the red-lettered score box. I watch the high-scorers' names and numbers roll across the screen. BOB 12,345,679/JLT 11,799,321 . . . then these words appear.

GIVE ME/SIGHT . . . BREAK/MY . . . EYE/BALLS.

And it is gone. I wait breathlessly. It comes again.

GIVE ME/SIGHT . . . BREAK/MY . . . EYE/BALLS.

Who's in there? Someone's trapped. Something's stuck. Devil-woman? The silver balls? The silver balls. I embrace PIN-BOT. I give it my all. Still, it is not enough. I sink down onto the smudged glass, drop my head. My face is cold there. Flat.

Gene is tugging at my arm. "Want to go?"

"Just resting." I smile. I push myself up off the glass pinball mattress, where my cheek lay and I listened to the hum of fallen silver balls.

"Dance with me," says Gene, and pulls me into his arms. "This is Buddy Greco. Off that album *Songs for Swingin' Losers*."

Greco is singing, "I feel so bad and that ain't good. One more kiss, it's more than I should."

"That's what my dad used to say to me when I first started falling for girls and getting my heart broken and told him about it. 'You feel bad and that ain't good,' he'd say, and laugh."

I don't want to laugh. I want to sink my fist into the mouth of the laughing father, all laughing fathers.

"Saw Greco six months ago in Vegas playing for free. Guy used to headline."

Every note Greco sings brings a wilting cigarette, a mournful pair of eyes with deep-dark circles underneath, a skinny alley cat winding around stumbling legs floating into the bar. My feet are so heavy the floor is mud, but we are turning and Gene's got his arm around my back and he's cradling the back of my head. I want him to strangle me with blue tinsel right now in his arms. But there's the Central American in white, bobbing his head to the smooth beat and leering at me, hoping I'm a transvestite, spittle showing in his teeth. The chili pepper lights sizzle, spice the air, I imagine skinny alley cats leaping over the bar and disappearing. The bartender keeps shaking up cocktails, pouring long minutes of liquid fire into waiting vessels. The ring in his nose belongs on a hitching-post.

I'm thinking I should go for it, tell Gene I want him. I'm thinking it's my last chance. Now or forever lonely. Gene's breath is hot on my neck and I'm so close I'm far away. A black corpse whirling on the pitted floor of The Blacklite. My chest is empty. The clock is ticking. Come back, come back, I plead with my heart, but the arteries swell uselessly. Stolen, and I have not reclaimed it. I don't know who or what I love anymore.

We sit down and all that's left of the Stoli is bare melting rocks. The water pools at the bottom of the glass. Tiny silver balls.

"Buddy Greco's the man," says Gene.

The pinball machine is quiet, only a few electric gurgles escape.

"He was a real showman, Greco," Gene says and stands up. Jades out his face, straightens his jacket. "He walks on stage, pointing his finger at You, You, You,"—Gene points at random spots in the dark air—"then backs off the stage pointing at You, Me, You, Me. Women call out, 'Remember Atlantic City, Buddy?' And he looks in their direction, real bored, looks down at his watch, points You, Me, You, Me, backs off the stage."

Gene's hands fall by his sides and he sits down, but I still hear his harsh voice, still see his finger, jabbing the air, pointing at me, pointing at him. Never pointing at both at the same time. It's impossible.

In the dim light, I look at Gene. His lips are wet from the Sharp's and shine dully. The mouth that blows a soulful blues harp, the mouth that kisses like jazz, slow and searching or frenzied and raw, the lips that part mine even when resistant. They've turned cruel again.

No more kisses after tonight. The last hurrah. Then we'll both be pointing, won't we. You, Me, You, Me. Until we both back off the stage into our own apartments.

Boxing

I wrap my hands in yellow: five times around the wrist, loop the fingers, criss and cross, around and around the knuckles, back around the wrist and Velcro seal; slip on the fourteen-ounce Perma-bilt gloves—fourteen, 'cause Coach says they slow me down and I don't swing so wild, or move so sloppy.

I see three girls giggling in the corner mocking my moves, the way I sashay sometimes when I swing. But when my feet are planted deep and light, and I cock my elbow just so, and the left hook swoops down, hawk from my shoulder, connects with Coach's outstretched pad and thundersmacks with drumming certainty, black on black, the world's a fist, and the fist is mine.

A Casa: A Day in the Life Of

Sirens wail and I hear them swooping up Ardmore Avenue. One, two, three white and neon greeny-yellow L.A. Fire Department trucks pull up in front of Father Armenia's place. Mother Armenia is standing plumply in the doorway, screaming and waving her hands. Father Armenia is pacing the sidewalk, calmly smoking a cigarette, while one of their nine sons hurls a mobile phone against the wall near where his mother stands. It does not shatter. Only a few hard plastic pieces fly off and the phone skitters into the foyer, its single antenna aiming dumbly. A passerby, his eyes on the Armenians, brushes against a Honda Accord. "GET OFF THE CAR!" mutters a disgruntled electronic guardian in halting mechanical monotone. It is a version of the starter's gun crack, for instantly the boy rushes toward his mother and throttles her around the throat. His bare shoulder blades are hunching butterfly wings working madly to escape the confines of skin. Father Armenia saunters wiry up the red-painted stoop and pulls the boy, seed of his loins, off Mother Armenia, and shoves him cheerfully down the steps. The boy, bare-chested and raging, paces, jaunts, grabs his khakied crotch, hits the white stucco wall, curses. A tear slides down Mother Armenia's face. All a Day in the Life Of. Not knowing this, the paramedics step out of their vehicles cautiously. There is a nervous crackle of walkie-talkies.

This is my neighborhood. I know these people. Father Armenia knocks knockety knocks on my door before eight in the morning if I've parked on the wrong side of the street. "You've got to move your car!" he shouts gruffly, saving me from a thirty-dollar ticket. Mother Armenia helps me carry groceries to my apartment when I have too many bags, chatters about her children, the recent fire up the street. The boys all wink at me when I walk by, sometimes whistle from the shelter of the foyer when I'm dressed for a Saturday evening out. I've even seen their only daughter get married right there on the stoop; I've seen the rice fall onto the small rectangle of grass and catch in the one twisted tree there; I've seen the daughter's white train trail down the dirty stoop and the flash of leg as she climbed into a shiny black Mercedes SL with her new husband who looked old enough to be her grandfather; I've heard the wail of Armenian music the brothers played as they danced on this very buckled sidewalk and cavorted in the sun-dried grass; I've seen Father Armenia laugh; I've seen Mother Armenia cry; I see them more often than I see my own family and I envy their stormy cohesion.

That's why I stare at the scene out the window.

I look through the cracked pane—that happened when the Santa Ana winds busted the windowpane wide open and the only way I could keep it shut was to duct-tape the sill and push a hand-me-down couch against the window—ignoring the raggedy-ass age-yellowed parchment plastic shades that were here when I arrived five years ago and I never changed, the rotten wooden frame painted white, stained and peeling, the two lower panes covered with Plasti-Kote glass frosting No. 33 that was supposed to keep prying eyes from scoping the apartment according to my old boyfriend Slim who had experience cleaning out entire houses when the owners were absent. One of the paramedics is inching his way over to Father Armenia.

I turn up the stereo, Celia Cruz, cross my heart, blankets the sound of sirens and the roar of the choppers. I talk on the phone, don't hear the Armenians scream at each other. I don't look out the window, see Mother Armenia in her nightie and nylon robe hurling slippers at Father Armenia. I don't see him skulking by the garage, cigarette glowing.

Jump for Joy

Outside the Hollywood Souvenir Shop, a thin man with Medusa dreads is jumping up and down, up and down. Great cork-popping leaps up from the sidewalk. Tattered parachute pants balloon in and out like lungs. Neon splashes on his shoulders and stripes his neck. Music booms from the store. Up, down, up, down, then skip one foot out like he's dancing, like he's sparring.

People pass by on Hollywood Boulevard, stepping on dirty star plaques, grinding their heels in celebrities' names, bodies hydroplaning over cement squares, they don't look at him.

He's nobody. No matter how high he jumps.

Also Yellow

"What's your favorite color?" asks this man I hardly know who sits across from me. We are at Farfalla, an Italian restaurant. Farfalla means butterfly and I wish I were one right now. At least I can flutter my lashes. We are on a first date. A time when questions spackle the gaps of unfamiliarity rather than poking holes in the delicate tissues of love.

"Ahm, don't know, don't think I have one. Used to be shocking pink when I was a kid, but I read in my mother's color psychology book that pink was gentle and geriatric, so I gave it up. You?"

"Yellow," this man says from the other side of the table.

"Yellow?" My breath catches.

"Yeah, Yellow Rose of Texas, you know."

"That's why?" I say. "Yellow Rose of Texas?"

The man sips his Pellegrino, looks at me.

I inch my plate over a spot of spilled wine. I am thinking how little he resembles Giorgio. This man looks like an Irish thug, a Reservoir Dog. He is raw-faced, unchiseled, authentic.

"Goddamn Texas, Big State boogaloo, you know? Big Sky, Big Hats, Big Women. Yellow roses clenched in every set of pearly whites."

I nod, imagine the two men meeting. It would be at Yuca's burrito stand, in the parking lot. Under the awning, the sun wouldn't beat down on this man and Giorgio, no, there'd be a little shade, a little carne sauce dripping onto and through the paper plates showing how fragile it all is. Giorgio would eat the whole carne asada burrito, mouth working, beans munching, and this man would take a few bites, watch closely, ready to run if the Italian guy got feisty, but Giorgio wouldn't. He'd think about clocking this man in the face while he was chewing on his burrito. He'd think about flipping the table up into the air and wrestling this man down to the asphalt ground for having laid a finger on his woman. And he'd add more Yucatán Green Chile Sauce, so much that it would burn his mouth and he'd have to order another lemonade, and by then it would all be too late. This L.A. guy would probably win. The son of a plater at a chrome plant would outpower the son of the Minister of Culture.

"My mother had a garden," this man was saying. "She could never grow yellow roses. Red, white, pink, purple, every other color, but not yellow. It was one of those tiny deals, surrounded by a wire fence. Small lot. She was trying to make the dump pretty. Fuckin' Downey, right? And we're the only honkies left, only ones who stayed after the Watts Riots, after the White Flight."

Thousands of snowy tissues wing up into the sky, the Big Texas Sky, take flight, flap weakly. Turn yellow, shot through with solar rays, form a great big V for Vulnerability. Sometimes I hate life. Sometimes I want out.

"Why couldn't yellow be sunlight?" I ask this man, my tongue loosened by the wine, the fragrant porcini mushrooms, the olive oil, the fresh bristles of rosemary. "You know. Globes of fire. Shiny plates. Golden balls bouncing down the wells of human mystery, the birth canal, the Tunnel of Love."

"Yeah," says this man, smiling. "I dig it."

For the first time that evening, I see him sitting there. His name is Gene. He lives next door. A band promoter, a blues harp man, a poet, a traveler, a white-knuckler.

Gene tells me a former girlfriend of his, now a writer for the *In Flight* magazine, just wrote a piece and mentioned him.

" 'My former lover, the punk rock singer who read me Arthur Rimbaud in bed, still lives in my heart.' Something along those lines.

So her husband called me, in tears. She's in Patagonia right now on assignment."

He pronounces it Paytagoneea.

"What'd you tell him?"

"I said it didn't mean anything. Said she was completely in love with him. Took two hours to convince the guy."

"Was it true?"

"No. She's still got a thing for me."

"And you?"

"Nothing. I don't harbor any feelings for her."

But I wonder, as Gene tells me the story, whether he does, or whether he is telling me the story to let me know he's desirable, he lodges in women's hearts and try as they might, even after marrying, they cannot forget him.

Bukowski Doesn't Live Here Anymore—He's Dead

I have met people who have met Bukowski, but I myself have not met him. Now he's dead. Tonight, a friend of Giorgio's, an actor, is reading poetry with Bukowski's ex-wife, or is it his widow. Giorgio says she's a wetbrain. Does any of this matter? I am not invited.

I met a man. This man was producing a movie about the space capsule *Apollo 13*, according to his business card. I held it so the edges dug into my fingers. I did not have a business card and still don't. We were at a cocktail party at a house in Malibu, owned by some writer who was out of town. This man was invited; I crashed. I was eating spinach dip and watching the sun set on the surf, minding my own business, trying to be antisocial, when he told me one night he drank with Bukowski at Musso & Frank's. He told me this proudly. At the end of the night, Bukowski scribbled GOOD LUCK, MICHAEL on a napkin and now this man has it framed. After he told the story the man asked me out to dinner. I said okay, but I never called him.

I made a U-turn on the Sunset Strip and got caught. I had to go to traffic school. The instructor, a failed stand-up comic, told the class how David Hockney was once a student, a bad student at that. Hockney was rude, did not pay attention, refused to answer questions of traffic safety or watch the crash video. Instead, Hockney spent the whole day biting, gouging, and scoring a Styrofoam coffee cup with his teeth, nails, and a Bic pen. The instructor now has the cup framed, if that is possible. Maybe I'm not remembering the story properly.

This actor I mentioned before, he used to be a lawyer, which makes him qualitatively different from most actors I know, and he is newly arrived from far west London, which also puts a new spin on things entirely.

Back to Bukowski. From what I gather, he was an ugly fellow, and proud of it. This is much harder if you're a woman. To be ugly. Think of it: Charlene Bukowski, or perhaps Brunhilde. Would such a face have been so adored? "Hey, baby, you're so ugly, you've got to sneak up on a glass of water to get a drink." I admit I am vain. Underneath the vanity is a fear that if I fail to attract attention, I will disappear off the pockmarked face of the Earth. There is also the desire to do just that. Once I was in Florence, at the leather market, where I bought a green and black leather beret. When I wore this beret, people said I looked like Marla Brando. I took it as a compliment. Maybe I was mistaken. After all, would Bukowski have given me the time of day? Booze and broads, broads and booze. Typewriter in the sky. On the scarred table, the puke-stained carpet, propped clumsily on the toilet seat. We would have hated each other, Bukowski and I.

My Uncle Otis, who lives in Albuquerque up near Signal Mountain where the scenic tram runs, once showed Marlon Brando some New Mexican real estate. Brando and my Uncle Otis drove around the center of the state, through Jarales and Polvadera, looking at land, eating homemade enchiladas and sopapillas bleeding honey, and farting. That's what my Uncle Otis says, then pauses. That's right, farting. Every time a fan recognized him at a diner and handed Brando a menu or slip of paper to sign his name on, Brando would fart, loudly, blasting putrid air, until the person backed away. I heard when fans approached Bukowski, he barked. Or stealthily retreated. He, like Brando, was easy to spot. I suppose that's really the point.

The Mayan Princess

I am at The Mayan downtown for an
Exposure party and am a guest of a guest of someone who knows
someone who works freelance for the magazine. I know no one, so
I order a Stoli and tonic and lean against a balustrade, studying the
crowd making occasional small talk with passersby and pretending
that I am at ease, nonchalant, self-contained, when really all I want
is some attention. I am lost in this grand ballroom done up like a posh
movie theater from the roaring twenties. Early on in the evening I
see Willem Dafoe in a black turtleneck and a cream-colored trench
coat, and I wonder if his tumbrel is really as big as everyone says it is
and whether I can capture a glance. But he looks furtive, not wanting to be recognized, and he leaves after merely ogling the scantily
clad sirens at the bar. He never notices me. Obviously I haven't
dressed right. All along the border of the ceiling, Toltec relief pan-
els of jaguars eating hearts, maize gods, rain gods, and long-dead
Mayan princesses stare down on me in pity. Ignoring them, I shift my
gaze toward the dance floor and watch people moving, but for once
I'm not in the mood. No one's sparked my burned-out eternal flame
with admiration or lust. I am a dead body, a casual corpse, dignified
and womanly in a loose-fitting vintage dress—high-necked, long-
sleeved necrophiliac black with elaborate white appliqué stitching on
the sleeves—funereal black stockings and mausoleum black spikes.
I'm bored with my drink and just about ready to find my friend and

beg to leave, when a rangy guy with mussed blond hair, wideset bolting eyes, and a rumpled linen jacket that gives him a boyish charm approaches me, and ignites the flame.

"Come upstairs and I'll buy you a drink," he says.

Upstairs, I sink into a red velvet chair for the test. He sits on the arm. Over his shoulder a relief of the Mayan death god with fleshless jaw grins at me, his protruding teeth glowing in the low ambient light of the club.

"Your dress isn't tight enough," he says.

The long-dead Mayan princesses sigh.

"Thanks," I say. Sounding tough, not wanting to but yes, accepting his poisoned barb into the softest flesh of my being and letting it quiver there.

We talk about this and that. He tells me he is a sculptor, he tells me he has trouble committing to women, he tells me he loves them all, but he is impatient as he talks. I can see it in the way he flicks ashes from his cigarette onto the carpet and takes quick swallows of Johnnie Walker, and I know soon he will either leave me or make a move. We have come to the crucial time when choices must be made and I am a brittle vase for sale in a store window, projecting silent ceramic screams to the potential buyer who flirts with my priced image. Then he leans in closer and whispers, "Let me tell you a story."

Finally, all his attention is mine. I nod demurely, gratefully.

"We are in a park and night is falling," he says. I inhale every word.

"I see you through the darkening leaves and I want you. I start to chase you and you run but you are wearing heels and your strong legs flash beneath a tight filmy dress and you are fast, but I am faster, and you are breathing hard and you feel my breath on your neck and I catch you and you fall onto the ground and you surrender."

He smiles at me, leans in closer to nip my ear. A woman in a rubber sheath walks by and his eyes follow her. A young woman with bared midriff and straight red hair walks to the bar, and his eyes follow her.

"So," he says without looking at me, "come to my place?"

"Wait," I say. "I have a story too."

He turns his head sharply toward me. His eyes are shiny and wet. Perhaps he sees me for the first time.

"Yes," he says, his voice suddenly eager.

"We are in a park and night is falling."

"Yes," he says, a little uncertainly.

"I see you and I know you're trouble, I know what you're thinking, and I start chasing."

"You wild one you," the sculptor says, a little breathlessly.

"Even in my heels I am faster than you. We're running through the park and the leaves are crunching underfoot, branches are snapping in your face and the sweat is coursing down your back soaking your cheap silk shirt, and you're running as hard as you can, your thighs are on fire, and still I catch you. I catch you and you stumble, panting, and I twist one arm behind your back, pin you down, then beat you with one of my high heels, and the black spike tears at your sweaty burning hungry hunter's flesh, and you sink down into the moist leaf-strewn grass and surrender to me completely."

"Let's go," he says, seizing my hand. "Now."

"Not a chance," I say.

He stands, puzzled, then turns his back on me, strides away into the bloody night rhythms of The Mayan, jungle temple in the bitten-up heart of L.A., where he will find other quarry. But the long-dead Mayan princesses and I know, even if he emerges victorious this Hollywood night, a broken-necked gazelle drooping graceful from his shoulder, my story has stained the smallest corner of his soul and will not, cannot be erased.

.

Undercover

Your lips are sweet like wine but under your arms is where I need to be. You raise these arms and surrender your secret smells to me. Sometimes it is rich and sharp with oils and musk, dung, cedar bark, and sugary smoke, like sap-covered pinecones heating in the sun. I hide in the cave of your underarms, I burrow my face there. Though always dense, other times the smell is sweeter, like berries in a dusty, dusk-leaved bramble bush. Maybe eucalyptus, maybe honeysuckle. Maybe there's a peach pit underfoot mingled with the warm dirt and earthwormed flesh and rainwater. The peach pit faintly echoes its former sweet-juiced fruit flesh, dried now, shards on a ridged pit.

This morning, Giorgio, you smelled faintly of sandalwood talcum powder and—is it possible?—popcorn (slightly burnt, butter and heat) like we ate last night at the movie theater. Sweet and burnt and warm like a field of bleached eelgrass in summer. All these things hang suspended in the mat of your underarms where I need to be.

Hide me.

Save me from her.

Flash Update: Larry Gets Foxy

My old buddy Roy and I are driving back from a party last night and he tells me that Larry Pitts walks by his office over at the Sony lot every day and says, "Hi, guy," every time he passes.

"What's he look like?" I ask. "Still that Blond Boy Wonder?"

Roy shakes his head. "Like hell," he says. "Dresses in black every day—black T-shirt, black jacket, black jeans, black lizard-skin boots. That's his shtick, you know. Hair's all stringy, bad complexion. I think he does drugs. Coke or something. He's fidgety and distracted, can't look you in the eye. You know the type." Who doesn't, I think.

Roy tells me Larry now drives a black Jaguar convertible and is producing a film called *Walker* with Alex Cox directing. "You know, the guy who did *Sid & Nancy,*" Roy says, never impatient with my lack of film lore. He says Cox's really good and so is the script. Damn, I think. The more horizontal I go, the more vertical he goes. Maybe it's a correlative function. What would happen if I made it? Would he plummet to the bottom of the heap, the metaphorical Mulholland car grave that lies below a treacherous curve, miles and miles of smooshed car strata—mostly Triumphs and Porsches and, of course, Jaguars. Looking far from sleek. Or would we end up taking yoga together, standing on our hands smiling at each other so it looks like frowns, because he'd have to acknowledge me then, upside-down decorum, power parlance? Or would we knock back a few cool, tall ones at the bar together and talk shop? Ew. Roy tells me Larry Pitts lives with Maria Wyeth, a gorgeous actress whose father was a famous rodeo rider. Says someone he knows says they go to the gym all the time together.

"You know, a guy like him, he wouldn't go out with anyone who wasn't a model." What guy wouldn't, in L.A., if he had the option.

Pretty as Italy

Hot tip: three-fifty for a little apartment up in the Hills, overlooking Lake Hollywood. Pretty as Italy. Same price as my downscale excuse for a domicile. Impossible, I think. But Isaac's gone and I'm living by myself on South Detroit Street—south of Wilshire where the vibes turn wiry—and I'm searching for an exit ramp that'll take me higher.

I'm a hamster in a filthy white-carpeted cage, in this dump where every move I make is registered by the Pablo Picasso's Dancehall disco hostess downstairs, Lorelei, who rings up when I've got a cold, "Puleeeze, can you keep that honking down, girl?" or when I'm crossing from my futon to the two-foot-high fridge and kitchenette snuggled squat against the front door too many times in one night, "Girl, I swear. I've got earplugs in and you're *still* working my nerves."

When Isaac was around, Lorelei chilled. If she complained it was all sweetish. I saw her popping out her triangles and wagging her high-rise watoosi at him every chance she got; but now, with Isaac out of frame, it's all-out warfare. Even my breath is not my own, so conscious am I of listening ears and prickly-ass nerves. I'm so sick of Lorelei and her wigs, and the sequins she leaves trailed on the oil-stained parking area below, I could even kiss that lemon tree good-bye—full with glossy dark leaves and fragrant with yellow fruit the size and shape of Nerf footballs—it's the one dash of beauty and hope in the whole damn 'hood.

Here, everybody's living in cubicles they call studios, and lots of them are stuffed with entire families. Most of the time I imagine I'm in a cartoon; everywhere the walls are so thin, I can practically see the sides of the apartments sway out and then in with the frantic scufflings, the roofs bulging off the eaves with caterwauling, the windowpanes popping with sonic blasts from radios all tuned to KDAY. I call it Chattertown, and if I don't get out soon I'm going to end up on the street barking hymns to the Almighty Dog and rattling a coffee can for spare pennies.

In other words, I don't belong here. I've come this far, clear across the country, away from the deadend streets my mother careened down in her battered Ford pickup. And here I am. No welfare for me, no food stamps, no two-bit jobs or sloppy lowlife for me. I am not my mother's daughter. I belong in the Hills, up there, straight north and a sloping vertical climb that's easy on the eyes.

I'm not a star, but I'm not a wig-wearing disco dancehall hostess either. I work at *Entertainment Tonight,* a show that millions of Americans watch with devotion. I've got my foot in the proverbial door, and I can keep smiling even though that door is pinching my shoe. I've got an idea if I can get to the Hills, I'll be able to kick that goddamn door down. Anyway, I'm around stars all the time and I still can't figure out what makes them so different from the rest of us. Except I do know they wouldn't be caught even driving on South Detroit, let alone shacking up here, although they might come incognito to pick up a tiny wrapped package or two.

I am lying on my belly on the futon that's flat on the dirty white-carpeted floor, thinking about how living in the Hills means a kind of success, a literal elevation of person in Hollywood. Like having a *terrazza* in Rome, my fantasy city where Fellini the God of all Gods makes his cinematic miracles. Surely height begets height.

I call Bob Arctor, the owner of the house.

"Hi, is this Bob Arctor?"

"Afraid so."

"Why afraid so?"

"Can't change it now. Been him all my life."

We make an appointment.

I conjure up misty vistas, faded rose walls, and creeping vines.

After work, the sky's already dark and shrouded. Gower north, right on Franklin, and then left up La Huerta into the fairy-tale land of Hollywood Hills. Once I get to Belden, the road narrows, so I squeeze my little car around the curves, between gingerbread houses, ranch houses, past minarets, cupolas, potted palms, spear-shaped bushes, Spanish tile and Southwestern stucco, New England wood frames, and sleek modern planar houses like flattened hatboxes. Christmas lights twinkle white or rainbow-colored from trees, eaves, door frames, garages. Sharp left on Flagmoor Place, then Dunbar Road, and finally Joyboy Lane. 113040. Right before the cul-de-sac with the gate that leads into Lake Hollywood path.

I park the car and get out. There is a high green wooden gate and I can see nothing beyond. I unlatch the gate and step onto a mildly sloping red brick stairway that winds through dark trees. Footing is hard because the bricks are jagged and broken. Still barely any lights. I pass through an arbored red-brick patio, pass a row of cylindrical lanterns peppered with small globular glass squares of dry Jell-O red, murky blue, and dirty ocher swinging strangely in the still night air, they are like hanged goblins with all their dead dingy eyes. I hear rapid barking, look down and see a dark sausage of a dog yapping toward me in short, jerky forward movements like it's popping out of its sausage casing. A tall bearded man steps out from a doorway.

"Tulku," he calls in a pleasant, whispery voice.

I tiptoe over a waterbowl scummed with water and then instead of a welcome mat there is another dog bowl, this one filled with chicken bones covered with shredded flesh. Some of the bones have fallen onto the red brick. I step over them into the house and am overwhelmed by the smell of stale air, body odor, dried dog piss, old spattered oil, unwashed sheets, dust, and sour skin. A flood of old memories. Life with Ma. Filthy apartments, decaying rented houses, seedy sublets.

I greet the tall slender man with the mellow voice. He is at least six-foot-seven and wears ragged Chinese canvas slippers, prune-wrinkled slacks, and a loose shirt thin from washings. His elbows are shiny knobs poking through. His face is that of an insomniac hound dog—long and narrow with sagging jowls and great pouches of skin below his droopy old eyes.

"Yes, yes, come in."

There are no lights in the house. Just two candles on the mantelpiece on either side of some maharishi yogi. I ask who's that, he says a polysyllabic name, then, "His body's dead but his spirit lives on."

As does my mother's, and I fear she's present. There is a sadness in the air. The carpet under my feet is thin, green, and soiled. I sit in a nubbly armchair with such a long seat my feet don't touch the floor. Tulku jumps into Bob Arctor's arms.

"What kind of name is Tulku?" I ask.

"Means reincarnation. He's the reincarnation of my other dog, Vranasat."

My nostrils are trembling, but I manage a smile.

"Do you have a dog?" he asks.

"No." I don't tell him I hate pets.

"You should," he says. "You're a warm, generous person."

"What should I get?"

"A Russian wolfhound." He winks. I think of Chekhov's lady with the Pomeranian, and am suddenly seized with melancholy. Is Bob Arctor so lonely he's conjured reincarnations of dogs and deceased yogi spirits, the better to see his imaginary companions in the dim light? And what if he knew of all the dead dogs in my past, the pets who met with one horrible, untimely death after another? Mostly run over by my drunk mother. There was Misty and Garm, Dandy and Butterscotch, Loki.

Named after the Norse God of Mischief, Loki was a good-natured German shepherd with great honey patches on his coat mixed with fur the color of chocolate fudge. He was afraid of cats and sitar music. Awkward, gentle, and clumsily mischievous, Loki was most attached to my mother. He would lope after her as she picked cranberries in the bogs, or nuzzle her legs when she was drunk. He was a faithful companion, riding in the back of her green Ford pickup wherever she went, with his leash tied to the side of the truck. He was always ready for a romp in the snow, or the water, or the woods. I can see his honey-colored forepaws dancing in the air as he jigged and lunged on the grass, egging me on with his tongue hanging out all dripping pink. Then, Thanksgiving Day. I was already at Mrs. Coggeshall's house waiting for my mother who was an hour late. The turkey was cool and the stuffing had formed a crust. Mrs. Coggeshall had only let me eat a dessert plate of boiled string beans and my stomach was growling. When my mother arrived, drunk, with a casserole dish of yams in her arms, she had orange streaks slopped over her jeans jacket and didn't even notice Loki hanging off the back of her truck, choked on his own leash.

No Russian wolfhound for me.

We go down the stairs to the apartment. On our way, Mr. Arctor shows me the outdoor kitchen.

"Got everything you need here—refrigerator, stove, sink, and microwave."

I nod mutely. The kitchen is covered by a roof, but open to the elements. There are dirty dishes in the sink, scummed over with rings of spaghetti sauce, soup, coffee, soda, and then frosted stiff. There are crumbs on all the counters, and the counters are piled high with newspapers, soup cans, coffee cans, boxes of Minute Rice, coils and strands of string, candles, matches spent and scattered, grease spots and sticky stains. It's an outdoor snapshot of the kitchens of my youth, where I never saw a pot washed, a chicken cooked, or a floor mopped, where linoleum crawled with a mind of its own, thick with a living coat of crusted crumbs, insects, dust, dirt, moss, and mold.

Around the corner, the apartment is the size of a small pool changing room. The thin carpet is blue, there is a bar, a tiny bathroom with a shower, no toilet. The room is not even large enough for my queen-size futon. And it is enclosed only by rickety sliding-glass doors.

"Here it is," Bob Arctor says joyfully. "Designed and built the house myself, y'know, whatever came to me."

Bob Arctor shows me the outhouse, up a flight of stairs. It is so dark I don't know how impressive the view is, and I don't care anymore. If I need Italy, I'll fly there.

"How much?" I ask him.

"Four hundred," he says. "What's your economy like?"

"Same as the country's," I say. "Kind of small."

"We can stretch it then," he says. "I think you'd make a good tenant."

I thank him and say how about if I come back during the daytime so I can see the view.

"Sure, sure," Bob Arctor says and tries to put Tulku in my arms. "Why don't you take him home, Rebecca?"

It is all I can do to keep the scrabbling reincarnation out of my arms. "No, no, he's yours," I protest too loudly, plucking dog hairs from my coat as I back out waving bye.

Back down through the Hills I get lost, and the quaint houses with their blurry strings of lights bend over the narrow road as if they will suffocate or snatch me away, hurl me into Lake Hollywood. Everywhere I turn I smell skunk. And once again I'm on the bumpy backwoods road going home after Thanksgiving, my face pressed to the window and my hands clutching the armrest and door lock, ready to jump out if Ma crashes the truck. Loki is in the back of the truck, wrapped in a dirty white sheet. The stench of skunk reeking from the dark woods on either side. She's tossing one Bud beer can after another over the seat, swearing to herself; the sound of all the beer cans clanking behind the seat is deafening. My brow is furrowed with the black tempest I carry for my mother, it is spilling tsunamis out my ears, williwaws hiss through my teeth, and I wish she were dead and every bump we hit, I close my eyes and pray for Loki to come back to life.

When I finally find my way out of the Hollywood Hills, concrete and smog take over. Everything is stripped down, wantonly grim. I am happy to live in the lowlands. On the surface streets. At right angles and perpendiculars, waffle-iron grids. Where the only view I get is by walking out of my apartment and tilting my head toward the Hills, toward the sky. This keeps me humble, like a head covering does for Jews and Muslims and Christians, keeping the distance between heavens and human, sky and scalp, the living and the dead.

L.A. Conversation

L.A. Conversation is the name of the coffee shop on Hillhurst where I went every day while I was in between film jobs and living off credit cards, unemployment, the kindness of friends, luck. Every day I'd get a double cappuccino and a raisin scone for $4.82. Siranoush, the Armenian counterwoman, always greeted me with a tale of woe: My no-good daughter-in-law left her son and grandson. Someone stole my car again, second time, even with alarm and the Club. What will I do? Already I borrow money from relatives to buy this new car. You want chocolate, cinnamon? Chocolate. Okay. And yesterday, right up the street, would you believe it? They shoot this homeless man on the sidewalk, in front of the newsstand. Who? I don't know, some kids. They want money, they want fun.

At this point, Siranoush will shake her head and stare at me with heavily lined, mascara-encrusted eyes, and I will remember, as I'm supposed to, that her husband left her for a young American woman when they came to America for a new life. And I will know she wants me to slide into the deep funereal grooves of her face. I will know she wants me to join her in renouncing the world and all false optimism, I know this voice too well (don't forget, you're fucked-up). And I will pretend to, but I will refuse. I will smile sympathetically, push the money over the glass-topped pastry case, but inside I will at that moment hug my arms around the warm, polluted world.

Place my lips on the soiled sordid face of Los Angeles and vow to love and cherish each carne asada burrito from Yuca's, each liquor/laundromat, every transvestite who struts and strolls Santa Monica Boulevard, even down to their tightass skirts and hurtful heels. And if they can smile. Well.

I sit at a table outside, sip my cappuccino so I leave a red-lip mark on the ceramic edge (leaving red lipstick marks on glasses, cheeks, napkins, noir-style, always makes me feel like a woman), chew, inhale exhaust from passing cars, and listen. Listen for the sound of a siren, an accident, a shopping cart, my friend Carla's gruff-growling Mustang that jars my nerves every time. One of the most soothing sounds in L.A. is near where I live, at the School for the Blind. They have blips for blind crossing. "Do-do, do-do, do-do." Double "do" for cross, yes cross. And "do . . . do . . . do . . ." for don't, not yet. When I get money from an automated teller, I always run my fingers over the Braille bumps while I wait for the bills to pop out, and I think about how it would be to touch my way through words. To hear my way across the street. What does the yellow skin of a banana sound like?

Carla pulls up in her broad white Mustang, a proud metallic steed of a car. Dressed in baggy overalls, a skimpy eggplant tube top, and Mexican boots with clownish toes—five dollars from Oaxaca— her thin arms the color of my cappuccino and lined with ropy veins pumping the air, Carla walks rapidly to the table.

"Hear about the rat that ate a kid in El Segundo?"

With her long skinny fingers, echoing her long skinny body— is that an example of a fractal?—Carla pincers a flake of my scone.

"What?" I say, almost spitting cappuccino.

"Yeah, this homeless couple was living in a car with their two kids. This one was only sixteen weeks old, and somehow, they must not have been paying attention and the rat gnawed the baby until it bled to death."

"Jesus, Carla!"

At the table next to us, a woman in a floppy velvet hat lowers her *L.A. Times.* "Hi," she says to Carla.

"It's Dee-dee!" Carla coos. "Did you read that story?"

Dee-dee shakes her head yes in disgust. "The worst is it was a pet rat. Is that a low-rent trend or something?"

Dee-dee, who is Dee-dee Disney, married a grandson of Walt Disney. Dee-dee and Carla go on to discuss details of the rat story.

I look away while they all talk, stare at the white pastry plate, the dull beige crumbs, and the shiny squeak-white. A Harley rips by and I imagine my flesh tearing, gnawed by noise, chewed by conversations I don't crave, or do I? The rat is loosed now in my mind. There's no peace in the pastry plate, no peace with the rat scurrying round. No escape from her.

Siranoush is wiping off a nearby table, her eyes glittering with satisfied despair. "Oh, yes . . . everything is terrible."

L.A.: Rrrrrriottown

This is my nightmare. Choppers rip through the smog-choked sky, tearing the seam of the city. Fires erupt from carefully aimed Coke bottles wrapped with gas-soaked rags of flame. While I am a scream captured in flesh, the city burns.

Johnny the Rocker

The first night I slept with Johnny the Rocker, thousands of flying ants streamed in the windows.

The next morning, tiny carcasses with gauzy black wings littered the futon and the walls nearby.

I met Johnny at a party of a friend of mine from *Entertainment Tonight* who had just edited a Meat Puppets video. My friend had a little Silverlake bungalow with low lights, strings of lit-up chili peppers, colored-glass Mexican votive candles with Our Lady of Guadalupe decals, Dia De Los Muertos paper cutouts of skeletons riding in cars, getting married, dancing, they were fluttering everywhere. My friend had a Mexican girlfriend named Perdita who wore Guatemalan dresses with strings of blue corn around her neck.

I was there to meet men.

The genuine Stetson on Johnny's long head of brown hair caught my eye first. Then it was the black leather jacket with one forearm scraped with zebra stripes. The other sleeve was stuck through with a monstrous gold nail. There was a Harley-Davidson patch stitched on the back.

"Wanna dance?" I asked him once I'd cut through the people between him and me.

He just nodded and started moving. My eyes drifted down his

shapely legs encased in leather pants. Biker boots. Minimum of dust on the toes.

When he smiled, when he swayed his hips a bit more loosely, my old engine gave a little purr, rusty from lack of use. It was three months since Isaac had headed for Tucson.

I called him Johnny the Rocker, even though he was a dancer by profession and a musician only by predilection.

The first night we hung out, we went to The Firefly on Hollywood Boulevard, had some Kamchatka vodka straight up. While the bartender doused the bar with clear juice and lit it on fire, Johnny told me all about himself. How he was a "downie," meaning he lived downtown in a loft with other artists. He had just quit his job at Le Sex Shoppe because things were cooking. He went on to tell me how he was good friends with Earle Shoop, a big-time choreographer who did Madonna's "Like a Virgin" video. How he just danced in the latest Pointer Sisters video. How he met Cher on her video and they hit it off, and she loved his leather jacket so much she asked him to get her one too and wear it in for her, which took about two months. How he used to date skate queen Tai Babylonia, did I know who she was? And how he was sad that hadn't worked out, how none of the girls he went with seemed to stick around for long.

The whole time he talked his gold nail kept slipping out of the black leather sleeve. "Damn," he would say, "this thing always slips out, then I find it in the weirdest places. One time it was caught in the drain. Took me the longest time to figure out what was blocking it up. Tai gave it to me," he said.

Flames were dancing on the bar. Smell of burnt gin, vodka. Spilt beer. Cigarettes. A tiny Filipina girl got up, shook her jeans-clad hips, and a bulky guy with a blond shag hoisted her up on the bar. She raised her thin arms over her head, tapped one foot on a nearby flame. Her high heel winked. Flimsy cotton shirt lifted above her stomach as she grooved to the jukebox and the handclaps, the pounding glasses and stomping feet. The fire flickered light over her skin, lit up the pores. I watched shadows streak over her belly, linger in the button, a true innie, deeply recessed and creased with lines. She couldn't have been more than sixteen.

Johnny kept talking, worked his arm around my waist. He didn't notice me stiffen. I saw sweat gather on the upper lip of the Filipina firefly. Her tits were like tiny snack puddings topped with cherries, nipples swelling against the thin cotton. I wasn't surprised when the blond shag bulkmonster reached up and tweaked one, or when the Filipina smiled back at him, baring tiny crooked teeth.

In the car driving back to my place Johnny played this one song over and over on the tape deck. "I'm Only Buggin'." The synthesizer sounded like an army of mosquitoes drunk on cheap wine, but the rhythm was catchy. I liked the way Johnny shrugged his shoulders to the beat, and moved his pelvis in the car seat while he drove so the vinyl squeaked. My jacket was still toasty warm from the bar's flames. Johnny said his Harley was in the shop.

After a pause he asked me what I wanted to do anyway. When I said I wanted to direct films he said great, he had a story we should write, wouldn't that be fun to do a script together and then I could direct it? I noticed then his eyes were more green than gold. I wanted to fuck him.

Upstairs, he stripped as he kissed me. Scent of ripe lemons drifted in the open window from the lemon tree below and mixed with faint traces of car exhaust. One sleeve, then the other, jacket on the carpet. T-shirt peeled off in one swift move. Two silver necklaces clinked against each other, against his skin. A silver bat with wings outstretched, a silver sword with a wiggly blade. He had a little trouble with the leather pants, so I helped him. Pulled them off, thinking about the time in junior high school science class when I tugged the skin off a frog we were dissecting. Formaldehyde stink on my fingers. Squeak of rubbery skin. The leather pants lay bunched on the carpet.

"What do you think?" he asked when he was naked. I was still dressed.

"I like your body," I said, rocking back on my knees. It was tight and lithe. A little pale, but he was a dancer which made up for it.

"That's all?" Johnny sat down on a chair.

"Oh, I like you too."

After that, fluid hips and moves were all a tease. Johnny didn't even push inside long enough to heat me up. Jerked himself off on my stomach like it was a tabletop.

I only saw Johnny a few more times after that. A gloomy twanged-out night in the murk of the Anti-Club. A body-crushing grope fest or two in the morbid dinge of Small's, former gay biker bar turned underbelly trendy. What killed the vibe for me though was the loft party where Johnny asked me to brush his hair, holding out a red plastic brush. Psychedelic Furs rasping through old speakers. Lots of people in black, swaying, staring at the walls, at the tops of each other's heads. I was so surprised, and so wanted to be loose and cool, I did it. Brushed his matted brown hair, tried to ignore the split ends, the dark oily curls dead in my hands. The cold of the red plastic handle. While Johnny sat on a stool and beamed. Said to a buddy pulling on a drink nearby, "This here is the life."

One night I stepped into Gorky's downtown for a caviar omelette with my friend Carla, and there was Johnny the Rocker behind the steam counter serving borscht. I hadn't seen him for a couple of weeks.

"Hey, Johnny. How's it hangin'?" I said casually.

"Cool," he said.

"What's new?"

Johnny ladled up a bowl of borscht for Carla.

"Got married," he said.

"What?"

"Yeah, last week I met this Ukranian girl, Irina, and, man, we clicked."

The white paper hat didn't look as good on Johnny as the Stetson.

"You kidding?"

Johnny pulled up his T-shirt.

"We got tattoos in Santa Monica," he said, showing us a Band-Aid diagonally covering skin where the appendix would be. Underneath, a fresh blue-green ankh with red puffy borders. Marriage tattoo.

Johnny handed Carla her borscht.

"We also got rings," he said, showing us a chunky silver ring in the shape of a honeycomb that turned into a skull with a grin.

"Oh," said Carla, "nice skull."

I shook Johnny's hand. It was wet with borscht.

"Congratulations," I said, jiggling my omelette around on the plate. "Was it for immigration?"

Johnny shook his head. "We just hit it off, y'know. Irina's too cool. Real skinny blonde, little diamond stud through her nose, she plays music too, kinda like L7. Girl rocker. Y'know, guitar and shit. She knows the band too."

He ducked his head and went back to arranging silver dishes on the steam table. The glass was so cloudy I couldn't see much of Johnny anymore. I don't know if he heard my last congratulations as I slid my yellow plastic tray of caviar omelette down the metal bars and over to the cashier.

A few months later I found his gold nail wedged between the carpet and the wall. I put it in the toolbox.

Wilshire Boulevard
Birthday Wish

This is why there's traffic in the right lane.

On the corner of Wilshire and La Cienega stands a woman. In the street. She is holding a placard.

BOB I LOVE YOU COME
HOME WITH ME IT'S MY
BIRTHDAY WE CAN MARRY
AND LIVE TOGETHER AND
I'LL TAKE CARE OF YOU

The writing is in black marker. Splintery letters. Underlined in red. It is rush hour. Her eyes are red-rimmed.

The woman watches every passing car closely.

The traffic is relentless.

Hollywood Cocktail

There it is, the HOLLYWOOD sign, planted like glamorously uneven teeth in the hills above where I park my yellow Toyota Corolla. Even though the lit-up sign is crooked, I am suddenly ashamed of my car and look to see if any other guests are around. Only when my Toyota starts sliding down the hill do I remember to cramp the wheels to the curb. I imagine my car streaking down the slope like mustard on the loose, which makes me think maybe I have a stain on my dress I didn't notice before, a stain so obviously crusty or wet or rank no one will even look me in the eye. They will know right away I am just another underpaid intern trying to get a real job.

"Really think I look okay?" I ask Isaac, turning on the car light and examining the dusty vintage cocktail dress for stains. There are none. But then I decide the dress itself is the problem. Probably no one in Hollywood wears a cocktail dress to a cocktail party.

"You look mahvalous." Isaac smiles, his white teeth a camera flash.

It is our first cocktail party in Hollywood. I take the tiny steps up the winding rock stairs leading to the house, careful not to sink my heels into a hidden crevice or grassy spot. Isaac bounds ahead, entering the candlelit house before me.

The party is a wash of glinting glass earrings, perfumes parrying with each other, shiny bodysuits, and skintight jeans. The men, dressed darker and more somberly, are the seaweed in a sparkling sea. Everyone looks vaguely familiar. Maybe I've seen them on the screen or in a dream, but it could just be nervousness.

A stout man with hair combed over a bald patch purposely bumps my shoulder and whispers in my ear. "Name's Gilbert, but you can call me Gil. You?" He glances quickly around the room before I answer, as if maybe he'd lost something and only now thought of it.

"Rebecca Roth," I say, grateful for the acknowledgment even from this man, and for a moment the swirl around me gels. I'm visible. I'm there.

A woman turns around from the couch and coos, "Rebecca Roth! That's one of my stage names!" She giggles. "I thought I made it up."

"You're kidding." I look toward the balding man, but he's already disappeared. Isaac is nowhere in sight.

"Nope. Had it, oh, hell, years now."

The actress turns her back to me and laughs a tinkly laugh that sounds like she's peeing halfheartedly into a tin pie plate from about six inches above.

"Hey," I say, then again louder, "Hey!" until the actress turns around, partway, so only a sliver of her profile is evident.

"I bet," I say, "you don't have a middle name."

She arches her eyebrows.

"I do. Miranda," I say.

"Oh, like Carmen Miranda?" she asks, rolling her r's and eyes at the same time.

I see Isaac in a corner flirting with a redhead wearing what looks like a fifties peignoir. She links her arm in his and leads him out onto the balcony where the HOLLYWOOD sign is glowing against the hillside. I can hear their laughter bubbling up into the champagne night.

"No, from Shakespeare," I say, marveling at the density and thrust, the unshakable authority of the ancient bard's name, something I'd never noticed before.

The actress closes her eyes for a moment, mutters a soft and blankish, "Hm," turns away for good.

I vow never to utter my middle name again to strangers. I'll keep my heart in my chest, not in my hand. I go out onto the balcony to get some air.

"Isaac," I call to my future ex-boyfriend.

Anastasia

Anastasia is a warm wafting breeze, a darting slender striped tigerfish, a shimmying splendor of hip and breast and tossing hair and shivering arms and puckered lips on the portable dance floor, her eyes flashing and flung wide open like windows at the first whisperings of spring, hummingbird speed catch her if you can, she is a sprite who squeezes out of your gaze out of your world without so much as a wave good-bye, slip blip byebye, leaving her lipsticked kiss on a napkin, a gift for you.

"My life is a sea of islands, and the islands are when I take lithium." So she says, my fragile friend, teetering on her shiny tightrope in her garage-sale-battered-and-creased Paul Revere buckled black shoes and floaty new mall dress compliments of Mom, refusing to take her lithium regularly, preferring to alternate between the ultra-shimmer and *Koyaanisqatsi*-speed of mania to the flatland valley vista of balanced days. That left lazy eye straying and betraying her split-level architecture, Anastasia might forget a planned meeting from one minute to the next, but she never recants her heart.

A Casa: Chinese Pop Guns and the Sound of Music in My 'Hood

Up the street a Liquor/Laundromat and around the corner, Day 'N Nite. Old men on the street playing checkers, sitting on seats pulled from cars, playing on cardboard boxes. Oranges, roses wrapped in cellophane, roasted peanuts for sale at Santa Monica/Western off-ramp. There are those who cannot drive. Griffith Park Observatory like a white girdle cutting into the Los Feliz Hills. Gray freeways unwinding like ribbons let loose from Los Angeles's hair, a city unbound. José selling empanadas for fifty cents. Batidos around the corner in the burned-out mini-mall. A looted gun shop is now a Lucky 13 Cards & Copies. Ice cream trucks. El Pinguino–flavored ice carts, bells jangling. Auto Pete's Used Cars. 99 Cent Stores. Families and children all around.

Two little girls on Big Wheels grind through the alley between apartment buildings, and the giggling and grinding of their plastic wheels on concrete is worse than nails dragged down a chalkboard. Before the fevered young racers' noises have faded, I hear a loud pop like someone's wrenched a massive cork from a champagne bottle tall as a person.

I just know it's a bullet, coming from somewhere on Kingsley near the crackhouse, near the liquor store that's around the corner. The girls' noises are fading in the opposite direction, oblivious.

Doesn't seem right that a gunshot should sound like a pop, not after all the THX wraparound sound we get in the theaters, where

235

the shots ring out like car crashes, like detonated dynamite, like trees falling and glass shattering, all at once.

I think about the Chinese pop guns I used to get when I was a kid, living in Manhattan. My mother and I would go to Chinatown to get them, shellacked wooden pistols with red handles you pull, then push and the air pressure pops the cork out on its string so it dangles like a broken, naked thing. I drove her crazy about those guns, because I would pop and reload them compulsively for hours until the string broke. Then I would bug her until she promised me we'd get another. I remember something I haven't thought of for years, how the Chinese shopkeepers would fall silent when we'd enter the store with the neatly dusted packed shelves, and I remember feeling a quiet hatred emanating toward me, and this is something I always link with those pop guns.

No matter how hard I try, I can't take that pop of a gunshot seriously. And if I did? I couldn't live here, and so I don't. It becomes part of the music, a jarring note, and then is gone, swallowed up by the cry of children, the jangle of an ice cream truck, a car burning rubber down the narrow street.

Close Encounter of the Cartoon Kind

Same rasp. Same sliding, hyper-bright eyes. Hair, even thinner, pulled back in a gnarly knotted mat.

"Stav. It's been years. You got a ponytail."

"I don't do this, see, my hair, it goes all over, some kind of crazy halo. Fuzzball. Hi. Hi. Good to see you. Sure. Ahm."

He snaps his fingers abruptly, trying to place me, trying. To catch a beat. A missed cue.

"Rebecca," I say.

"Good, good. Yeah."

He claps me on the shoulder, hard, his eyes darting around the foyer outside the Bandini Studios screening room where we are gathered, coincidentally, to sneak preview a film. Everyone's late. Later than us.

"What're you . . ." I begin.

"I'm doing this thing, this thing, this bucaneer flick, present day, yeah, it's great, great," he growls, his eyes ping-ponging the walls, sweeping flash-searching the still-empty stairwell. "Wrote it, directing, acting too, the whole. Hey." He jabs his finger at a blown-up black and white photo of a musketeer on the wall. The musketeer is wearing tights, mid-thigh boots, and blousy white shirt. His hair is the same length as Stavros's. Dark. It also flops in his face. The musketeer's right leg, shod in soft leather, is charging toward us, threatening to break the barricade of frame. Or so it seems, the way Stavros is staring bug-eyed at it. Wishing it were another guest. A distributor with deep pockets. A dame. Anyone but a former assistant/ slave.

"That's a swashbuckler," says Stavros. "That's me. Hey. I'm a pirate."

He keeps his jabbed finger frozen in the corporately conditioned air.

"Yeah, yeah, well, almost," he says.

Stavros turns abruptly, sticks his face close to mine. I can see a large blackhead swelling on the left side of his nose. When he stops talking or moving, his face sags, I've seen it, but he never does stop. Not tonight. Not after all these years.

"Somedays we've almost got the money to go, then we don't," he says. Swashbuckling. He pinches his index finger and thumb together. "This close. Yeah." He shakes his head and wisps of bent black hair fan into his eyes. Hardly any hair remains in the rubberband.

"That beautiful woman I saw you with some years back. The one in the coffee . . ."

"You mean those Spics. Married her, we were married, ding-dong bells and every . . . it was amazing, incredible. Only lasted ten days. God, she was, see, we'd be in bed, and the kid would come in, want to climb in with us, we were naked, see, the son wants to . . . 'My old boyfriend used to let . . .' she said. Hey, the kid, he was six years old. Ten days. What do you . . . those Spics."

Stavros shakes his head, grins. Gets stuck. The rubberband falls to the floor, bounces briefly. His hair, loosed, it's like a ring of black marsh grass circling a pond, a pate, the invisible wind lifting and blowing each blade in separate directions. He starts pulling at his shirtfront. Tugging at a wrinkled collar. Looking caught. Primed for spontaneous combustion. Nerved out. Sprung. Not knowing what to do—I never did—I take his hand. Pump.

"Great, great to see you," he says, withdrawing his hand, right.

He drifts backward, toward the cluster of guests rising up the stairs, his feet doing nervous little two steps.

"Yeah," he says from a ways, I can hardly hear him. "I remember you."

A Casa: Inferno, or Which Inner Circle Is This?

At nine o'clock on a warm Saturday night I hear footsteps running through the alley and out onto Ardmore. Almost immediately the footsteps race back down the alley and disappear over the garage roof. Kids, I think, going back to combing my wet hair. There is an explosion, sudden sound and fury. I go to the living room, look out the window. An empty VW Rabbit convertible parked right in front of the Villa Ardmore is in flames. The top's down. A great ball of orange fire erupts from the upholstery. Sparks of yellow spray into the air.

It's October and the Santa Ana winds have been blowing for the last week. During the day the temperature's risen as high as a hundred and eight. Last night the winds blew out all the stoplights on Sunset Boulevard. Everything's prickly and dry, chafing. Prime time for fires and rash acts.

"Maratruca," mutters Father Armenia, who is standing near the car. He is always the first at the scene of an Ardmore crime, accident, mishap. Flames cast a glow over his short body, transform his dark hair into a radiant furry cap. He drops a cigarette and grinds it into the dark street. People appear at windows, wander outdoors, watch, mumble, point. Soon a group gathers around Father Armenia. Someone calls 911.

Maratruca is an El Salvadoran gang. All over the neighborhood MAR, the gang's nickname, is spray-painted on walls, discarded couches, newspaper machines, sidewalks, street signs, garbage cans. Many of them live one street west on Kingsley, where gunshots come almost every night. I thought they kept to Kingsley.

Fire trucks arrive and put the fire out. A stream of water subdues the roar, sizzles, sputters. No one claims the car. Twisting columns of smoke jet up from the steaming metal carcass. The fire trucks leave. Half an hour later a friend picks me up and we go to a party. I don't tell the story of the blazing car to anyone at the party; I don't need to see the raised eyebrows; I don't need to hear the tongue-clucks of dismay, the sharply hissed reprimands, "Why are you living there? You should move." Instead I chat, flirt, charm, pretend. Can't they smell the burnt gasoline, oil, melted plastic, hot metal, smoke, and murder in my hair?

The next morning I run into my neighbor and friend B+ on the street. He is standing next to the burned-out car. On the grass nearby lies a jumble of charred clothes, a singed purple T-shirt, scorched white jeans, loose socks, and bras. A blackened running shoe sits on the ledge above the backseat where the vinyl top lies accordion-folded. The body of the car is scarred with spots, flame tracks, bubbles, and warps.

"What the hell?" I say.

"Salvadorans torched it," he says. "That's the latest thing, dude. It's my friend Mona's. Not even hers. A friend of hers. She was moving and she had all her shit in the trunk."

"Christ," I say. "Insurance?"

"Lucky the friend just had electrical servicing done, so they're going to say it was that, right? Check this, last year Mona had her car stolen from across the street there." B+ points. "I don't know. Things aren't happening between the Salvadorans and the Armenians, dude. Two nights ago three Salvadorans were shot outside the liquor store around the corner. Two died. There's a lot of tension. I don't know, dude, I think it might be time to leave."

"Leave!" I say. "Leave the Villa Ardmore?"

"I'm gonna scope it for the next month, but the vibes aren't good, not good at all."

I peer into the dead Rabbit. Blackened seat coils, naked tubes, wires, it looks like a barbecue pit. The windshield's blown out, shards piled on the hood, a spiky deck of fifty-two pickup. B+ picks at a loose strip of silver metal lining on the windshield frame. The silver flakes off in his hand. A gust of Santa Ana wind lifts a layer of ashes from the interior and scatters it on the old, warped sidewalk.

Later that day, the car is gone. I see Father Armenia in a white shirt and black cotton trousers digging in the yard in front of his apartment.

"No cars today?" I say.

"The landlord won't let me work on cars anymore," he says in his gruff, smoky voice. "I'm digging up these flowers to take to Valencia."

"Valencia?"

"We're going to move. The landlord's raising the rent. Won't let me work. I'm going to Valencia." He winks. "Quieter there."

"But you've been here twenty years!"

"Maybe time for a change." Father Armenia smiles at me, lines in his tanned skin forming parentheses at either edge of his mouth, crinkling darkly alert eyes. In all my years at the Villa Ardmore, I've never seen Father Armenia smile before. There is something familiar in his mouth, the way the lips curl richly at the sides and seem so ready with laughter.

Yes, I think.

Hollywood YMCA

Some people say the Y is shabby. The machines are old and stiff, out-of-date. Members look like street people.

There are no pink walls here. No hip-hop music, no disco, only the heavy perfume of exercise. No canned music, no frills, no spandex, no bullshit. The mirrors all around are for rigorous self-awareness, not self-admiration. The sweat-stained walls are more solid, more human than stained-glass windows.

The Y is my temple, my shrine, my church, and my mosque. It is my purification rundown. My dirty dahlia, my darling.

I look around and see a Mexican gang member with MAMA QUERIDA tattooed over his chest, a barefoot street person in cutoff polyester pants toting bags with him from one Nautilus machine to another along with the putrid smell of a sea-rotted buoy, a European backpacker who speaks no English, a Rastafarian with a FIGHT THE POWERS THAT BE T-shirt, white grunge musicians with pierced nipples, a Midwestern white kid with Bermuda shorts and white tennies, a hip film actor, a police academy trainee, a Thai kickboxer, a road worker, an Italian film director, a professional basketball player whose head grazes the doorjamb while he signs autographs, a transvestite who primps and readjusts his/her bangles as he/she watches the boys hoof it down the court, identical twin porn stars who bare their midriffs as they train, little kids with little sneakers darting this way and that like minnows, and old white men with tummy bulges— former athletes with muscular veined legs and hair dyed brown or red—flirting with the ladies on the Stairmasters.

I set the Lifecycle for Level Seven. My legs pump out so many revolutions, life, death, life, death, I fall into a trance. Strenuous movement that shifts into stasis, stillness, calm—this is what I seek. The sweat pours down my face and neck and collects in the cleavage of my black lycra sports bra, streams down my back and stains my T-shirt like a watery wound. After a half hour, I am ready to submit.

I am sweat-drenched before the drinking fountain. A clear rainbow of water splashing down my throat and my spirit is refreshed.

For a moment I listen to the pounding of feet down the court and the harsh bounce of the ball, the shouts, the buzzer sounding. A sweet swish from the outside corner, a clean jump shot, a smooth steal, a strong half hour on the Lifecycle, these give us momentary peace and pleasure. All part of the preparation.

Another splash of water, then I climb the stairs to the roof.

On the first step I poise my black Converse All-Star high-tops halfway over the edge, toes gripping the crosshatched lip that sparkles with mica or maybe flecks of diamond. I let my heels drop and my calves sing in readiness. My left hand rests lightly on the metal railing that slants upward toward the sky, city sky.

I climb. Two, three, four, all the way up to twenty and I am halfway. I reach the landing. On my left a room for EMPLOYEES ONLY. Pay no attention to that man behind the curtain, those air ducts and boilers and ventilator shafts lurking in the gloom, awaiting Penitentes. I am Alice in WonderLAnd, rising. I turn toward the light, toward the right. A tiny wood-floored room. The chapel. YMCA DANCE CENTER painted on the floor. A fleet of bodies, bellies on blue mats, their arms and legs rising and falling to the bark of an instructor. Flopped, their faces to the ground. But when they raise limbs up, their bodies arch in sweaty supplication.

The steps are worn smooth like the toes of statues in the Vatican. Kissed and trampled so many times by so many sneakers.

My hand skims the railing as I climb the next twenty steps and think of the two staircases in Piazza Venezia in Rome, the one steeply climbing upward to a church, and the other sweeping grandly to the piazza of the Capitol. The medieval staircase narrow and troublesome, one hundred and twenty-two stairs. Built in thanks for deliverance from the Black Plague by the ones who believed life was a weary pilgrimage leading to heaven. The other, designed by Michelangelo for a visiting emperor, spoke for the glory and greatness of the world.

The stairs at the Hollywood Y are not too steep and not too grand.

When I pop out the door, I'm on my own personal *terrazza* overlooking the city. Hands laced behind my head, I start walking out my legs when I notice I'm not alone.

"Hello," says a new maintenance worker.

"Hi," I say. He's sitting on the weathered wooden floorboards with his back against the chain-link fence that surrounds the workout area. I bend down to touch my toes, stretch my hamstrings.

"Why do you do this exercise?"

I stand up and shake my legs out. "Makes me happy," I say.

"I don't do anything and I'm happy," he says, getting up to leave.

I stand tall and sweaty on the rooftop of the Hollywood YMCA. I circle the caged-in rooftop workout spot, twenty times prancing legs up in front, left, right, twenty times flexing legs in back so they hit my butt, left, right, this is my ritual dance, my cooldown tradition.

Weathered boards give beneath my feet, the air duct blows hot breath on me. I grab the fencing all around. Fingers curl through cool metal chain link. Beyond the fence, red tar paper where the track used to be until they found out the roof was dangerous and stripped it away. Sunset Boulevard spread below. To the right, the Hills, and

Frederick's of Hollywood with four magenta banners. Choppers no bigger than mosquitoes float through the air, cutting gray clouds. A Big Mac posted on a billboard floats meat in the air. The HOLLY-WOOD letters on the hill, a crooked diadem.

I walk to the other side and survey my city eastward, toward Little Armenia. East away from the Pacific that borders the coast like a liquid skirt, and into the choked-up bodice of the city.

I climb over the fencing and stand on the edge. Now I can see the Sunset Landmark where the Hollywood Athletic Club is, trendy with pool tables and hipsters and valet parking. Used to all be a warm shade of pink like the sweater my father's ex-wife gave to me, the one I wore when I played Gloria Upson in *Auntie Mame* and all the boys craved me. They ruined it. Painted the whole Landmark pale yellow except for the very top, the pink nipple, exposed to all the elements. I lean over a little farther. My sneakers grip the tar paper. A plastic bag scutters around the parking lot below, blows this way and that. The pigeons flash their sooty gray wings and scrabble around the air duct.

If I threw myself from the rooftop, I would make sure to keep my eyes open the whole way down.

Two Tales of a City

Fiona Molloy rolls the bottle in her palm. She studies the tiny white pills, how they shift and tumble. For a long time, she does this. The Girl Who Everybody Loves. There are a lot of tiny white pills. How many, she's not sure. Fifty, a hundred. But enough. When she uncaps the bottle and shakes them down her throat, she chokes a bit. Goes to the fridge and drinks from a jug of spring water from the French Alps, leaves her lipstick on the rim.

There is the Boy Wonder, ensconced in his faux Italian villa atop Mulholland, behind electronic gates with eyes and triple-bolted doors and shuttered windows, sunk down low in a black leather armchair, sucking from a pipe. In darkness, except for the bluish-gray haze from a wide screen and the blue smoke curling up around his ears, Larry Pitts presses ghostly white fingers against his damp brow. No longer blond, his dirty brownish bangs pasty on the boyish forehead. Fingers shake as he removes them, reaching for an open bottle of silky cognac on the deco side table. Faltering, the hand hangs strangely in the gloom, uncertain. Wearing only a dirty silk jacket, thin legs drawn under him, he shivers, stares dully at his own movie. Pale blue eyes glazed over like they've just been fired in a kiln.

An Epilogue Wrapped in Smog

And yet . . . I am still here in the town that throbs with celluloid and videotape. Something keeps me. What do I cling to? For all the city's smog, its choppers, sirens, gunshots, snarled traffic, and ego-tripping monsters, there is comfort here. Apocalyptic authenticity. Raw urban urgency. And what about the connect-the-dot mutability? I create the city as I choose, plot my course through terrible terrain, even as the Biz wizards spin their own maps of media dreams and fantasies, the dollar signs trembling in their eyes. This is the only passion they are capable of. Leaves me room for mine.

Yesterday I saw a bumper sticker that said:

I ♡ YOU CALIFORNIA, WITH ALL YOUR FAULTS.

Over the last word was an earthquake split, a tremor ripping at the letters' seams. And when I drew up to this bumper, my mouth creased in a faint smile, one of guilt and uneasy complicity, a recognition that quietly spreads, as if the driver and I both shared the same terminally diseased lover.

Today I stand outside the Villa Ardmore. A gust of Santa Ana wind sends dry palm fronds scuttling down the street behind me. I couldn't catch them if I tried.

Mama Querida

In the grave, I sit with my back against the damp earth. I have chosen Hollywood Memorial Cemetery for our meeting. I think of the display of dusty funereal flowers in the Cemetery Shop. She will appreciate the carved animal sculptures that crown plots here and there. A squirrel. A miniature horse for a dead rodeo rider. A watchdog, ears pert and stony. A replica of a sphinx. The stone wall built in the old-fashioned way, stacking and fitting, will please her. The way moss spreads wantonly over the wall and archways. The scent of newly mown lawn, turned earth; rotting carnations and lilies, gifts to the dead. Barely discernible hint of cooked corn and stewed meat from a Mexican joint nearby. Exhaust.

There is a stub of root sticking in my back. Six feet above me, not a star is visible in the sky. It hasn't rained in months. I rest my palms on the dirt floor, attempting to relax, but almost immediately I feel movement. The undulation of worms right beneath the surface? A truck passing by on the boulevard? A small earthquake. First, dirt will sift from the walls over my head. A quiet shushing, a low growl. The grave will jerk from side to side, then the walls will fold in on themselves, cascading over me, filling my nostrils, and ears, and sleeves, and eyes, until I am completely buried.

The desert gets cold at night. It isn't long before I start to shiver. I pull my sweater closer around me. A siren starts in the distance. A low wail, getting more shrill as it comes closer. A wash of red light floods the narrow grave. Red light drops down in layers. Maybe it's the shape of the grave. When I can't stand it anymore, I squeeze my eyes shut. The siren must be long gone now, but I can still hear a faint wail. Very close.

I only open one eye, partially. Through the narrow diagonal slit, I see her. There, opposite me, mirroring my pose. She too with her back against the wall. Knees up. Fleshy in later life, she is the same here. Grotesquely so, since the flesh seems to keep shifting from place to place on her body. She is completely naked. The goose-bumps are clear, and also seem to be moving. Her mouth is not open, but the wail, low and steady, is surely coming from there. Before I can help it, I see her eyes. Pale blue as I remember them, but flung wide as if propped with invisible braces. I do not see her blink before I wrench my gaze away. Then, somehow having avoided it, I see her neck. The flesh shrugs along within its shape, some kind of clayish color, until it gathers round the neck. There it shifts into a gradual deepening violet and finally to black. Here too I rip my eyes away and they fall upon her breasts, which lie flaccid on her stomach, their nipples also stained black. The wail, almost inaudible, circles around my head, my ears, and I am frozen.

This is not what I expected. Where is the translucent robe, the diaphanous ghostly cloak, faint trace of wasted beauty. For a moment I am almost angry. Then I shudder. On my knees, before I know what I am doing, I am crawling toward her. The Earth is tilting. It is an earthquake. The walls begin to slide. I am thrown, or do I throw myself around this wretched thing that is my mother, and I press my lips against her wounded neck.

I take my hands and squeeze. Everything I have is in my hands as I grip tightly. I am strangling my mother.